MACK BREAKS THE CASE

MACK BREAKS THE CASE

John Holmes

Published by Happy Self Publishing
www.happyselfpublishing.com
writetous@happyselfpublishing.com

HAPPY
SELF PUBLISHING

WITH THANKS TO:

Meredith Nason for editorial advice

Alex Shucksmith for initial cover design work

Members of various writers' groups in
Brighton and Retford for advice and support

and

HSP for making it happen

'I said "Be careful, his bowtie is really a camera."'
(Simon and Garfunkel: America)

'When I leave now don't you weep for me.
I'll be back, just save a seat for me.'
(Love: Maybe The People Would Be The Times or Between Clark And Hilldale)

To Maggie

who patiently encouraged the writing,
listened attentively to early drafts, and who,
when informed the book would be dedicated to her, replied,
'I would think so.'

Contents

Chapter 1

A Body In The Pool

Paz Wheat was running late. Noise in the street in the middle of the night had kept him awake. He had a new missing person's case to review and a fraud report to study, but as he was rushing out of the flat, he received a call from Charlie Kibbs. He never knew what to expect from Charlie. It might be a tip or the answer to a question he'd asked him three months earlier. Charlie had been a hustler most of his life and had the attitudes and ways of a hustler. He was never dull. Paz didn't want to hear whatever he had to say at that moment, but ignoring the phone only made him more persistent.

'Yes, Charlie.'

'I need you to come over. There's a body in the swimming pool. Dead.'

Paz had heard some strange stories from him over the years but not quite this. A dead body in the pool? Of course there was. Paz was still dreaming from lack of sleep. 'Is there blood? Is it a drowning?'

'Come and see for yourself.'

'Have you contacted the police?'

'No.'

'Charlie, I don't need to tell you...' Such obvious things were not always amongst Charlie's immediate thoughts.

'I want you to come and see it first.'

'Why? To be clear: I'm not a priest. You must—' But it was like talking to an awkward child. 'What's your address again?'

Paz drove straight to Charlie's, but as he approached the village, he was delayed by farm traffic. He found the street easily enough. Just off the main road, apart from a few older, smaller properties, it was all new large detached houses - self-consciously exclusive and yet all the same in their tawdry luxuriance. The only way to afford living there for someone like Charlie - with no regular income - was as a lottery winner or crook.

When Charlie opened his front door, Paz saw he was in an agitated state. 'Late! Wasn't sure you were coming,' he chided, all scrawny, harassed, and in old pyjamas. He was smoking a roll-up cigarette, drawing hard on it repeatedly.

'Have you called the cops yet?'

'Like I said, I wanted you to have a look.' Maybe Paz owed him before, but Charlie certainly owed him now. 'See if you recognise him. I think he might be one of yours.' He meant a PI. There were too many possible reasons why he could be right.

Paz walked out through the French doors at the back of the house into the garden. The air felt especially cool and fresh. He approached the pool tentatively but found it empty - both of water and bodies. Only leaves at one end and the odd branch or tree blossom. He turned round to look at Charlie who was squinting at him. Paz gave him a glare of bewilderment and gestured to him with his open hands. Sheepishly, Charlie approached on his bare feet.

'Is this a joke?' said Paz. 'There's no-one here. What's going on?' Charlie gave him a look of disbelief. He peered into the pool and then beyond that. He walked around to the other side of the pool and sauntered across the rough grass towards the trees thirty feet beyond on a slight incline. Paz followed him. They stood at the low wooden fence gazing across the fields. No sign of anyone. 'So what's it all about?' he said. Charlie looked at him as though he were questioning his sanity. He explained how he heard a commotion outside, rushed towards the pool, and saw the body lying face up. Paz asked, 'Did you take a photograph?'

'Why would I need to do that when he was dead? He wasn't going anywhere, or so I thought.'

It occurred to Paz this might all be a subterfuge to keep him away from the office. He walked away to call Jane. 'Everything OK?' he said.

'Yes. Why? Where are you, by the way?'

'Over at Charlie Kibbs' place. Out Lewes way. Anything I'm missing?'

'Want me to do that insurance case?'

He winced. He'd forgotten about it. 'Nisbet? I'd better do it, thanks. New client. You know what I mean.'

'OK.'

As soon as Paz ended the call, Charlie ushered him back indoors. He said, 'I had another reason for dragging you out here.'

'Really? Am I surprised? Well, usually "another" means two things. Here it means one.'

Charlie peered at him, oblivious. 'I've got some stuff coming any day. Maybe tonight or tomorrow. Fine arts. Thought it might be something of yours. You've had some fine arts cases lately, haven't you?' Paz looked hard at him. Charlie was suffering from some serious stress. Or was it merely drugs?

'Interested?' Charlie said.

'I don't think so.' Paz was annoyed with him for wasting his time. He'd told him in the past that insurer clients did not do deals on stolen property.

'Shame,' said Charlie.

'Tell me when you've got it,' Paz said, realising he'd probably sounded harsh a moment earlier. He liked to know, even if his clients wouldn't want to buy it back.

'Not that simple. I'll sell it. I just thought—'

Paz walked out. He'd had it with Charlie's games.

He set off for Brighton. As he drove it occurred to him that he had not even been at Charlie Kibbs' house. He lived at a different, much smaller house in the same street, and he had no swimming pool. Why had he not realised that? And what was Charlie doing there? Or had he come into money and moved house for the pool? Surely he would have said.

He drove into Lewes town centre. He needed food for the insurance job because he could easily spend hours waiting for dear Mr Nisbet to appear. He decided to park up and go to a coffee shop. Besides, he wanted to have it out with Kibbs about his charade, about there being no-one in the pool which wasn't even anything to do with him.

'Charlie, listen to me,' he said as he sat waiting for his Americano to cool. 'What were you doing in that house? It's not your house, is it?'

'Did I say it was? You're a little slow on the uptake, Paz. House-sitting. I'm house-sitting for a friend of mine. They had to leave suddenly. Family emergency. That's what you do for your friends, Paz. You do them favours. You might not know—'

'Leave it,' said Paz tersely, and he rang off.

His journey out of Lewes was delayed. The traffic was snagged up in the narrow oneway street he was forced to take. A helpful pedestrian told him that just ahead a young man was threatening to jump from a third floor window. Paz had to sit and wait. He rang Jane. He said, 'You can have that new case. I can't get there. Traffic jam. Someone threatening suicide. It's not a difficult case anyway. Nisbet, it's called. It's just a new one to us. He claims a bad back. Serial claimant. They want him for fraud. Could be more work from them if we nail him. Any news I need to be aware of?'

'Breakout at the prison.'

'Where? Don't tell me — Lewes?'

'Yeah. Late last night. Only one got away. Last seen on the Barcombe road.'

'I was around there earlier. With Charlie Kibbs, my favourite person. He claimed there was a dead body in his pool and it turned out there was nothing. Not even any blood. I felt I was being played but didn't know why. Or how.'

'Unless this Nisbet's one of his mates.'

He'd half-suspected chicanery by Charlie but hadn't considered that. 'Jane, please don't jest. They'd have had to hack into our system. But imagine it: Charlie creates a diversion while Nisbet robs a bank or something. A raid that, because of his bad back, he couldn't possibly have done. Maybe we should watch for any bank jobs out Worthing way today. And jewellers' shops. That could be it: "Get old Charlie to fence the proceeds." No, in all seriousness, I don't think there's any connection.'

The police persuaded the young man to step away from the window just as the traffic was backing up and being diverted. It wouldn't be the end of his saga. Paz imagined there'd be endless trouble in that family. Just maybe no more inconvenience for the likes of him.

There were no bank raids or jewellery heists that day. Jane made it to Nisbet's place, but when he emerged he was hobbling heavily. No obvious signs of malingering, she said. Paz told himself he would have caught him. Experience brought its own luck. For him it was a quiet day in the end, spending time on the new missing person's case. He already had a couple of leads to follow up.

As for Charlie, his travails that day were not over. Around eight, while he was cooking his favourite steak dinner, a young thug forced open the kitchen door. Charlie was on heightened alert from the previous 'incident' and, knife in hand, chased him out into the garden. In the confusion and dark, the intruder fell into the pool and broke his leg. Charlie called out the police and ambulance immediately.

The police later told the press they believed it was a case of mistaken identity, and the target was the man who owned the house. Paz savoured the thought that Charlie would have felt insulted.

Chapter 2

A Surprising Appointment

Chaos always secretly appealed to the well-ordered Paz Wheat. Here in his office without prior warning or approval had suddenly arrived a woman in her early twenties. She was tall with long red hair that ran down her back - Pippi Longstocking without the braids - and wore a garish yellow top, scruffy denim shorts, fishnet tights, and biker boots. She looked to be recovering from a hangover or overdose. What did she want on a Wednesday at nine a.m. at the Brighton premises of Wheat Investigations? How had she even got in? What was security up to?

She'd wandered in through the open door of his private office and was now sat down with her legs crossed. Paz surmised she'd been up all night.

'Have you come about the job, by any chance?' It was absurd, but he trained himself to never assume anything. He was joking, though.

'Eh?' The question startled her. She stared at him the way a drunk examines a strange aquarium fish.

'How did you get in?'

'Er, someone opened the door... downstairs, and I just... walked up.'

'And the job?'

'Um... could I possibly have a glass of... water?'

He felt slightly afraid. Or rather, he thought he should feel afraid but chose to dismiss it. It had been a dull week so far in his work-exclusive life, and here was a spark of the random, the surreal, and it was almost welcome. It could mean the flash of a knife or the start of something beautiful. Most likely, it meant so much of nothing, and she would go on her way as soon as she'd drunk her water. Having lived in Brighton for twenty years, after moving from the States for a change of scene, he was used to the unexpected. Security downstairs would need to be admonished, but that could wait.

Paz had a water cooler in his office, and obtaining his visitor's drink meant standing with his back to her. That would be her best time to strike if she were going to. He got to his feet, accepting whatever his fate might be. Everyone had their time, he told himself, and then he smiled at his own grandiosity.

There was no knife in the back. The creature merely gawped at him from the moment he rose from his chair to his return and the gentle transfer of the small carton from his hand to her sweaty palm. She smelt of alcohol which her deodorant and perfume could not hide.

The young woman now had what she'd come for, although she would probably have appreciated more of it. She drained the carton with one gulp before he'd even reached his chair. Noticing this, he gave her the other carton of water, untouched, that he'd poured for himself. She remained where she was. Had she not been oblivious, she might have wondered at the incongruity of her sitting there in the private office of a man maybe a decade older than her father, short, a little overweight, slightly stooped, balding, whiskery, round of face, and with the unhealthy look of someone who did not get enough sun.

As best he could, Paz ignored her. She had not come about the job and hopefully she would just leave. He had work to do. He had another missing person's case to read up on. They were his favourite kind, even though they usually had a sad outcome when the person was found dead. But he always liked to believe that the next case would be that rare one in which the missing was not only alive but wanting to be reunited with those seeking them.

He could not concentrate with a stranger in the room. She fidgeted, began swaying her legs, and he'd decided it was time to send her away, which he would achieve in the most diplomatic yet firm manner. But not at this moment; he would force himself to concentrate. Besides, his assistant Jane would arrive in the main office in the next few minutes, and she would be as brusque as he was gentle. With her, no random person off the street would be allowed to sit down in the office, and certainly not given water, even if they were desperate.

'Yes.'

The creature had spoken. Paz peered at her for a moment, and seeing nothing in her expression to indicate she would add anything further any time soon, he continued the ritual of reading up on the case. Jane had conducted the initial telephone conversation with the couple about their daughter and he was looking through her notes.

Then the interloper said, 'Yes. I'm interested.' He caught her glance which he immediately knew was fatal. Her soft eyes and face and gently warm voice conveyed such appeal that it triggered something in him - affection, perhaps - and he sensed danger. He lived alone, with the only intimate intrusion in his life of work being occasional nights and weekends with an escort he'd known for many years, and he was vulnerable to needy glances from pretty young women. But more than that, although he could be ruthless and uncaring, his main motivation was kindness and a desire to help good people better enjoy their lives. He decided, based on no evidence whatever, that she was a good person, and he wanted to help her.

'I'm interested.' He was sceptical but the fact she was prepared to feign interest appealed to his vanity. 'Tell me about it, please.'

It was that word *please* that made it seem her interest might be genuine. The water had woken her up and there was almost an urgency in her tone. But he needed time to think. 'I'll get you more water,' he said. 'This time, a proper glass.' As he left his office to go to the kitchen he paused to see if she moved - she could yet be a thief - but he observed she merely took out her phone. He felt oddly serene. If she did steal something he wouldn't even mind, provided it was nothing serious. He knew he was a sucker. Why would she be interested in working in a private investigator's office? He must talk to security downstairs, he reminded himself, as he looked in the cupboard for a suitably large glass. He'd talk to Jane about it when they later discussed the missing person's case and shared a laugh about this latest 'visitor'.

As he returned with the pint glass of water, he saw Jane enter the main office. She removed her coat and he immediately saw her baby bump, a reminder of his own failure: prevaricating about maternity cover which he'd thereby made unnecessarily urgent. They waved greetings at each other. He said loudly, but with an air of helplessness, 'Got someone with me.' Seeing her also reminded him he had a call arranged with loss adjuster Fran Owens for ten thirty, a dubious pleasure he always had to prepare for psychologically.

He decided the visitor would need to quickly sort herself out and decide whether or not she wanted the job, and if she was unqualified, he would have to send her on her way. As soon as he'd sat down, he started rambling about the vacancy but then paused on realising he did not even know her name. He asked her.

'Alison MacKnokaird.' Please call me Mack with a "k".'

'OK, Mack with a "k", I'm Paz Wheat if you—'

She smiled. 'Wheat, OK.'

'The reason for the appointment is that I need to have cover for Jane, who incidentally just walked into the office.'

Mack instinctively turned to look but couldn't see her from her chair. Then she said, 'I'm sorry, Mr Wheat, but do you have any Paracetamol?'

'Erm. I don't know.' He had not anticipated an interviewee disclosing having a headache, but then she was not the average interviewee. He scrambled around in the desk drawer until he found a packet with the last two tablets in it. He gave it to her.

'Thank you,' she said, and she smiled again.

'Where was I?' She did not answer, apparently unaware of what he'd been saying previously. He was disappointed at himself, and at her for pretending to be interested and wasting his time. As soon as the conversation had dragged its sorry self to an end, he would ask Jane to contact the agency, which she would want to do anyway. 'Ah yes: Jane is due to give birth in just a few weeks.'

'Really?' Mack was nearly asleep.

'So the job involves basic admin and secretarial, and also searches.'

'Searches?' She stirred again.

'Yes, online searches.'

'Oh, right.' She grinned. Paz wondered what other notion of 'searches' she'd had in her addled brain at that moment.

'On missing person's cases. Social media. Directories, publicly available information. That kind of thing.'

'Missing persons? OK. I could do searches.' Mack must have realised she needed to put a trifle more enthusiasm into the proceedings. With apparent difficulty she asserted, 'I just want the chance.'

He was startled by this latest remark. 'CV?'

'Eh? Oh, I didn't bring one.' He figured, she didn't possess one.

'Education?'

'A-levels. English. Psychology.'

'Uni?'

'Durham. Psychology... Not completed.'

'Why?'

She shuffled in her seat a little. 'Er, life, I guess...' He took this as an oblique reference to drugs or drink.

'OK. Work experience?'

'Just bars, shops.'

'What do you do now?'

'I don't. I live with my rich girlfriend. Well, rich compared to me.'

'Interesting. OK. So why do you want to work now?'

'Play my part, you know.' He noticed she now had a sad expression, as if she at last realised the absurdity of the situation. She then gingerly rose to her feet, as if to leave. It seemed she had given up and he felt a pang of regret, as though it were all his fault. 'Do you need to be somewhere else?'

'I can be,' she said.

'No, you can stay a little longer if you wish.'

She sat down. He then asked her to excuse him and he left the room. She returned to looking at her phone.

Jane looked harassed.

'I've got someone in who's applying for the job,' Paz said, thinking she'd be happy. 'Quick, eh?'

'Certainly is. Especially as the ad's not even up yet. And I haven't told the agency.'

'Anyway, could you have a chat with her? She's a bit...'

'Nervous?'

'Bohemian's maybe the word. I rather like her.'

'Well, that's the main thing,' she said stiffly, looking away.

'But I wouldn't want to employ someone you weren't confident in.'

'OK,' she sighed. 'I suppose you want me to show her the job. It's a shame I didn't know about it before because I wanted to get that report on the Simpson case done.'

'Don't worry about that. I can do it if necessary.'

'I know. OK, I'll be nice to her. She can get me a coffee for a start.'

He took out a twenty pound note and placed it in her hand. 'Me too.'

When he returned to Mack he found her crying, looking at her phone. He took some tissues and handed them to her. 'Did you want to go home?' he asked sharply.

'No,' she said, embarrassed. Perhaps she realised that crying in the office would kill her chances in his eyes. He gently led her from his private office and introduced her to Jane who tried but failed to hide her disdain.

Paz returned to his room and, distracted, sat down to read papers on a new case. This concerned a suspected fraudster who had a penchant for marrying old ladies in care homes who would soon die, preferably without close family, leaving him as sole beneficiary in their will. A care home manager had contacted Paz because she was suspicious of a man she'd seen on the premises. She recalled seeing him at a previous home she worked at, where he'd married one of the more frail residents weeks after meeting her. He'd now shown up at her new place and was visiting a woman in her eighties almost every day. Paz found it an interesting situation which, like much of his work, left him with sadness at human nature, coupled with a determination to do enough background work to get the police interested. All he'd need was a client to pay for it.

On checking his voicemail messages, he found one from Fran Owens' secretary advising that her boss had cancelled their phone appointment. Paz was delighted. He didn't mind Fran in the smallest of doses but loved the feeling of suddenly having more time than he'd anticipated.

His joy was short-lived. He looked up and in front of his desk stood Jane frowning. She said, 'It's been twenty-five minutes since she left. I couldn't take that long if I crawled there on my knees. I wouldn't bank on you getting your twenty pounds back. I'll go and get ours from Derrick's.'

'OK.'

'Not looking good,' she said cheerfully.

'Give her a chance,' he said. 'She'll be back. OK, so it looks like she screwed up getting coffees, but we wouldn't employ her to do that. By the way, don't Derrick's deliver?'

'Paz, seriously, I think she's on something. I mean, you know, could be class A.'

He sighed. 'OK. That and the alcohol - I know she'd been drinking heavily - and I found her crying earlier. I can't have that.'

'Then why?'

'I see something there.'

'Yes, a pair of legs. No-one comes to an interview dressed like that. It's always the same with you, Paz. You fall a little bit in love and it's fatal. A bit wild, a bit bohemian, and a look of "Daddy, please help me," and you're hooked.'

'Please.'

'It's true. Look at the others we've tried when we needed extra help. All useless and you wouldn't even fire them. We had to wait for them to get bored and leave. Shall I ring the agency?'

'Not yet.'

Observing Mack's arrival back at the office, Paz noted she looked completely flustered. When she retreated to the toilet, he went to see Jane. She told him how Mack had gone to Mickey's, contrary to what she'd told her, forgot what the order was, guessed and got it wrong, bought some cookies (which neither of them would eat) and, out of a sense of guilt, given her back the twenty pounds. The latter point was perhaps cause for hope.

'Shall I order a taxi for her?' said Jane. He did not reply, mulling it over. She said, 'If she can't get a coffee order straight, what use is she going to be?'

'OK.' On hearing the door open he merely said, 'Give it until lunchtime,' and turned away so as not to see Jane's reaction.

As it transpired, it was not Mack returning but his ten forty-five appointment. He wondered whether Mack had simply fled in embarrassment. He sighed, satisfied he'd made a mistake over her, and returned to his private office to greet a severe-looking gentleman in a dark suit who proceeded to advise him of his concern about his aged father's investments. Paz could not help thinking that his main concern was not his father's financial or mental health, but the fact that he, as the son, stood to lose his inheritance from his father's rash decisions.

The man said, 'You come highly recommended.'

Paz smiled. 'We like the flattery here but can't promise anything, you know. Have you talked to the police, or is it still too early?'

'They wouldn't do anything.'

'Well, nor do we normally. It's not something we're really geared up for.' This was a message he always hated conveying. 'But maybe we should. We're getting more enquiries.'

Paz felt as disappointed as the visitor looked, although he suspected this was the latter's natural state. 'I tell you what, though: Give me or send me details of the scheme and I'll keep an ear out, and if I hear anything that might be useful, I'll let you know. The thing is, if it's a Ponzi scheme and he cashes out early, he might be able to get his money back in full, maybe with some interest. If he tries to get his money out and gets the runaround, or they ask for money for fees or taxes or any other nonsense, then you know it's a scam.'

The man appeared buoyed by this. 'So if I can get him to withdraw... The trouble is, to get him to do that I'll have to come up with an alternative. Costa Rican forests, or wine, or God knows what.'

Paz cheered up. 'I'm with you. I'll see if I can find something out about it. Send me what you have.'

Paz mused that maybe this was why people recommended him. He always offered hope, realistic or not. Maybe this type of scam was something the new person, whoever it was, could get their teeth into. The man appeared contented when he left.

At lunchtime Mack departed, and as soon as Jane saw Paz was off the phone she went to see him. She had a smile on her face that he always found ominous. 'OK, hit me with the bad news,' he said.

'Admin: hopeless.'

'Letters and so on?'

'Right.'

'OK. Something to work on there. Searches?'

'Alright actually. Quite quick.'

'Alright, you say? So if she could do four to your one, would you say she was almost adequate for the job?'

She laughed. 'But the truth is, we don't know anything about her. She could be a scammer for all we know. When I return from maternity,

I want to find I still have a job, not that the place has been scammed out of existence.'

'I think I know quite a bit about her, as a matter of fact, and I believe I can trust her. But I know what you mean. She says she has a rich girlfriend. Any idea who it is?'

'I think it's friends with benefits at least.'

'Why was she so upset?'

'Do you really want to know?'

'Of course.'

Jane raised an eyebrow. Paz was not normally interested in staff's personal affairs, finding them an embarrassing distraction. She told him about Mack telling her how she and girlfriend Lily went out on the town, and coming home they were accosted by some young men, felt at risk and ran away, but somehow she lost Lily. Mack ended up being dragged off to a party by two girls, and now was unable to contact her.

'Drink, obviously,' he said.

'And more. This morning, she tried again and became frantic. Still hungover herself, she went looking for her. Feeling ill from her overindulgence, she sat down on our doorstep.'

'I see. So she never intended to apply in the first place. But I knew that anyway.'

She smirked. 'Indeed.'

'But now she does.'

'So she says.'

'I see something there. Something that could be good for us.'

'Paz?'

'Yes.'

'Can I say one thing?'

'Go on.'

'It's your company and you do what you like—'

'I do try to involve you, though,' he interjected, sensing where the conversation was heading.

'Yes you do, and I appreciate that. But please don't make a project out of her. She's not some genius fallen on hard times. She's not in need of saving. A knock-back might do her good, sharpen her up.'

'So it's a No from you then.'

'Not No. A heavily qualified Yes.'

'I know I'm not good when it comes to these things. She must send in a CV, we will offer the going rate, and she'll be on probation for the whole, say, eight month period. That means, if it doesn't work out I can easily fire her.'

'OK. Not that you would.'

He paused for a moment, like a boxer caught by a surprise punch, but responded in bold fashion: 'To be candid with you, I've been thinking about the future. We need to get more digitally clued up. Look how many hours this insurance surveillance stuff takes.'

'It's our bread and butter.'

'It is, and maybe always will be, but it's keeping us small. If we could get better geared up, we could get more work done. We could get involved in some of these scam cases the police can't cope with. This chap I saw this morning is a case in point. He was worried about his dad's investments. I don't know if it's a fraud. It sounds dodgy as old hell, but how would I know? It's not something we've got involved with. I'm old school and behind the times. It's the same with evidence: I find it, but others plant it. That's never been my way.'

'I understand you now about her, but I still think we could find someone more promising. Someone who at least can write a letter.' She chuckled as though this was so obvious there was nothing to discuss.

'I hear you, but I'd rather take a chance on someone who's not going to get so many opportunities. She dropped out of uni and we know she has her problems. She maybe just needs the encouragement.'

'Dropped out of uni and most likely would stay here five minutes and then leave if she's any good.'

'Let me think about it overnight.'

In fact, he thought about it all afternoon. Principally, he thought about Mack's girlfriend Lily. Was she missing? Did Mack need help finding her? Were the police involved? He knew he shouldn't be thinking about it but couldn't help feeling protective towards Mack and her friend.

Fortunately, strict deadlines forced him to focus on a couple of reports for insurers: One on a surveillance matter, the other for Fran Owens on a suspected arson case. Whilst waiting for someone to answer his call to a potential new client, Paz wondered whether his senses had left him. What was he doing employing Mack? Jane clearly thought it crazy. Should he not at least consider other candidates?

He noticed Fran Owens had sent him one of his annoying emails. He said the insurers had questions on Paz's investigation report on a theft case. Fran always liked it when Paz got questions from insurers; it deflected pressure from him.

Next day, he was out on a surveillance case when Jane phoned: 'What are we doing about Mack? She's phoned up three times. What do I tell her?'

'Well, what's she saying? Is she desperate to know because she's got other job offers but we're top of the list? I've heard it all before, you know.'

'You're grumpy. What's the matter?'

'Just Fran Owens. He's sent me a bunch of questions from insurers he knows the answers to. He just likes to put me in my place. In fact, I'm pretty sure all the answers are in the report.'

The real problem was that he knew Fran Owens was keen to hire Jane for his ever-expanding operation. Paz was always the one staying small.

'So what do I tell her?'

'We never got a CV, so No.'

'Yeah? I thought you wanted to give her a chance.'

'Then tell her Yes, subject to CV.'

'References?'

'Them too.'

'But what about terms?'

'I don't know. Fifteen grand annual salary? Eight or nine months, or left open? I'll let you decide. I'll go with your decision. What do you think?'

'It's all a bit of a rush. And it's a rush because you didn't deal with the issue before. You didn't want to hire anyone to begin with.'

'Alright. Alright.' She was giving him a headache. First, Fran Owens, now Jane. 'OK, tell her I'm dealing with it,' said Paz. 'I will contact her.'

He gave up on the surveillance and made his way back to the office, managed to see a couple of his regular informants about one of his cases but drew a blank on new information.

By the time he'd arrived back he'd decided what to do. He couldn't face the whole hiring and interview process. That's why he'd put it off in the first place. His gut instinct told him to hire Mack and hope for the best, his head told him it was mad. He sent her an email offering her the job to start from Monday but reminding her he wanted to see a CV. He didn't bother about references.

He received a glowing reply, accepting.

He told Jane, 'She's thrilled. Though I sense you're not.'

'I don't know.'

It made Paz defensive: 'OK, so she's maybe not the best possible candidate. But then nor were you.'

'What?'

'You were late for the interview, for a start.'

'That wasn't my fault.'

'Exactly. When it happens to you, it's not your fault. When it happens to someone else, it's because of some flaw in their character. There's a psychological theory on that. Read it up. Better still, ask Mack about it. She studied psychology.'

Jane was furious. Paz realised he'd been insensitive, but after his initial twinge of regret he shrugged it off.

Thus it was that Mack who wasn't even looking for a job, was hired by Paz Wheat who didn't even want to employ anyone.

For Paz the weekend was typical. This meant work - writing reports, a little surveillance on malingerers, and visiting a couple of contacts around town who might have information on missing people he was looking for. In the afternoon, he went to cricket at Hove where he read and wrote emails while watching the game. Back at the flat he did stretches to exercise videos online and cooked himself a straightforward pasta meal from a recipe taken from the previous week's Sunday Times Magazine. The fact he had no-one to share it with didn't bother him. He had no close friends, and he was content with that. On Sunday it rained and so he went to Duke's cinema. As was his habit, he fell asleep during the film. In the evening, he prepared a list of priorities for the week. With irritation he noted that Mack had not yet sent him the CV he'd insisted on.

Monday morning arrived, but Mack failed to show up. Jane had specially made a point of arriving early. She didn't say anything, and Paz sensed that her satisfaction at being proved right outweighed any irritation. But he knew such satisfaction would be short-lived, for although Jane liked her judgement vindicated, her overriding concern was for the business. She had a lot of admiration and affection for Paz and did not relish what she saw as his inevitable disappointment regarding Mack.

Paz felt let down. He did not like to be made a fool. By ten o'clock, not a word had been heard from Mack. He rang the number he had for her, but there was no answer. Annoyed, he told Jane he was going out to canvass various shops and contacts on a missing person's case.

He drove into the town centre and started exploring. He visited a couple of coffee bars and encountered one of the beggars he knew. He gave him a cheese roll he'd bought for this purpose, but the man didn't recognise anyone from the photographs he showed him.

Frustrated, Paz stayed out for lunch and delayed returning to the office for as long as possible. Still nothing. It was not until three thirty when Mack, sounding what Paz later described to Jane as 'spaced out', phoned to say she was ill. Mack did not elaborate. He was so fed up he merely said, 'OK' and rang off.

Next morning, he went out early to meet a prospective client in Shoreham on a fraud case. After an ultimately disappointing conversation, he was approaching his car when Jane phoned: 'Nothing heard from Mack again.' She was not amused. It was eleven already. 'This is nearly another week wasted. How are we possibly going to hire anyone quickly enough?'

'OK, we'll contact the agency tomorrow. Perhaps I should leave it to you to decide who we employ in future.'

'What's wrong with her?'

'I don't know.'

'Paz.' There was a strong tone of admonition in her voice.

'I hear you.' Nothing more needed to be said.

He turned his attention to a surveillance job he had to do. It turned out that this led him to a road near where Mack lived. He asked Jane to check the paperwork on Mack's application for her exact address because he thought he'd call in. It was a smart apartment block in a quiet street near the seafront. Feeling a little nervous in anticipation of an argument, he rang the doorbell. There was no answer. He almost kicked the front door in frustration.

When Paz arrived back in the office after a late lunch, Jane said, 'She's taking the piss. Half past two when she phoned. And she sounded completely out of it.'

He said nothing. Once at his desk, he began drafting an email telling Mack in the politest way he could conjure that she'd been fired.

He hated doing it. He fretted over the individual words, deleted some, added others, then put back the words he'd taken out. He looked at it over and over. Realising he could spend the whole afternoon agonising over it, he sent the email at about four o'clock. There was no response by the time he left the office at six and he felt relieved.

He disliked unexpected visitors but especially in the evening. They always meant trouble. Either they were in it, or they brought it with them, or both. He liked privacy. He was, after all, a *private* investigator, and he didn't like people knowing where he lived. Often doing his work for clients meant putting someone else's nose out of joint. Someone who might call on him if they knew where he lived.

Whoever it was ringing his doorbell at six thirty before he'd even thought what his dinner might be was pretty inconsiderate. They rang a second time. He had the chain across, so the door only opened a couple of inches. 'Yes?'

'Paz, it's me.' A young female voice. He recognised it but not who it was.

'What do you want?' It was Mack. 'What are you doing here?'

He opened the door and she walked in and immediately sat down in his lounge, drink-addled Pippi Longstocking no more. She was wearing a black leather jacket and smart denim skirt. There was a cold, determined look on her face, and she smelt not of booze but the subtlest of scents that flew straight to his unconscious. 'I've come about the job,' she said. 'You gave me the chance and then you took it away again. I want it back.'

He was riled. 'You didn't turn up. Believe it or not, the way it works is that the job entails turning up.'

'I rang you and told you I was ill.'

'You weren't really. Drunk or on drugs, admit it.'

Now she was upset. 'How dare you! I was ill.'

He chose a softer path: 'How did you know where I lived?'

'Oh come on, Paz, I wouldn't be much of a PI if I couldn't work that out.'

'But how did you?'

'I waited outside your office with a bike I borrowed from a friend and followed you home. I lost you at first, but then caught sight of you at the lights and managed to trail you all the way to the car park. After that it was easy.' His name was not listed at the main door and how had she got in? She must have asked another resident, but she wasn't saying and anyway he was intent on throwing her out.

'What about your CV?'

'What about it?'

'I need it.'

'Why?'

'It doesn't matter why.'

'Are you insisting?'

'Yes. If not, you can leave. In fact, you should leave anyway. How dare you invade my privacy like this!?'

'OK, you asked for it.' She then gave him the shock of his life by pulling up her T-shirt to reveal her naked breasts.

'Please stop!'

'Go on, have a good look. They're smaller than I'd like but they're not bad, are they? When I was a cam girl at uni, guys like you paid to see them. You get to see them for free.'

'Please!' He was flushed.

'Are they OK for you?'

'Please pull your shirt down.'

'And do you like my legs?' She let her T-shirt fall and pulled up her skirt to reveal the top of her thighs. 'Well, do you?'

'Yes, I love them.' He said it without thinking.

'Oh, so you love them. And you fancy me.'

'Stop it.'

'If you didn't fancy me, you would never have employed me in the first place, would you?'

'I saw something there.'

'Really? Well, you've seen a lot more now.'

'I mean, potential. What are you: a scammer, a blackmailer?'

'My girlfriend suggested I set you up for sexual harassment. I've a recording device in my pocket but I switched it off. I don't want to set you up.'

'Girlfriend?'

'So you want to know about her, do you? Not Lily. She's an angel. It was Jude. She's a hot little devil.'

'Lily? Jude? How many girlfriends have you got?'

'Two. Three if you include Jude's friend Scottie.'

He wished he hadn't asked. 'Please put your skirt down.'

'I will if you put your arms around me and tell me everything's alright about the job.'

'I can't do that. I won't say anything until you pull your skirt down.'

She complied. 'I'll formally apply for the job if necessary. Look, Paz, I just want the chance you promised me. Please.'

'You already applied.'

'No I didn't. Not really. You know I didn't. But now that's my job and I want it back. I was so happy to get it, but then you took it away from me, you bastard. I mean, Mr Wheat.'

'You just said you weren't even there for the job.'

'It's true, but when I found out what it was, I knew I could do it. Please, Paz, Mr Wheat. Is it that Jane?'

'No.'

'I'll prove you both wrong. If you knew how useless I feel right now, you wouldn't hesitate to say Yes.'

'What will you do if the answer's No?'

'Same as I do now. Sex, drugs and poncing off the woman I love. Or go back to camming. Not really. So where's the wife then? Working?'

'There is no wife.'

'Oh, divorced?'

'No. I've never been married.'

She looked baffled. 'So what do you do for, you know, companionship?' She sniggered.

'I live for my work. No girlfriends.' This was not true, but he wasn't going to mention his escort 'friend'.

'Sad,' she said. 'I'm sorry I blew it about the job.' She suddenly stood up and walked towards the door, then stopped and faced him. 'And, by the way, I lied. I wasn't ill. I was stoned. I'm sorry for lying. You were right to sack me. I've learnt my lesson.'

It was his turn to feel sad. 'So which girlfriend will it be tonight, then?'

She didn't like the question: 'What's that got to do with anything?'

'Well, you asked me about my wife.'

'If you must know, from now on if I'm working, it'll be Lily. She likes to snuggle in. If not, it'll be Jude, who wears me out. There, you can get off on that.'

Undeterred by her rebuke, he said, 'Make it Lily, then shall we?'

She paused before replying. 'Really? Are you being serious?'

He smiled nervously. 'You'd better be there. Tomorrow.'

She stepped forward and wrapped her arms round his neck. 'Oh, Paz, Mr Wheat, I will, I will!' She kissed him on the forehead, causing him to blush again. She immediately left, perhaps in case he changed his mind once more.

Afterwards, he wondered what he'd done. Jane was right; it was a risk employing her. He sensed the bigger risk, however, was that he might fall in love.

Next morning, Mack was in early, demurely dressed. When Jane arrived, she made straight for Paz's office. She was not happy. 'Why is she here? I thought—'

'I gave her another chance.'

'What happened?'

He hesitated to respond. She merely stared at him. To break the deadlock he said, almost as a whisper, 'Personal approach.' Jane merely continued staring to extract an elaboration. He said, 'She came to my place and made her appeal.'

'Did you give her your address?'

'She says she followed me on a bike.'

'You're kidding. This is ridiculous. All this nonsense going on while work's piling up.'

'We can hire a temp.'

'Cost!'

'We're OK. I'll take less salary.'

'You hardly take any anyway.'

'We'll get a loan. Whatever. Let's make it work.'

She was silent for a moment to take it all in. 'So you got the CV then that you were so worried about?'

He hesitated again. 'Yes.'

'Is it OK then?'

'Yeah.'

'So was it what you expected?'

'Erm—'

'Did you want to show me, since you supposedly value my judgement so much?'

'I haven't got it with me.'

'Paz.'

'Yes.'

'What's going on?'

'What do you mean?'

'Personal approach - what does that even mean? Has she compromised you in some way? Be honest with me.'

'No she hasn't.'

He then announced that he needed to go out on a case straight away. Jane said, 'So what do I give her to do?'

He had no idea but was suddenly inspired: 'Give her the Marshall case.'

'The missing person's file? But we spent ages on it and never found any leads.'

'Give it to her to play around with. And get her on drafting letters.'

'So what was on her CV?'

'It's a bit embarrassing.'

'Why? Was she an escort or something?'

He decided to tell her straight. 'She said, "Here's my CV" and pulled up her shirt to show me her breasts. Then she showed me her legs all the way up and said "Do you like my legs?"'

'Bloody hell!'

'Indeed. But that's where it ended.'

Jane started laughing. 'I've got to admire her. Huh! Blimey. So tell me, did you like her CV?'

He was pleased he'd told Jane about it. He felt he'd won her trust again - just about. He said, 'It was certainly a first. And as CVs go, it was probably the only truly honest one I've ever seen.'

Chapter 3

Vanished

Over the next couple of days, Mack demolished the Marshall case, given to occupy her in the same way one might give crayons to a child in a restaurant. Using only online sources she established that Stacy Marshall, who was English, had got married in Australia to a man then about to emigrate to the US. The biggest breakthrough was finding her on a Colorado Jane Doe website of unidentified deceased females. Working with an American websleuth, she established from photographs that one of these unfortunate women had the same unusual teeth pattern as Stacy. Timeline and geographical location also matched up. The excited websleuth declared that, with Mack's help, the case was effectively solved. She would liaise with the police to establish precisely how Stacy came to be where she was found. Paz's clients, Stacy's parents, had long given up thinking she might be alive, but nevertheless, informing them of the latest findings would not be easy.

With Jane's last day in the office approaching, she said to Paz, 'I still think she could be a problem, but I have to hand it to her: that was good work. No-one had made those connections before.'

Paz merely grinned as he waited for his latest potential clients to arrive.

Sol and Marie Stiversen were a gentle-looking couple in their early fifties. Americans just arrived in the UK, both casually dressed, he was tall and grey-haired with kind blue eyes and a ready smile, while she was short with wiry blonde hair and a quiet, appealing air. But there was steel there; you couldn't run a thousand acre cattle ranch being soft-hearted. Theirs was a trip they hadn't wanted. Never in Europe before, they'd heard of Paz Wheat through American connections. They wanted to find their daughter Annette whom they hadn't seen for six months.

What had prompted their visit was a card, postmarked Brighton, which had a distinctive arty design depicting a lyre bird. The card said Annette was fine, having arrived in England from France several weeks earlier with her boyfriend Richard, but she was on her own as he'd now returned to Paris.

'So why are you so concerned?' Paz asked.

Marie said, 'We don't know how she's living as she's burnt through her savings. We know she has nothing in her checking account because she's been getting overdraft letters at home. We added money a couple of times, but it was taken out immediately. We believe she wants to come home but can't afford the flight and doesn't want to ask, and we're tired of putting money in her account. We thought Brighton was not a big place and we might be able to find her here.'

Paz wondered how difficult their parting might have been. 'I like to speak plain; it saves time. Are you sure she'd be glad to see you?'

'Yes,' said Marie firmly. 'Things were a bit tense between us before she left, admittedly, but I'm sure we've all forgiven each other now.' She produced a photograph: 'This was taken shortly before she left.' It was a close-up. A round pretty face, light brown hair, green eyes, petite nose, no real distinguishing features - the face of many thousands of young women. Paz might see her every day and not remember her.

He said, 'So you want me to help find her, assuming she's still here?'

The couple glanced at each other. There was something else. 'The thing is,' Sol said with a deep frown, pointing at the card, 'We're not convinced it's her writing.' They produced another card for comparison. Paz didn't notice any obvious difference. Seeing his puzzlement, Marie explained, 'Superficially it maybe looks like her writing, but it's different. First, every capital is larger. She wouldn't do it like that. Plus the capital R: see how she puts a little flourish on the end.' She showed him and Paz now saw the difference. 'And the latest is less neat,' she said.

'Could it be the stress of being alone in a strange city got to her?'

'Possibly. Or the boyfriend wrote it,' she said.

They were silent as Paz digested this notion for a moment. Then he said, 'Is it something he'd do? How could he send it from Brighton when the message says he's in Paris? That makes no sense.'

'He's a bit of a prankster, a joker. I wouldn't put it past him to say he's gone to Paris and not go. Or he could have written it and posted it before he left. But it seems odd and, whatever the story, we feel it's time she came home. And we believe that's what she wants. We won't force her, just give her the chance.'

They talked some more and the couple left him various items, including cards Annette had previously sent from other places across the world, and photographs of the boyfriend, Richard Polson, who was about twelve years older than Annette. Marie said some of the other cards might not have been written by her. 'We're not even convinced she's in Brighton,' she said at last, 'so we'd like to try and clear that up.'

After they'd gone, Paz discussed it with Jane. They identified some shops that might sell these particular postcards. She and Mack also began initial internet searches on Annette and Richard. Paz couldn't resist the theory that a jealous Richard had pretended to leave and returned only to find his fears of Annette being unfaithful realised and, as a consequence, she was no more.

In local missing person situations like this, Paz and Jane usually split visits to likely shops between them, but this was hardly appropriate due to Jane's condition, so she delegated her share to Mack except for one near the car park she regularly used. As an overall strategy, Paz liked to start his investigation in and around the main railway station, especially, as here, where the missing person was less likely to have a car. After the station, his investigation would spread out. He had a loose collection of contacts across the city - janitors, bar staff, newsagents, taxi drivers, beggars he supported with food - that he could approach to see if they recognised faces in photographs. Over the following days, he would begin going through these various contacts.

Next morning, Paz began work on the Stiversen case in earnest. He called in at various retail shops in and around the station and showed the photographs to the staff. One or two people seemed to recognise Richard but then hesitated and corrected themselves. Results were negative in every instance. He also visited coffee bars in the vicinity but without success. Then, after a positive response on Richard Polson from a young beggar on Western Road in Hove, he tried several shops in the immediate area. In a small general store, the shopkeeper said Richard had been in a few times but not in the last ten days. She did not, however, recognise Annette. Other shopkeepers, including one selling cards like Annette's, also recognised him but not her. He speculated this area was close to where they lived, although a nagging concern arose because Richard had a vague resemblance to a famous film actor, and it might be him they unwittingly recognised.

He tried a café where once again one of the baristas recognised Richard but not Annette. At that moment, he wanted to sit down and study the latest email just in from Fran Owens, which contained insurers' questions on one of Paz's jewellery theft reports. He had a coffee there, sitting in the window in case he glanced up to see either of them, knowing that was a long shot.

He did not linger in the café; it was a warm afternoon with clouds already building up for the expected rain, a time to be outside to enjoy the fleeting sun.

The following morning, Paz met the Stiversens at the office to update them on what he'd learnt to date. He concluded, 'So there's sightings of Richard, maybe, but none of Annette. I intend to make door-to-door enquiries around that area.'

Marie said they'd spent time at the station, looking at people leaving and arriving, talking to ticket collectors, observing people getting on the bus and hailing taxis. 'Why don't we hang out in that café?' she said. 'The last one where the barista recognised Richard?'

'Sure.' He gave them the details. 'Now I have to tell you that Jane and Mack who work with me have done some research on the couple, and we understand they both have criminal records.'

They blushed. 'Yes,' said Sol, not making eye contact. 'Drug offences.'

'She likes the bad boy type,' said Marie.

'Can I be frank?' said Paz.

Sol said, 'Sure.'

'There's playing at bad and there's being bad.'

'I think we understand you.'

'Richard has convictions for cheque forgery, violent assault, and attempted second degree murder. Were you aware of that?'

Their expressions showed they were unaware and were embarrassed. Sol quickly recovered his composure: 'It just emphasises why we must find her. Please continue your enquiries - whatever it takes. And please show us that coffee bar and we'll make that our base.' He turned to Marie who nodded.

Accordingly, Paz took the couple to the Ambassador coffee bar. They sat at a small table by the window. Paz liked the place which, despite its grand name, was unpretentious, cheap and therefore popular. At one point, Marie, who spent the whole time looking through the window, stood up as though recognising a face, then hesitated and sat down again. Paz asked them if they'd had any contact with Richard's parents. They said they never had, and according to Annette they'd both died in a house fire, cause unknown. Paz kept his immediate suspicions on that to himself, merely adding this latest fact to the criminal record and the issue of authorship of the card.

Having other work to do, he left them. When outside, perhaps because of their conversation, after a few minutes he thought he'd just seen Richard and almost bumped into him. He called out 'Richard!' but the preoccupied man did not stop. Instead, he hurried on his way, suddenly crossing the road, narrowly avoiding being hit by a van, then running into an alley. By the time Paz reached it, the man had disappeared.

The clients went to the Ambassador every day. Sol would pace up and down the nearby streets just to tread where their daughter had walked, visiting shops she may have gone into, calling at bars she may have frequented. Paz continued enquiries, checking faces he passed in the street but without success. He called in at the Ambassador to see the couple and had only just sat down when Marie rose to her feet. She looked as though she'd seen an apparition. 'I'd recognise that necklace on that neck anywhere.' She rushed out, almost knocking a brimming cup of chocolate from a man's hand, and ran up the street, disappearing from view. 'Exciting,' Paz said, but Sol merely took a sip. 'She's been doing that all week,' he sighed. 'Don't hold your breath.' He clearly wasn't in the mood to chat so Paz checked emails on his phone, learning a new case was in from Fran. Paz then heard the door open and looking up saw Marie, red-faced from running, and behind her a younger woman, pale and emaciated and with a torn bandage on her right forearm. The latter reminded him of someone recently released after being locked up, still acclimatising to the light. She and Sol hugged awkwardly and Marie talked excitedly and formally introduced Paz to Annette who looked nothing like her picture; wasted from poor diet and, he suspected, drugs. She was nervous. He felt as though he were intruding on a private family scene and, with other work to do, thought it time to leave.

A few days later, the Stiversens settled Paz's account. They wanted to take him out to an expensive dinner, but he politely declined. He felt glad to have assisted, but it was rare he celebrated a case's resolution, knowing it risked the whims of Fate. He did, however, make a point of seeing them off from their hotel when they left.

It was Annette who'd sent the card. She'd been 'homesick and inebriated' at the time. Richard had gone to Paris, saying he would not return as he had a new girlfriend. The parents were relieved he'd gone, as was Paz. Above all, he was relieved her parents had come looking for Annette.

Weeks later, there was a reminder of the dangers that lay in wait for someone in her situation. A body was discovered by foragers in a shallow grave in a remote wooded area on the outskirts of town. Police suspected foul play. That the body could not be identified added to the poignancy. There was a photograph of the deceased in the Argus. If it had been Annette, no-one would have recognised her, nor would they know this person's name. Paz didn't recognise the face and put the paper aside, but then Mack ran into his office, insisting she knew who it was.

Paz stared hard at the picture. 'No it can't be,' he said. It was hardly a film star face, but he had to concede it was indeed Richard Polson.

He felt proud of Mack, and she was full of herself, bubbling with ideas about what had happened and why. She seemed to think she could crack the case herself. He quietly reminded her that this was now a matter for the police with all their resources. The private detective running rings round Scotland Yard was a creature of fiction.

Paz took his file to the police. In the subsequent weeks, a local man was arrested. It transpired that Annette had been in a love triangle. Her new lover killed Richard while under the influence of crystal meth, and she was terrified, realising she'd gone from one toxic relationship to another. Mack pointed out this had been one of her theories, to which Paz responded that she'd had so many it was likely one would prove correct. She countered by saying she believed Annette guilty too.

The mystery of the postcards was solved. Fearful of revealing the truth lest Richard discover what she'd written, Annette became adept at creating an imitation of her own handwriting distinct enough to trigger her parents' concern. Eventually, this strategy worked. As for her family, joy at finding their daughter would be followed by years of travail through the courts, but at least she was never charged with anything.

Chapter 4

Jude

One Friday night, several weeks after Jane had gone on maternity leave, Paz was in his study reviewing a surveillance video, when he heard a familiar voice outside: 'Paz, please let me in. I have nowhere to stay tonight.'

He went to the door. It was Mack. She was standing in the same clothes she'd worn to the office. The only difference in her appearance was that she'd been crying.

'You'd better come in,' he sighed, unable to pretend the intrusion was welcome. He couldn't stand tears so he'd insist there be no more of them. But as she followed him through to the lounge with the holdall containing her clothes, he softened. He prided himself on always being open to a client's needs, so why not someone who worked with him, and on whom he relied, and who now needed help? But then, clients never expected to stay over at his small flat.

He retired to the kitchen to make tea and acclimatise himself to the idea of her being there. It was the latest in a relationship that had already become uncomfortably close from his perspective, ever since Jane had departed. Mack's arrival at his place reminded him of the previous time she'd visited, pulling up her shirt to win back her job. Now, weeks later, here she was once again in his shabby lounge with its tatty furnishings. All the years he'd worked with Jane she'd never visited his place, nor he hers.

He could not have turned her away, but it felt weird. His place was not exactly in a proper condition to play host to anyone, least of all a young woman he worked with. The spare bedroom was cluttered, mainly used for storage, but as he quickly tidied it up, he made a point of not grumbling. He could not reject her at a time of need. He just hoped she wouldn't get too comfortable and decide to make it permanent.

She hadn't eaten and she offered to cook them both a meal. She'd expected there to be an abundance of food, but was immediately disabused of that notion on opening the fridge. He therefore treated her to a Chinese takeaway. He was now pleased she'd chosen to come to him. It stirred paternal feelings. Jane would have been appalled, but he didn't care what she'd think. He waited for Mack to explain the reason for her sudden visit, the latest episode in her own soap opera. He went over in his mind its plot so far.

Since first working with Mack, he'd gradually become caught up in the wild ride of her relationships. It was an anathema to him, since he had no real personal life himself and had no interest in what she did outside work. But to her the two were interwoven and she was keen to keep him informed, as though providing a prior excuse for any future lapses in work performance. Once resigned to such conversations, he began becoming interested. He asked her about her relationship with Lily. She explained they'd been close school friends as young teenagers, gone their separate ways; then at Lily's instigation, they'd become close again. By then, Lily had become a successful businesswoman and was able and more than willing to support her financially. He surmised their relationship was, as Jane described it, 'friends with benefits' and was open. Certainly this would explain how Mack could be in a relationship with another young woman, Jude, apparently in the knowledge and with the acquiescence, if not the acceptance, of Lily. He had to admit to himself, he'd become intrigued by the dynamics between the three of them.

In the office, he'd observed Mack becoming increasingly affected by Jude and her demands. He always knew when she'd stayed at Jude's because she'd be in late next morning and be less sharp than usual. He did not admonish her over this, for he could tell she was unrelaxed about it, and later she would work harder to make up for it.

The stress point in the Lily-Mack-Jude triangle had come when Mack asked Lily if she could have Jude stay at the flat, which was a luxurious one, while Lily was away on business. Lily said No. Mack protested, but Lily was adamant. Jude, however, who was behind the request, was not so easily put off. Accordingly, they did stay at the flat and, not only that, at Jude's insistence, they made out in Lily's bed and, unbeknownst to Mack, Jude left a note of thanks in lipstick on the mirror of Lily's personal bathroom. The outcome was that Lily threw Mack out of the flat.

It was after that, Paz noticed a disappointing decline in Mack's performance. She was so tired she would fall asleep at her desk, which he did not need to remind her was unacceptable. This began to cause tension between them. He hated this, but she had to understand she must manage her personal relationships so they did not impact on her work. Although he felt bad telling her off, he appreciated the fact she made it easier by not arguing. She knew she didn't need to. Jane was right: he hadn't it in him to fire her. Even if she sat popping Ecstasy tablets all day, he'd find a way to excuse her. The result was that Mack opened up to him. She felt Jude was trying to take over her life. She'd already sabotaged her relationship with Lily, and now she wanted to ruin her job too. Why? In order to make Mack more dependent on her. All this made him uncomfortable. He had a business to run. And that business did not involve relationship counselling.

But whatever he thought about it all was irrelevant now she'd turned up at his flat unannounced. Jude had told her she was leaving that very evening and Mack would never see her again. This had thrown her into turmoil. Lily was away and, following the debacle last time, had changed the locks. Mack had nowhere to go.

As they talked, Mack revealed that she'd fallen deeply in love with Jude and it had been like a strong drug. Now she realised Jude had no feelings for her, merely wanted to make her dependent and then dispense with her, which she'd achieved. Mack could see their relationship had been an illusion. She'd had growing doubts after the 'Lily's bed' incident, and these had reached a pinnacle with Jude's 'Venice' idea which she now described to Paz.

He listened with amazement as Mack described how Jude had wanted to steal Lily's car - a brand new Nissan Skyline - sell it to a buyer she had already lined up, use the funds to set up in Venice, find a rich, frail, solitary old man, get to know him, live with him, make him write a will in their favour, then they'd 'fuck him to death and collect the inheritance'. Mack said she couldn't believe it. She told Jude she could never do such an evil thing, could never have sex with a man anyway, and would never want to hurt Lily by stealing her car. Jude was unmoved. She said, 'He dies happy, we live happy, and Lily collects on the insurance. No-one hurt.'

Paz was glad she appeared comfortable telling him about it, and she said she was relieved to be able to unburden herself. She felt 'clean of it' now, having felt dirty before. She said that her rejection of the Venice plan was partly why Jude broke off the relationship. The other reason was that Scottie was ill and— 'Who's Scottie again?' he asked. Scottie was Jude's best friend who was with Jude when they picked Mack up after her night's drinking with Lily. That was the night Mack tried to get Lily drunk, succeeded, then unintentionally abandoned her in the street when Jude and Scottie whisked her away for their own drug-fuelled hedonism. By morning, worry about Lily had turned into panic and, after checking back at the flat, she wandered around looking for her before ending up, 'rough as toast' at the four-storey building containing Wheat Investigations.

Jude had now told Mack when dumping her, that she'd never been seriously interested in her, was not even gay, and the whole thing had been a piece of situationist art, an experiment. A psychological experiment to see how far she could influence a random person to do what she wanted. It was that phrase 'random person' that hurt Mack most. 'There,' Jude said. 'Now you know everything, how do you feel about it?' Mack merely looked at her in shock. Emotional breakdown followed, quickly replaced by anger.

Mack could not understand how she'd been so easily conned. Paz asked her if she thought she had an addictive personality. She said she'd never thought about it, but maybe she did. He asked her what was wrong with her relationship with Lily. 'Wrong? Lily? Why, nothing.' So why did she need to explore other relationships? She explained that Lily was straight and sometimes had boyfriends, that she had asked Lily to marry her multiple times but Lily had always declined, and she believed that was because Lily did not want to be thought gay. She said, 'The problem is, she wants a man. Until she realises all men are worthless, she'll never commit to me. If she would, I'd never stray for a moment because the truth is, we love each other as much as any two souls ever did or even could.'

As the evening wore on, Paz began to feel more uncomfortable at her being there, and she was aware of it and it amused her. 'Don't worry,' she said, 'I won't be wandering about the place naked. Or does that disappoint you?'

'No.'

'I'm the vulnerable one here, don't forget.' Then she laughed. She knew she was safe with him, although what kept his vanity exercised that night was the fear this was because she assumed he was impotent.

Next morning, Saturday, Mack asked him to drive her over to Lily's flat to see if she'd returned and would allow her back. Relieved, he readily agreed. When they arrived, he asked if he should stick around. She said not to. 'Not if she's there. You'll hear swearing and then she'll let me in. An hour later, all you'll hear is her whimpering. No man can make her feel loved like I can.'

Lily was there, and Paz immediately left.

A week later, Lily's car was stolen. She and Mack had been out for dinner, and on their return they found it gone. Mack wondered whether Jude was behind the theft.

Any thoughts Paz had that her recent visit to his place would not be repeated were soon extinguished. Soon it became 'Can I stay over, as Lily's boyfriend will be at the flat?' He allowed it because he enjoyed her company. Later it became 'Can I stay over as Lily's away?' Why did she want to stay with him? He didn't ask. As long as she didn't distract him too much he didn't mind. Of course she did distract him, but he was gracious enough to pretend she didn't.

Mack was now sure Jude was a serial fraudster. When Jude had said she was an artist, to Mack that meant 'scam artist'. She wanted to hurt her and wanted Paz to help her. He made the mistake of telling her she was just sore because Jude had tricked her into a love affair that was fake and she got mad with him. Although he knew he was right, he apologised and wished he hadn't said it. After this he encouraged her in her 'Jude researches'.

Mack was able to track down Jude on a dating site. She was determined to make her onetime lover suffer, and it showed Paz how ruthless she could be. She decided to approach Jude in the guise of an old man with a terminal illness based in Venice, looking for young female companionship. This was exactly what Jude had told Mack she wanted to find. Was Jude in Venice? Mack preferred to think she wasn't, so that she would feel compelled to leave wherever she was in pursuit of her Venetian dream. Paz asked her whether Jude might not realise she was being deceived. She knew that Mack worked in a PI's office, after all. Mack said that although Jude was clever, she had a blind spot. Her desire to get what she wanted overrode everything else. In the same way Jude was a drug to Mack, Jude's ambition was a drug to herself. When high on her ideas she could not see even what was obvious.

After the initial back and forth on the dating site, Mack asked if they could move on to email. Jude, who was clearly excited, agreed. Mack set up a fake account and, when asked for a picture, used a photograph of an old snap she found in a flea market. She kept in reserve a second snap of the same old man, should that ever be required. Jude claimed to be in France but Mack was wary, suspecting this was a ruse to extract money; Jude would likely say next she was broke, so could 'Sven' (Mack's persona) pay for her flight and so on? This prediction proved correct. Jude asked for all her travel costs, her own 'modest' accommodation (this was unexpected) and a food and clothes allowance (likewise). Sven, however, was adamant that he would not pay for travel and would only consider paying for anything once she'd arrived in Venice. Sven added, 'I am known for my parsimony. If that is an issue for you, I can easily find someone else to be my companion.' Jude then made a rather pathetic and squalid claim, so Mack thought, about her sexual experience and tastes. Sven responded that he did not want a 'harlot' and if she thought he did, she was mistaken. 'The important word,' Sven insisted, 'is "companion".' After this there was silence.

Mack was pleased. She'd got Jude's hopes up and dashed them again. That was enough. It was time to forget her now. She became so happy she devoured work. Paz could hardly keep her busy enough, such was her speed and attention to detail. But finally she did receive a message from Jude: 'Whatever you want. However much, however little. You are the master. I am your slave.' Mack now became worried. She wondered whether Jude had sussed out who Sven really was and was plotting a deadly revenge online, accessing Mack's personal information to make mischief with it. She told Paz, 'I don't like it. I don't trust her. What has she been doing, except getting someone to hack into my computer?' Unsaid, although he read it in her face, was the concern that the hacking operation might extend to the company site. He knew he should be worried too, but part of him was always half-looking for the excuse to give up the office and go and live abroad. So he remained sanguine about the possibility of a cyber attack; rather less so, however, at the thought that from the company's site the hacker could possibly work their way into bank accounts, both corporate and personal.

Mack became jittery, and her work began to suffer, for she was certain Jude knew. She felt guilty because she thought Paz would get caught up in it. She said, 'Paz, if this all goes to bad for you because of me, I will want to kill myself.' He told her not to think like that and how he was confident (even though he wasn't) that nothing bad would happen. The fact was, however, that some action had to be taken in response to Jude's latest. Mack's idea was to establish a second fake persona to 'warn' Jude about Sven, saying he was a rapist and dangerous fraud. Paz thought this would make Jude more suspicious that Sven was fake. They couldn't agree, but he felt she should do what she thought best, and told her so. But before she did anything further she received a message from Jude saying she was now in Venice and requesting Sven's phone number.

They decided the best response was silence. Let the messages from Jude keep coming. When these started to become frantic Mack decided 'Luigi' would respond on Sven's behalf. Paz said. 'Who the hell's Luigi?'

'Sven's manservant.'

'What!?'

She assured Paz it was easy. Luigi would reply, saying Sven had been taken desperately ill and could not respond personally. That would kill it. Jude would know it was too late to enact her plan and, besides, now she would have Luigi to contend with. 'Perfect,' Mack purred.

But it didn't work. Jude now turned her attentions to this new person. She obviously surmised that Luigi would inherit from Sven and might be interested in a young woman like her in his life. She could drain his bank account while looking for a new victim. Jude must have sussed them out.

Luigi fobbed her off, assuring her he needed to devote all his time to his 'poor master' who was 'on his very deathbed'. Mack was tempted to let Luigi ask for pictures but decided against it, concerned as to where that might lead. But Jude had the same thought and began sending pictures anyway. Nothing pornographic but suggestive - cleavage, short skirts and lingerie. And then there were close-ups of her face. When Mack saw the latter, she suddenly burst into uncontrollable tears. Paz put his arm around her to comfort her. She was inconsolable. Mack had taken some of these pictures herself when they were intimate and she was high. She wept for her more innocent self deceived by this woman who promised so much. In his clumsiness he asked her, 'So do you love her still?'

'No,' she said. 'I never loved her. The person I thought I loved was an illusion. No more real than Luigi.' She had a bit more of a cry, then dried her eyes, and as she blinked she smiled and said, 'I'm so lucky. I've got Lily and I've got you. One day I'll have her all to myself. You know, she forgives me everything. And so, I like to believe, do you.'

'Nothing to forgive; just one question,' Paz said. 'What will Luigi do now?'

She was composed, businesslike. 'That's the easy part. Luigi, you see, is a very religious man. He won't appreciate receiving such pictures when his 'poor master' is dying. He's married anyway. He will simply not respond. I know what you're thinking: How far will Jude go if she gets mad? Well, she won't. She's not in Venice and I doubt she's even in France. She'll be in bed in Glasgow with Scottie and a laptop, smoking a joint or eating peanuts, wondering whether her "dating game" experiment has worked.' She pointed at Jude's picture, 'What did I ever see in that?' She had a few more impromptu tears and then smiled again and said, 'Now let's talk about something else.'

Chapter 5

The Suitor

Paz welcomed a brother and sister, Tosh and Jess Manders, into his office, although he soon couldn't resist taking a dislike to them. In their mid-thirties, they were both well-dressed and superficially attractive, but their eyes were dull and they seemed agitated, as if from lack of sleep or excess of caffeine. Tosh in particular seemed overly urgent in manner and somewhat arrogant, as though regarding Paz merely a necessary nuisance.

Paz's client list, if based on personal liking, would be a short one. He dealt in human failings, and that applied as much to his clients as anyone else. This pair appeared almost wilfully unprepared for the meeting, as though anticipating likely questions was a concession they were unwilling to make for such as him.

Their problem, however, fascinated him. Their father had died leaving millions to their mother, and since then she had been swept up into the arms of an American businessman, by name of Strenger. The siblings were worried that he was only interested in her money. They said Strenger had been married at least twice before and had 'mislaid' both known wives in strange circumstances.

'Apart from it seeming odd to you, do you have any real grounds for suspicion?' Paz asked.

Tosh said, 'Our mum's unworldly and easily hoodwinked. We want to believe in him, but we don't understand, apart from the money, why he'd be interested in her. We believe he learned of her inheritance before he met her.'

'I see. And what do you want me to do exactly?'

'Find out what you can about him.' Tosh was already on his feet, indicating he was keen to be somewhere else.

'Hopefully all bad, right?'

Tosh could not prevent a slight smile but then said hurriedly, 'We are genuinely openminded. We're just keen to know the truth and protect our mum.'

Paz did not believe they were openminded, but he saw it could be lucrative work. If the evidence didn't support their fears and hopes, they'd keep wanting more until it did. That's if they could afford the fees. But he was disappointed at himself for thinking that way.

After they'd left, Paz and Mack had a look at Strenger online. There were YouTube videos about a financial services company he ran. He struck Paz as a typical amiable conman, always so impressive at presentations. If he had money to play with, he might, in a weaker moment, have been tempted himself; but he didn't, so was not at risk. He was expecting to find a racket, but it was not an obvious one. There were no fake-looking testimonials of people saying how they'd got their promised returns on time and were now investing twice as much. There was no-one complaining about being cheated out of their savings, or 'experts' warning against the company. But Paz couldn't see the business had any function beyond pushing the investment.

Of greater interest to him and Mack, their clients, and various true crime aficionados, were the deaths of Strenger's two former wives. His first, Amanda, had fallen down the main stairs of their house. She was known to have been suffering from depression, and high levels of tranquillisers were found in her blood. The accepted narrative was that she had fatally injured herself whilst heavily sedated. Strenger claimed he did not see or hear her fall. He was out in the garage when a neighbour called round and asked him to help him start his car, which he did. The neighbour confirmed this was correct. Whilst still out of the house, he noticed a child had been injured in the street, possibly from a hit and run, and rushed to help, then waited with the family until the ambulance arrived. By the time he'd returned to his garage, done some tidying up, gone into the house and discovered his wife, she could have been at the bottom of the stairs for an hour and a half. He was crying down the phone on the 911 call, and the story he later told detectives sounded persuasive, neat and plausible; he had answers to every question and alibis who could vouch for him.

Paz was inherently suspicious of such people. He could easily imagine Strenger telling one of his investors, with an entirely neat and plausible explanation, how their fund had dropped one hundred per cent overnight to nothing, and make it sound like he'd done them the biggest favour ever, full knowing they would put even more money in. People like Strenger were a pain. They sold you a dream and made you think the dream was what you really wanted; you lost but you had fun doing so. He'd gladly steal your shirt, sell it back to you and still keep you happy - and everyone else too, it seemed, except his potential stepchildren and a few websleuths. Paz fully understood his clients' concern. Their mum might easily be coerced into marrying him or conned into giving him all her money, and the family couldn't afford any financial reverses. Their own business was in serious trouble, according to Mack's research.

Strenger's second wife had also suffered a fall, although this was more dramatic. A hiking trip in the Santa Ana mountains had ended in tragedy. She lost her footing, stepping backwards in preparation for a photograph he was taking, and fell a hundred feet to her death. Exactly as he'd been over his first wife's demise, he was distraught and, once again, no blame attached to him. He had told her to step forward but she'd stepped back instead. He even had a witness who confirmed seeing her lose her footing. It was tragic, but Strenger's story was so neat and plausible he attracted great sympathy. He was one of life's unfortunates, destined never to have a long marriage. It was not only sympathy he attracted; women felt the need to comfort him and look after him, this attraction not in the least associated with the million dollar life insurance he had on his second wife, nor the two million dollars her employer's accidental death policy paid out. He was not a lavish spender. He lived well but not ostentatiously. His house was comfortable in a smart part of town, but even the most Spartan of critics would not find it extravagant. This made Paz wonder whether the life insurances, including that on his first wife, were used in the main to keep his financial enterprise afloat.

Enquiries confirmed the police did not have an open file on either death. To them Strenger was simply unlucky, or more particularly those who married him were. Paz thought he would not want a loved one of his to marry such a man. Life with Strenger, it seemed, offered an agreeable if not overly exciting experience with a sudden ending.

After a few days, Paz reported back to the clients his initial findings, adding that he proposed to continue investigating. They were impatient for results so insisted he continue but 'as quickly as possible', lest their mother be flown to Las Vegas for a quick visit to a wedding chapel.

Further research revealed that the family of one of the deceased wives was dissatisfied with the outcome of the police investigation and was pressing them to reopen the case. This was invariably what happened with mysterious deaths; someone always wanted the investigation to go on. Paz reached out to the family of Barbara, the wife who'd fallen in the mountains. They had appointed their own investigator. This person had a thorough reputation and was someone he knew. Paz rang him.

He told Paz the witness to the accident had been compromised. He hadn't seen the fall. He was a very isolated person who was wary of human contact. That was why he'd originally said it was an accident with Barbara instinctively stepping backwards. She was physically smaller and probably felt intimidated, as indeed did the witness who was afraid of Strenger. He told the investigator he saw Strenger step forward towards his wife and believed he pushed her but could not be certain because his view was obstructed by rocks. He'd been afraid that if Strenger saw him he might push him over the edge too. The investigator planned to speak to the police to persuade them to reopen the file, as well as that on the death of first wife Amanda. This was not without risk; Strenger reportedly had family connections who were criminals and could easily hire a hit man to fix the investigator. Private investigators often had plenty of actual or potential enemies, as Paz knew well enough.

In the following weeks, the investigator was successful in that the police reopened their files on both deaths. This information was exactly what Paz's clients were hoping for. They were delighted, and even more so when their mother broke off her relationship with Strenger after she heard about the files being reopened. At her children's insistence, she returned to the UK. Their mother, and, indeed their future inheritance, were safe. Five million pounds sterling and more.

But neither mother nor inheritance remained safe for long. Ostensibly to flee the police investigation, Strenger pursued their mother to the UK, and with persistence was able to rekindle the relationship. He began staying at the family house, while the loving couple made plans to hire a car for a trip to explore England, which he claimed he'd always longed to see. All this threw Tosh and Jess into a panic. They warned their mother against it, but by now she was completely under his influence.

The night prior to leaving for their trip, their mother and Strenger were to attend a cocktail party in recognition of her work as a philanthropist, but Strenger surprisingly developed stomach pains and cried off. Consequently, Tosh agreed to take her in the hire car, as she'd requested. Tragically, on the way into town the car veered off the road and crashed into a bridge wall. The mother was killed when her air bag failed to operate; Tosh was injured.

Tosh and Jess wanted Strenger charged, claiming he'd tampered with the air bag, but the police did not arrest him and he slipped back to the US.

It was the third suspicious death involving Strenger and it was obvious to the British tabloids he was responsible. The circumstances played on Paz's mind. Strenger was no fool. Unless he was a psychopath, which he might be, he had no obvious motive. But then Paz discovered through his clients that Strenger had already obtained life insurance on her, and it all fell into place.

Paz couldn't avoid feelings of guilt, however. His assignment had been intended to save his clients' mother from harm, and he'd failed, even though he couldn't think of anything more he might have done. Strenger had not been charged with anything and was a free agent.

The unease he felt remained until Jess arrived in his office one morning. She looked as though she hadn't slept for a month. Paz gave her his condolences and she burst into tears. She sat down and he comforted her as best he could. Suddenly businesslike, she said she'd come to settle his account and apologised for not paying it earlier. He was tempted to waive it but then remembered the size of some recent bills; indeed, he thought she might be insulted by such a gesture. She thanked him for his work and revealed her next stop was the local police station. She said she had new evidence. When he looked at her for elaboration she added, 'Please don't misunderstand me. I'm grateful for what you did, Mr Wheat, but if Strenger had been driving that car my mother might be alive today.'

Paz was aware of his eyebrows raising. 'Really? What does your brother say about it?'

'We're not speaking just now,' she said. 'It's too upsetting. He's still in hospital but will soon be home.' With that she stood up.

'I'm sorry to hear that. Grief can—'

'It's not about grief, Mr Wheat.' She turned to leave.

'Wait,' he insisted. 'Please explain.'

She turned on her heel and faced him, her eyes hard. 'To be a successful criminal, I suspect you need to keep your mouth shut. The likes of Mr Strenger know that. My brother, however, does not. It was he who tampered with the air bag, Mr Wheat, not Strenger. He told me he believed it right in order to save our inheritance. Of course I could never condone such an utterly despicable act.'

Chapter 6

Junk

One afternoon, Paz arrived back at the office to find Mack talking with his nemesis: the loss adjuster Fran Owens, in his unbuttoned honey-coloured trench coat and looking more condescending and august than he remembered.

'Ah, Mr Wheat, my favourite Anglo-American,' he said.

'This is a surprise.' Paz was suspicious: Fran preferred the phone and rarely visited. He wanted something Paz would probably rather not give. It was unlike him to arrive unannounced. No doubt, Mack would soon receive a job offer.

The two men shook hands stiffly. 'Good to see you, Paz.'

'Been a while,' Paz observed. They retired to his private office.

'I'm hoping you can assist me,' said the unwanted visitor, who decided not to remove his coat.

'Always keen to help someone on the same side,' said Paz, gesturing him to a chair. 'I assume it's something local. Not just in town for the sea air.'

'I'll get straight to the point. I'm sure you're almost as busy as me. What do you know about Freddie Hiseman?' Paz felt that 'almost'.

'Of Freddie's Emporium fame? Been in business longer than I have. Or you. Married, three grownup kids. Drives an old MG. Good reputation. His prices - what he pays and what he sells for - are considered fair by those in the know. So he doesn't make a lot of money. What have you got on him?'

'An artwork to find. My insured reported it missing, insurers paid out, but then my insured got a call to say it had shown up in Fred Hiseman's shop in Brighton. Fair enough, but then it's not there and, to cap it all, he's denying ever having it.'

'What sort of value are we talking?'

'Thirty thousand pounds.'

'Really!? You're joking, aren't you? That's not Fred. Thirty thousand cobwebs more like, every one intact. Police?'

'Not enough for them to work with. I thought maybe you could assist with this curious situation.'

'Be glad to.' Work was welcome, even from Fran.

After the adjuster had gone, Paz discussed the case with Mack. She said politely it would have saved time if he'd let her attend the meeting with 'Mr Owens'. This irritated him. She immediately brought up a picture of the artwork on her screen because Fran had already told her about it. This annoyed him further, but he was determined not to show it, especially if Fran had sown the seed of alternative employment with her. The picture was by the artist Charles Berriman who produced smallish cityscapes with surrealist flourishes, especially using words, such as a man being attacked by a gang of French verbs or a murmuration of English pronouns. Mack also showed him a press article indicating some of the gentleman's work was missing, meaning: not in the hands of galleries or known collectors. The piece in question had first come to light within the last ten years but had never been formally confirmed as a Berriman.

Paz decided to pay Fred a visit. He found him rather like his shop - dusty and tired with the odd flash of brightness. What he immediately noticed on this occasion was that Fred was inundated with stock. 'So much junk, I don't know where to put it all,' he complained. 'I've got a room at the back I'm having to open up for it now.' Paz asked him about the Berriman.

'Not you as well!' Fred exclaimed. 'I might have guessed this wasn't a social visit.'

'Sorry, Fred.'

'You're the third person to ask about it. I've had a loss adjuster, that Mr Owens, then a woman from High Wycombe on the phone.'

'Was she from a gallery?'

'No. So far as I know, an antiques collector who'd heard I'd got it. I don't understand it. I never had it in the first place. It's not the kind of thing I sell. I wish it was. She told me to let her know if it came in. It was before that Owens called round. I was going to tell him, but I didn't like his rather accusatory manner, and I was hoping the issue would just go away. Now you've showed up, I'll give her details to you.' He had a look over his desk for the phone number and then consulted a shabby old book. He couldn't find the number. All he remembered was the name: Hogan.

When Paz returned to the office he had Mack see if she could find a Hogan in the art or antiques world in High Wycombe. She found one running an antiques shop in the area. Paz rang Fran Owens to let him know. It transpired he already knew of Hogan's interest though he didn't reveal how, and he said Fred was wrong; this Mrs Hogan wasn't in High Wycombe at all but West Worthing, only a few miles from Brighton. Had Fred merely made a mistake, or was he trying to mislead? Paz concluded they ought to start a little surveillance on Fred because he knew Fran would insist on it. He talked to Mack and they decided to try one of the freelance investigators he was interested in using for straightforward cases. Meanwhile, he would visit Mrs Hogan in West Worthing himself.

When he arrived he found her shop shut. Not merely for the day but, it appeared, closed down for good. He looked through the barred windows. There were only a few objects he could see in there: a couple of large vases on the floor, a desk. He assumed there was nothing of value. He tried the door. No joy. There was a metal staircase next to the shop, and he followed it up to a flat. The name written next to the bell was the one he was looking for. The door was answered by a middle-aged, nervy-looking woman smoking a roll-up cigarette. 'Mrs Hogan?'

'Everyone's asking for her, it seems. Have you come about antiques?'

'Yes.'

'I regret to advise that Mrs Hogan has passed away,' she said without emotion. 'I'm her niece.'

'Oh dear.' He paused for a moment. 'I'm very sorry for your loss. Had she been ill, then?'

'No, all quite sudden,' she replied brusquely. 'Can I ask the nature of your business?'

He handed her his card and explained he'd been asked to investigate a missing artwork by Charles Berriman which her aunt had apparently been enquiring after. The woman revealed that a collector had asked Mrs Hogan to try and obtain it for him.

'Was your aunt an expert on art?'

'She knew a bit.'

'Was there a particular reason the collector asked her? Had they bought other things from her?'

'Possibly. I know she didn't like dealing with him because he was so persistent.'

'Was he local? I assume he must have been.'

'I don't know. I'm thinking, maybe Portsmouth? I suspected he was hoping for a relationship with her. Not purely business. That's what I wondered. His various requests were more like an excuse. But any interest he might have had in her was not reciprocated. They never met. I don't recall his name, but I can look in her contacts book. I haven't it to hand so would have to hunt for it. I can get back to you.'

Paz thanked her. He felt he'd imposed enough on her at a difficult time so he left. He wasn't optimistic he'd hear from her.

When he arrived in the office, Mack told him there'd been a setback. The freelancer he'd chosen had advised that he could not take the job. Paz thought maybe the reason was a conflict, but if so he could at least try to pick his brain. He phoned him and the man revealed he was a personal friend of Fred Hiseman so could not do surveillance work on him. He added that Fred had been under a great deal of pressure lately and he didn't want to add to it.

From the man's tone, however, Paz sensed the friendship had perhaps deteriorated, so he asked, 'What kind of pressure?'

'Divorce,' he said. 'That and drink. He's losing it. Both literally and metaphorically. It's not impossible Fred had the artwork and simply forgot about it, even forgot to record having it.'

'Hard to believe. Are you sure?'

'Absolutely.'

Before Paz left the office that evening he received a surprise call from Mrs Hogan's niece: 'I thought I'd let you know, I heard from that man again, the one asking after the Berriman. I don't know why he rang me. I'm not in the antiques business.'

'So what did he say?'

'He asked me, was I absolutely sure my aunt didn't acquire one? He also asked me to let him know if I heard from anyone about it, anyone having located one, or enquiring. Obviously, I didn't tell him about you. His name's Hawker and he's in Pulborough.'

On the way out, he noticed in the window of the bookshop at the front, a volume of French poetry, thinking it a possible present for Mack's birthday. The owner, Mr Cairns, was a habitual drunk but also the landlord, so Paz bought the occasional book to show his support.

That night, the warehouse where most of the late Mrs Hogan's stock had been stored was raided by burglars. Paz phoned the niece next morning. No answer. He figured she was busy with the warehouse owner and the police. It was late in the afternoon that she returned his call, informing him nothing of her aunt's had been taken. It made him wonder if she had a proper handle on the inventory. 'So other people did suffer losses, right?'

'Some fine arts, tapestries, silverware, the odd painting.'

'Paintings? Who by?'

'I don't know. I know the man who owned them, so I can ask.'

'No, don't worry.' When he got off the phone he was surprised to see Fred Hiseman in the office. He did not look in a good mood. 'Fred, this is a nice surprise.'

'Not for me, it isn't. I want to know why you're following me. I've known you for years. I've even put work your way. Why would you do this to me? You want to know something, you ask. I told you I didn't have anything on that damned artwork. Don't you trust me?'

Paz tried to console him. 'Fred, Fred, we're not following you. We haven't been asked to. I'm not saying we would anyway, but no client has asked us.' This was strictly true, even if highly misleading.

'Well, someone has asked someone because I've seen him. He's not very discreet.'

Fred continued complaining, but fortunately Mack came in with an urgent message on another insurance case - one that was going to court - and at this point Fred decided not to wait, leaving looking harassed and confused.

'What do you make of it?' Paz asked Mack after relaying his brief conversation with Fred.

'It can't be Mr Voller, can it?' she said, referring to the freelancer who'd declined the job.

'I bet it can,' he said. 'I bet he's retained by the wife, Fred accosted him, and he told him he was working for us. So he starts being nice to Fred while he's really working for the wife and passing on all his secrets to her. See how it works? See what you're getting into?'

She grinned. 'I like it.'

'Believe me, there's no trust in this game.'

Mack tracked down Hawker's location and Paz went out to visit him in Pulborough. It was an impressive-looking house set back off the road. The door was answered by a young woman who had the kind of distracting beauty that almost made him forget his age. He explained who he was looking for, and it transpired that Mrs Hogan's niece had been mistaken: it was a *Ms* Hawker who'd phoned, her voice just sounded like a man's. She was tall and had long straight brown hair, large blue eyes, a relaxed smile, and cherry-red lips. She walked slowly and sedately as she led him to her study. 'I was expecting you,' she said, as they sat down. This took him aback. He could only think that Mrs Hogan's niece had told her.

'So do you know where this piece by Charles Berriman is?' she said.

'I wish I did. I don't like mysteries. Until I've solved them, that is, then I love them.'

'You're working for Fran Owens, aren't you?' He nodded. 'Dear Fran,' she said.

'How come you know him?'

'You know him, so why shouldn't I?' She took a card from the top drawer of her desk. She was a private investigator, too.

'Oh boy!' He was pleased to be sitting down.

She brought out Cuban cigars and offered him one. He demurred and then watched her cut one and light it. 'I've done work for Fran too,' she said. 'I'm the opposite of you - a Brit working in the US.' Paz pointed out he was a dual national and she said, 'Oh, excuse me,' sarcastically. 'You must be telling people that all the time.'

'Only when it matters. Aren't you living here, then?'

'Only temporarily while I sort this out - which I will. This and a couple of other matters, also for insurers. But don't worry, I'm not after your patch.'

'Believe me, there's enough work for a hundred patches.'

'But I only work for insurers,' she said, 'although I don't know why. They can be terriers when it comes to fees. I think you work for all sorts.'

He let the snobbish dig pass. He wasn't in the mood for a spat with a fellow PI. She ordered coffee and a maid brought it in. His guess was that although her stay was 'temporary' she or perhaps the young woman (her daughter, he wondered?) owned the house. He could almost smell inheritance money. 'So you're on this case too. How can we both be working for insurers on the same case?' he said. 'Are there different insureds involved?'

'Indeed there are,' she said, 'and only one of them, my client's insured, is the rightful owner. Your clients' insured never owned it. So your clients paid out incorrectly, based on dear Fran's recommendations. But Fran's OK. He will be able to report to his insurers that they're due their money back and make himself a hero. The only loser is you, because you will have nothing to investigate.'

'I beg your pardon, Ms Hawker, but the artwork is still missing.'

'That's not your concern. I will send documentary proof to Fran that my client's insured, a highly-respected businessman, is the rightful owner, and Fran will then ask you to close your file.'

The sad thing was that he would be unable to hear their conversation. Fran was an ornery bastard and he would challenge any documents put before him. 'Why don't you phone him now to let him know the paperwork's coming?' said Paz.

'And I can put him on speaker so you hear his reaction - what a good idea. No thanks. I know what he's like. He'd argue like the devil over ten cents. No, I can't let you have the pleasure of hearing me grappling with him. He can't argue with the documents.'

'He can. He can ask to see the originals in his office. And until he hauls me off the case I'll continue to work on it, and obviously I'm honour-bound to tell him of this conversation. And, through my various contacts, I might still find the thing before you do.'

She relaxed. She clearly liked to spar a little. They stopped talking about the case and chatted about others they'd been working on. They even exchanged a couple of contacts they'd found useful. One of her specialities, she said, was marine work, which was maybe why he hadn't recognised the name at first.

One person who knew Hawker's work well was Fran Owens. 'She's even slower than you are,' he said. 'At least you send in your reports just about timely. I can never get them out of her.' Having told Fran that Mrs Hogan's 'enquirer' was in fact another investigator, Paz introduced him to the allegation that his clients' insured never had the art to lose in the first place. His reaction was suitably fierce, and when Paz asked him if he could continue to investigate he became annoyed: 'Yes! And hurry up and find something. I don't need someone to not find things. Anyone can do that.'

Paz told Mack they had to prioritise the case, although in reality they had nothing to go on. At that moment he received a call from, of all people, Voller, the freelance man shadowing Fred Hiseman for his wife. Paz had used him a couple of times, Jane had found him good, and despite him setting Paz up by telling Fred that he, his old mate, had him under surveillance, with all the embarrassment that caused, he wouldn't rule out using him in future. Consequently, he asked to meet him. Although it was clearly not Voller's preference, he agreed, and so they met in a pub near the office, one which usually gave plenty of opportunity for quiet chat.

Voller was a tall, lean man with black-rimmed spectacles and long hands. He was a little nervy and Paz believed this was the way he normally was, rather than any apprehension about meeting him in such circumstances. When Voller had bought the drinks and they'd ordered food, he apologised profusely over the embarrassment concerning Fred which he said had been unavoidable. Paz wasn't so easily convinced and let his expression make that clear, but he was prepared to give him the benefit of the doubt. Voller was intense and Paz figured that following people was merely an extension of what he did anyway; he reportedly walked around town looking at everyone and everything with the same close attention even when not working. Paz would have preferred someone less tall in a freelance team, but he had a reputation, with Jane at least, of being thorough. Voller then explained the surprising story of how Fred let this supposedly valuable artwork (nominally thirty thousand pounds, way more than anything he would normally hold), in and out of his hands without even knowing it.

Voller had learned, through working for Fred's wife Miranda, that her erstwhile lover, a man called Mayberry, was something of an art connoisseur, or at least fancied himself one. Mayberry had heard through criminal contacts that the Berriman was available, the thief being keen to dispose of it. He also knew of someone interested in possessing it. Mayberry therefore bought it, with a view to immediately selling it for a worthwhile profit, except he did not want to be identified in any way in these transactions. Accordingly, Mayberry arranged with Miranda for the artwork to pass through Fred's books. This they did when Fred was on one of his routine business trips. They put it briefly on display in the shop, photographed it there, then sold it on to the buyer already lined up. Mayberry kept part of the profit and left a thousand for Fred which was then reflected in the shop's books. When Miranda informed Fred, somewhat obliquely and without details, about this uncharacteristically large transaction, Fred, who wasn't exactly making real money from his shop, was happy not to ask questions.

'Maybe I'm missing something, but why photograph it? Was that not incriminating?'

'Incriminating for Fred if he ever became difficult over it.'

'OK. You said "erstwhile lover", so this man's out of the picture. Is he contactable?'

'He's changed his phone number and dropped off social media.'

'He hasn't been nobbled, has he?' said Paz, half-joking.

'Could be.' He gave Paz a sceptical look. 'What would the motive be? This is not America. This is not your Wild West.'

'OK, OK,' Paz replied wearily. 'Unless Miranda got mad with him, thinking that he maybe used her. I don't know.'

On his way back to the office, Paz called in on the bookseller / landlord and asked him how many customers he'd had. 'Three,' he said, heavily boozed. 'Two hundred pounds, though.'

'Make it four,' said Paz on seeing a Sherlock Holmes book on a dusty display stand, and he gave him five pounds.

A few minutes later, Paz was talking to Mack about what Voller had said, only to be surprised when in walked the man's client, none other than Miranda Hiseman, spouting fury. She appeared in a bright blue and crimson dress, and with her red hair she reminded Paz of a freshly lit bonfire. Her mood was of that ilk too. 'Why are you making enquiries about Juan Mayberry!?'

'I'm sorry,' he said. 'I didn't know I was. I assume you are referring to the Berriman matter.'

'The what? That painting? All above board. What is it you want to know?'

'I've been asked to track the item down for insurers who paid a claim on it. They are entitled to its recovery.'

'Juan never did anything wrong. Not over that, at least. He's a rat alright, but that's nothing to do with it.'

'Who did he buy it off and where is it now?'

'I don't know the answer to either question, and I don't even know where he is. He was living out Hastings way. That's where he was when I met him.' Her tone softened. 'All a bit of a whirlwind, it was.'

'I see,' Paz said. 'And what does Mr Mayberry do for a living?'

'He buys and sells. Sharp, he is. Very sharp. He doesn't like to hang on to things long. Lives out of a suitcase, so far as I could tell. Has no premises. Uses his hotel room as an office for a week or so, then off he goes again. Does everything on his phone.'

'And is Mayberry his real name?'

'I don't know. He has lots of names, I believe. Mayberry, Maycock, Mayflower, Mailham. He was staying at the White Hotel.'

'Do you have a picture of him?'

'No, but his business is now on Facebook under Mailham Enterprises.'

Either Voller hadn't known that, or was concealing it. 'Show me,' said Paz. 'He handed her his laptop and within a few moments she had the page up. He then handed the laptop to Mack who could extract all the data they might want. Mrs Hiseman left soon after, leaving a business card bearing Mayberry's name.

From Mack's analysis of Facebook, Paz decided that Mayberry's next destination would likely be Whitstable. From the picture he'd created in his mind about the man, he surmised Juan would choose a hotel on the seafront with a balcony and spectacular views. The latest Facebook photograph he'd put up supported this and Mack settled on one particular hotel. Paz concurred.

Mack persuaded Paz to take her with him. When they arrived at the hotel in the early evening she told him she had a plan to find Mayberry's room. She seemed determined, so Paz decided to let her. He would take a seat in the lobby and observe.

Mack walked to the front desk and asked for 'Mr Juan Mayberry'. When the young clerk hesitated she showed him the man's business card and then entrapped him with an appealing glance. The clerk, unnerved, said he could neither confirm nor deny whether Mayberry was staying there. 'But he told me he was,' she complained loudly and tears began to appear in her eyes. She told him she'd met Mayberry in a bar the night before and he'd invited her to dinner, saying he was staying at this particular hotel and she should meet him there. He hadn't known the room number because he wasn't checked in. 'I'm his dinner date,' she insisted, giving the name Tina, her voice rising.

Flustered, the clerk asked her to step away from the desk and please sit down. She did so and began playing with the business card between her fingers. She and Paz did not communicate with each other, even by glance. Paz was impressed.

A few minutes later, a puzzled Mayberry, lanky-looking, in his forties, appeared and walked to the desk. The clerk pointed out Mack, and a bemused Mayberry came over, 'Tina?' he enquired.

It was Mack's turn to look confused. She told him he wasn't the 'Juan Mayberry' she'd met in the bar. Was this some kind of joke? If so, she didn't appreciate it. She started to make a scene and Mayberry snatched the business card from her and retreated to the lifts. This was Paz's cue and Mack, still performing the deceived victim role, marched outside and then took up a position from which to watch the front door and car park should Mayberry leave.

Paz stepped into the lift behind their target. He had already decided the man would not be too handy if it came to violence. When Mayberry exited on the top floor, Paz followed him but hung back a little. Then as he entered his room Paz rushed towards the door and pushed his way in behind him.

Mayberry was bewildered. Paz showed him his own card. 'What do you want?' the man said. In his haggard face Paz saw up close decades of petty betrayals and running from consequences. At first Mayberry looked about to fight it out, but then he wilted. 'Tell me what you want.'

'I'm investigating the theft of a piece of artwork by Charles Berriman which I believe you know about. I believe you have sold such a piece.'

'Are you with the cops?'

'The police are not involved but they may be later. I'm working for insurers. I believe you sold it through Fred Hiseman's shop while he was away on business and that you shared the profit with him.'

'Profit?'

'Come on, Mayberry, you're not going to suggest to me there was no profit involved.'

'OK,' he said mournfully. 'I assume you want to know where it is now.'

'Correct.'

'I can't recall. It'll be in Fred's book.'

'Look, I didn't come all the way out here to be told you can't recall.'

The man didn't know what to do. He was cornered. If he tried to punch Paz out - an unlikely prospect - he would have to flee to somewhere else. If he called the police, out would come the fact of his handling stolen goods. 'OK,' he said nervously. 'The company that bought it is called WDR or BDW or something like that.'

'Come now, a name please. You're not telling me you go around using acronyms all the time.' Paz pursued him around the room. He didn't want to strong-arm the guy but his patience was running out. 'What's the problem?' he said. 'If you did nothing wrong, why the secret?'

Mayberry gave up. He had no choice. 'Wace,' he said. 'Ronald Wace. A military man.'

'Address?'

'That I don't know. It was sold through the shop, as you know.'

'I don't know anything,' Paz replied. 'Just hearsay.'

'I believe Wace is a regular at Fred Hiseman's.'

'Excellent, Mr Mayberry.' Then his reluctant host told him he remembered the buyer's name was not Wace, but Waites. John Waites.

Paz was enjoying himself. 'OK, Mayberry, one other thing: Who sold you the item in the first place?' At this Mayberry grabbed a glass ashtray and went to throw it. Paz put his hands up to his face. Mayberry charged for the door, catching Paz off balance. He was out and on the stairs leaping his way down while Paz was still in the room doorway.

Paz reproached himself for his complacency and slowness. Maybe he'd been working out too much, or too little. He decided not to pursue him but instead use the opportunity to look through the evidence left behind.

First, he rang Mack to warn her Mayberry was on his way to the exit. If he went to his car she would catch the registration number, although ultimately they probably wouldn't need it. Mayberry had left a few phone numbers on the table. He put them together and took a photograph of them. He didn't learn much else. Mayberry's case was locked and since Paz already knew he wasn't the main interest in the matter, he wasn't going to damage his personal property.

Later, in the car Mack did a quick internet search of the phone numbers Paz had found. This told them the next place Mayberry was likely to grace with his presence was Hull. They decided they did not need to wait for his return to the hotel.

Next morning, back in Brighton, Paz and Mack went through the various John Waites. They settled on one in a small village twenty miles away; he had a website dedicated to art. Paz decided they'd both go. He then hesitated, wondering whether to give Fran Owens the opportunity to tell Captain Waites he'd bought stolen property. But maybe Waites had himself sold it on. Collectible art could change hands multiple times. Because they'd had a sudden influx of new work in the office, Paz thought about phoning Waites instead. He would merely find out if he had it, then report back to Fran. No, that was unsatisfactory; he always said there was no substitute for physically being there.

Waites' house was a pretty little mock-Elizabethan place that was obviously worth millions. Mack remarked on how the path and garden conveyed a sense of order and tidiness. Paz rang the bell. After a long pause a small raddled woman came to the door. Paz asked to see the Captain, explaining they were investigators on an insurance case. She became visibly nervous. 'I'm afraid my husband is not well; he is not up to seeing visitors today. Perhaps you could call another time.'

'May we ask what's the matter with him?' said Mack.

'It's PTSD. He saw some terrible things in his military career and it has wrecked his health. Some days he's better than others. Today is a bad day.'

'I see,' said Paz. 'Could you tell us whether he recently bought a painting by Charles Berriman?'

'I don't know. He's an art collector, I can tell you that, so it's quite possible he did. It would have been a reputable dealer.'

He made a point of not looking at her. By no stretch of his imagination could Juan Mayberry be considered a 'reputable dealer'. She was looking to end the conversation, but Paz wasn't conceding just yet. He and Mack kept her talking, playing for time until the moment came they were waiting for. Eventually, there was a shout from upstairs, 'It's alright, Maisie, send them up. We might as well get it over with. They'll only come back.'

Reluctantly she led them upstairs to see the Captain. Like everything else they'd seen inside and out, his study was extremely tidy. Behind a large desk sat a withered man. Glancing at the proud soldier Paz saw in the photograph on the wall, he felt a pang of sorrow for the hollow wretch now before them. Paz produced a business card but the Captain did not look at it. 'What have you come about?' he demanded, even though it was obvious he knew. He merely wanted that little extra time to prepare himself. Paz explained why they were there.

'My wife is correct. I do suffer from PTSD, and today it is particularly bad. Perhaps, however, it is made worse by circumstances. This visit by yourselves will not serve to alleviate it, I'm afraid.'

'I'm sorry,' said Paz.

'Oh, I'm sure you are genuinely sorry. I'm afraid I have been rather... foolish or unfortunate, I don't know which. I unwittingly bought a piece of stolen property. I had no idea. Not at the time anyway. I bought it in good faith from a man called Mayberry. I didn't trust him, but I am a collector of Berriman. Or at least, I have been; I may give it up now and sell what I have. I have never had this situation before.'

'When did you first learn it was stolen?' Mack asked him.

'Someone came to see me. Just like you coming to see me now. They knew I'd bought it because I'd mentioned it on my blog—' Paz heard Mack sigh at having missed this '—and I was known by fellow collectors of Berriman. They told me the story behind it.' Paz wanted to ask who'd visited him but let him continue, 'It was an awful meeting. They said they were reporting to insurers. I didn't know whether to believe them or not. I insisted I'd bought it in good faith but they brushed that aside. I had stolen property and had to give it back to the rightful owners. They became quite aggressive about it. Then they said, to avoid prosecution I could swap it for another Berriman that was fake. The man then went to their car and returned with something in a similar style to what I'd bought, and he explained how I could tell it was fake, a piece of junk. I felt foolish because I thought I should have known already.' The Captain then produced from behind his desk the picture and showed them how, according to his visitors, to tell from the signature it was fake.

At last Paz understood. 'Tell me more about who it was visited you.'

'A man and a woman came. The woman talked in a deep voice. I think the man was there mainly as a threat, although they didn't actually threaten me physically.' He then gave a description of the woman.

Paz thanked the Captain profusely, said they had information on the seller they'd pass to the police and they'd do whatever they could to help him recover his money. As soon as they were in the car, he phoned Fran Owens. 'Fran, I'm pretty sure we've located the Berriman artwork.'

'You have?'

'Yes. Your friend Hawker. Ms Hawker.'

'No friend to me.'

'It's alright, I meant it ironically. We've met the man who gave it to her in return for a fake. You can bet your life she's either left the country or is about to.'

Fran sounded pleased, which he rarely did. Paz was so gratified he promised to treat Mack to an expensive lunch.

On the drive back to Brighton, Mack talked excitedly about the case and Mayberry and the Captain and the fake piece. She said, 'I know there's a lesson in all this, but I'm not sure what it is.'

Paz replied, 'To me it's that we compartmentalise too much. I saw Hawker as an investigator only. It never occurred to me she could be a collector as well. Or, more particularly, a con artist.'

Chapter 7

The Fringie

Paz had known the Fringie, by name of Stony Lake, for several years, although not closely. He'd seen him around town at odd times - slight, mid-thirties, always a little offbeat, with his moustache and goatee beard, and dressed in denim jeans and buckskin jacket. Paz had chatted with him a few times. He always had a story to tell. He knew what was going on in the city and was a brilliant reader of the street. Paz felt he could learn much from him. But Lake was solitary by nature. He'd see him sometimes with another person, usually only one, or perhaps on the edge of a group, but he always seemed to be the outsider observing, analysing. He was a mystery and that was the way he liked it. Brighton was his base, to the extent he had one. He appeared rootless. He travelled abroad often, though Paz wondered how he afforded it.

On this occasion, the Fringie had just come from India, so Paz heard him tell a couple in the Three Jolly Butchers pub. He'd been at an ashram, though Paz doubted he would have been taking much spiritual instruction. He'd have been on the periphery, playing some practical role: looking after the gardens, driving to pick up groceries. He never had any money because he preferred a situation where he could work for his keep. Then he'd be back in Brighton, selling artefacts he'd picked up cheap, presumably to help fund his airfares, and scrounging off friends for a place to stay.

Then Paz heard a rumour that Stony had suddenly left. A few days later, while calling about something else, Paz asked mutual friend Zeke

Brown, a freelance investigator he sometimes used: 'Seen old Stony lately?'

'Stony Lake? He was around last week but he's gone again.'

'That's what he always does, isn't it? I don't know him well but that's my impression.'

'He told me he'd be around for a while. But I guess he's always on his way somewhere.'

That was the thing: how would you ever know if he'd disappeared? The fact Zeke hadn't seen him either bothered Paz. He felt protective towards the Fringie, even while he guessed Stony would resent that.

A few days later, Zeke appeared in Paz's office. He was tall and lean with a wide smile. Mack seemed transfixed by his appearance and beamed when he said, 'You must be Paz's delightful new assistant I've heard so much about. You know Paz is technically dead, so any life you breathe into the place will be welcome.' She laughed, but only politely as she did not want to hurt her boss's feelings.

'Alright, Alright,' Paz chuntered. He was used to Zeke's digs. It was Paz who gave Zeke his first job, and underneath the banter there was much affection and respect. When they'd sat down together over coffee, Zeke told him there was growing concern about the Fringie. People who knew him best said they were certain he'd intended to still be around in Brighton, but he wasn't in his usual haunts.

Paz said, 'You know, putting out a missing person search on him would be pointless. He could be anywhere. The police wouldn't get involved.'

'I don't know,' said Zeke. 'It doesn't feel right.' Paz asked him if Stony had any family in the area. 'I don't know,' he repeated.

'Where does he normally stay?'

'At a friend's out First Avenue way.'

'Know the address? We could go over there now. I've got surveillance to do in Hove and I can do this first.'

They drove west along the front to First Avenue. The still sea was mesmeric with the path of sunlight upon it. Paz never tired of it. He reminded himself this scene was one of the main reasons he liked living in the town.

Zeke couldn't remember the number of the building or the name of the person he was looking for, but then he saw someone he recognised getting into a car. It was a middle-aged woman who was a little disconcerted at him approaching her. But after the initial embarrassment, she became engaged in trying to establish with him who it was he and Paz were looking for. After their discussion, Zeke thanked her, turned to Paz and indicated where they needed to go. They strode along the pavement until they came to the smart-looking five-storey apartment block. The name they wanted was Stewart. They quickly found her flat number.

Mrs Stewart lived alone. She was about fifty, Paz guessed. She dressed extravagantly and colourfully like a rich Marrakech hippie. Her flat was decorated with many artefacts of 'tribal' manufacture. Paz took a slight dislike to her after sensing she felt negatively towards him. He was used to it as a PI. After his friend had introduced the subject of Stony Lake, Mrs Stewart said, 'I know him, obviously, but he hasn't been here lately. He has a girlfriend in Hove. I met him years ago at a spiritual retreat. We hit it off. He amused me and, I think, I amused him. He has stayed here a few times when he has nowhere to stay.'

'What can you tell us about him?' Paz said.

'Why do you want to know?' She gave him the impression that protecting Stony's reputation, almost as much as her own, was a major concern.

'We wonder whether he's in some kind of trouble,' said Zeke. 'If you're worried about him, Paz here might be able to find him.'

'I see,' she said. 'Well, I don't know anything about any recent trouble, but someone like him knows a lot of people, and I suspect some of those people are not going to be kindly disposed towards him.

I was with him at a couple of ashrams, one in the US and one in France. He was what is known as a fringie.'

'I know the term,' Paz said, 'though I have only a vague idea what it means.'

'He was on the edge of the group. He's very practical, you see. You've got those devout followers who want to be close to the centre, close to the swami or whatever, and then you've got others more on the edge who do work for the community and in return get exemption from some of the restrictions, like watching TV. And some of them are also on the edge of criminality - buying drugs and so on. And that puts them at risk. Do you understand what I'm saying?'

'I think so. Wherever there's drugs there's going to be trouble. Was he running away from someone?'

'I don't know. You'd need to talk to the girlfriend about that.'

'And how do we do that?' Zeke asked.

'She works at the town hall. Her name's Emerick.'

Zeke had to return to Brighton, so Paz went alone to speak to Ms Emerick. At the town hall, Paz showed the receptionist his card and asked if she'd ring her for him. After a few moments, the question came back, 'Is it to do with Mr Lake?'

He asked if he could speak with her direct. After checking, the receptionist handed him the phone. The girlfriend's first name was Helia. 'Are you from the ashram?' she said. She sounded nervous.

'No. Speak to Mrs Stewart if you're worried.' She said she didn't need to and asked to meet him. They arranged a rendezvous in a restaurant down by the beach. Paz did his surveillance job and then went to meet her.

Helia was a short, quite bubbly woman in her late thirties, and she struck him as very different to what he understood of Stony since she appeared very ordinary and down-to-earth. 'I was worried you might be from the ashram,' she said, 'so I did speak with Julia. Stewart, that is.'

'OK. Why are you so worried about the ashram?'

'It's not the ashram itself. It's someone whose wife was there.'

'Ah.'

'He threatened Stony, you see.'

'How do you know this man's here in Brighton?'

'I don't. I think Stony lied to me. I'm not even convinced anyone from the ashram is after him.'

'Why would he lie about that?'

'Smokescreen. He's done something, I've no doubt.' She told him Stony had wanted to buy a piece of land and was going to grow cannabis there, and he'd got an 'associate' to put up some money towards it. She said, 'An old school friend. But he didn't buy the land in the end, and he didn't give the money back. He said he would but he hasn't, and I don't know where he'd get it from because he's probably spent it and he never does normal paid work.'

'Where do you think he is then?'

'On a commune somewhere - doing carpentry, driving tractors, but getting nothing for it.'

As they came away from the restaurant he couldn't help thinking she was not entirely believable. He felt she was hiding something. As they walked he said, 'Could you be mistaken?'

'Anything's possible with me.' She then surprised him by asking if he would like to come to her flat for a cup of tea. He accepted.

In her surprisingly untidy flat - he had expected her no-nonsense approach to be illustrated in her living space - she surprised him again, this time by offering him a joint. He declined and then felt annoyed at his own priggishness, but he had to drive back to Brighton that evening. 'When was Stony here last?' he said.

'Stony doesn't stay here,' she replied. 'He has a friend over in Portslade. We go there.' Then she said, 'He's my other boyfriend.'

'I see.'

'I guess I'm not quite what you expected.' She sat smiling on the sofa opposite him as she opened her legs to reveal she was wearing no underwear. He knew it was time to make his excuses but decided to stay anyway. He therefore accepted her second offer of a joint, and the several glasses of Cabernet Sauvignon, and the chance to stay over, and everything she offered after that.

Next morning, in the office, with Mack's help he found the likely identity of Stony's old school friend who'd put up the money for the 'business venture'. He had a criminal record for drug offences. A dangerous character when you couldn't repay a debt to him. Paz talked to Zeke about it. He knew this person. 'I didn't know about the debt, though,' he said. 'But it doesn't surprise me. I can take you to his place.'

'What do you think?'

'I don't think he'd seek rough justice, but money can do things to a person.'

'Plus, if he killed Stony he'd have no chance of being paid back,' said Paz. 'Let's go and see him.'

Zeke drove Paz out to Stony's old school friend's place, which was a motor home with a little vegetable garden outside. This man with an untidy goatee and dressed in a T-shirt and shorts greeted Zeke but said, indicating Paz, 'Why's he here?'

'He's looking for Stony. As am I.'

'Well, I'd sure love to find him because he's got my money. He told me he had a wealthy benefactor who was prepared to support a grow operation on two conditions: she was not the only person in it and there was no reference to her in any document. He asked me for ten grand. I'd sold some dodgy artwork and don't like holding cash so agreed to it. It was madness on my part.'

'So where do you think he is?'

'Since he has no normal means of income, he always needs someone to support him, like a lonely rich, old widow who needs a chauffeur. When he gets tired of that he'll find an ashram, then back to Brighton for a while, a new girlfriend, and so the cycle begins again. And once in a bright blue moon he'll give me five-hundred pounds he's bummed off someone else.'

Paz concluded there was nothing to be done. Certainly if Stony was murdered his name didn't show up in the press. It was only weeks later when he encountered a beggar in his thirties near the office, that Stony's name arose again. 'You'll never find him, you know,' the quietly-spoken man said. 'Stony Lake, I mean. I heard you were looking for him.'

Paz was bemused. 'How do you know I won't find him?'

'Because I killed him.'

Paz thought the addled fellow just wanted a drink or food; he took him into the office despite the smell he brought with him. He made him a cup of tea and gave him biscuits and half a Bounty bar he'd bought that morning. The man said, 'Stony Lake as such no longer exists. I helped him. He owed money all over. He wanted a new identity, and I helped him get it.'

'You did? How?'

'I wasn't in this predicament then. I was making money off creating fake IDs. I had a small business doing it. But a month ago, a drug gang stole all my equipment—'

'Oh my God!'

'—and I lost my regular job, and the landlord served notice because they wanted to redevelop.' He took a sip of tea. 'And suddenly I was out on the street.' Paz looked hard into his sunken eyes; he was telling the truth. 'Needless to say,' said the unfortunate, 'Stony never paid me a penny for it.'

Chapter 8

The Cure For All Ills

Paz received a call from an old friend in the States who told him a disturbing story about a missing person's case he had in Europe that was causing him concern. It involved an American family, the Stapleforths. They had been on a cruise in Europe some months earlier and their teenage daughter Sally had gone missing on the ship the night before the stop at Marseilles. The next morning, the ship docked and passengers started disembarking. The parents reported Sally missing and the ship's security staff began enquiries, but the disembark was completed and many people left the cruise. A full search of the ship was later conducted at the captain's direction. The Maritime Gendarmerie became involved because it was believed Sally had gone overboard, although there was no formal evidence to support this, nor evidence of foul play. The parents were naturally distraught and, to make matters worse, Sally had been in an argument with them the night she disappeared. Against their wishes she had gone to a dance and spent several hours with a group of other young people. Naturally this group became the focus of enquiries, but the hastily-conducted on-board investigation was to no avail. All that was established was that she was very drunk but not in any obvious distress. Sally had not been heard from since.

As was often the case in such situations, there were many possible 'sightings' of Sally and, as was even more often the case, these sightings increased after the family posted a generous reward for information leading to her safe return. There had supposedly been sightings all over

France, and even in Spain and Italy. The parents had been to Europe four times to follow up on some of these. The FBI became involved but found no leads.

The sightings continued and they gradually grew more sinister. Whereas initially one of the theories had been that she had disappeared of her own volition in a wild act of defiance against her parents, with time the only viable scenarios became either death or kidnap. Such cases were heartbreaking for the family, who were vulnerable to frauds as a result.

Paz's friend in America had phoned to tell him that the focus of the investigation had moved to the UK. There had been sightings on the south coast of England including Brighton. This latest development also preyed on one of the family's worst fears: that their daughter was in the hands of sex traffickers who were moving her around Europe.

Paz was expecting his contact to tell him he was to be the person to investigate this latest scenario, but he was in for a surprise. The person the family had chosen was a man called Spraggs.

Spraggs had made a name for himself after successfully busting a kidnap gang in Germany. His approach was marked by a heavy reliance on violence or the threat of it. He gathered a team of 'consultants' together as and when required; in other words, he employed thugs. Nominally a private investigator, he scoffed at the more customary approaches used by people like Paz. He'd met him once at a meeting at which Spraggs disparagingly referred to Paz's type of investigator as 'lardarse Poirot wannabes'.

'He's scamming these people,' the contact said.

'He may well be, based on his reputation, but what do you want me to do about it? I'm not some alternative police force. As you know, I have to have a client. Who will I be working for?'

'I want you to find out what Spraggs is up to and report back. I'll make sure you get paid, if that's what's worrying you. The Stapleforths have already spent plenty and you'll be saving them money.'

'I haven't come across Spraggs in a while. Do you know where he's based these days?'

'In South London somewhere, I believe.'

Mack did her customary research, which she then discussed with Paz. He looked up Spraggs' operation online. The unconventional PI promised 'direct no-nonsense solutions to extortion and kidnap' and claimed a team of hand-picked experts and twenty years of successful operations. One of his hand-picked experts was someone Paz had worked with on a case in the past, by name of Rick Holman. He was another PI, though not one who advertised his services in the media. Word of mouth was how he got his assignments. High profile divorce cases were what he liked best, ones where you didn't so much find dirt as create it. He wallowed in it. He was envious of the rich and famous and obtained a vicarious pleasure from seeing all their tawdry private dealings dragged up in court. But lately he had become involved with Spraggs' antics. Paz phoned him.

'Paz, long time. Still down in Brighton, I hear. Don't tell me one of your clients is at war with mine. I sure hope for your reputation that they're not.' Always the big man talk.

'I get all the clients I can handle,' said Paz.

'All the little stuff. Well, if it pays the bills.'

'It does, thank you. I heard you were working with old Spraggs these days. Is that big enough for you? I heard he was on the Sally Stapleforth case.'

'You know I can't discuss that.'

'I don't know, actually. And have ever heard of me breaching a confidence? No, right? So is this job Brighton-based?'

'In the south, that's all I'll say.'

'Do you seriously think she's here? What is she now - a sex worker? A drug mule? The poor kid probably went overboard and was never seen again. It was probably those others she was with. You know the chance was lost after the disembark at Marseilles. You and Spraggs are taking money under false pretences.'

'*I'm* taking it? I'm just doing a job. If you want to make a noise about it, talk to Spraggs. I'm sure he'd be delighted.'

Paz went to see the man in question. It was hard to track him down and he was reluctant to meet. Paz found him staying in the house of a friend in Littlehampton. He had a couple of rooms there and saw himself as some kind of military commander always on the move, a guerrilla leader with an aristocratic moustache, army fatigues, and a big cigar that always made him cough. 'What do you want?' he barked. 'Run out of Miss Marple cases? How's the knitting?'

They argued about the propriety of what he was doing. 'You know that girl's dead,' Paz said. 'You're just exploiting those people.'

'I need funds for my work and I take my guidance from God.' He tapped the black cover of the Bible on the desk before him. 'This is important work and "those people" as you rather disrespectfully call them - Mr and Mrs Stapleforth - will get their reward.'

'Just not the reward they want,' said Paz.

He bridled. 'We're conducting an operation next week. Come along if you want. See how it's done. You can stay in the car like an old lady, playing Cluedo while we do the real work.'

This narked Paz. 'As a matter of fact, I would like to,' he said. 'I want to be able to tell the Stapleforths where their money's gone.'

'The raid's on a place in Nottingham.'

'I thought it was supposed to be in the south.'

'I run this operation, not whoever you've been talking to.'

'I'd like to come along, just gathering facts. That's what I do. You do the action man stuff if you want, but I'm gathering evidence.'

'I used to be like you,' Spraggs said contemptuously.

'And I wanted to be like you - for five nanoseconds.'

Spraggs and his men went in two minivans to the scene of the operation late one evening. One vehicle would take the girls away, Spraggs travelling with them to the police station, and the other was for most of his 'team'. There were seven in the team in all. Paz was the only person not carrying a weapon.

The operation started badly. The house they went to turned out to be the wrong one. An old man answered the door and it soon became clear they needed to be three doors along. Paz gained the impression this was not an unusual mixup from the old man's perspective. Spraggs' tetchy apology was accepted with remarkable grace.

The embarrassment merely invigorated the team. When the door to the correct house was hesitantly opened, they powered in. Resistance from the occupants was quickly overcome. The girls were 'liberated' but there were so many of them that some team members had to take taxis. Paz remained outside throughout, thereby inviting more derision from Spraggs. He took photographs of the terrified girls as they emerged from the house. For all they knew, they were being kidnapped by just another band of violent men. To any of the girls that might conceivably have been Sally, he shouted her name in case it triggered a response, but it didn't. After the team had left with the girls, the police arrived to make arrests.

Spraggs' operation had been successful. Of course amongst the group of mainly Eastern European girls there was no Sally Stapleforth. Paz told Spraggs there would be no more games, no more new leads from out of the air, and he needed to return the money the family had paid him. If he didn't, they could sue him for fraud. Paz had no authority to say that, but he knew if he didn't press Spraggs he would wriggle out of it.

Spraggs was grudgingly amenable to Paz's pressure because he secured a huge win. Amongst the latest harvest of girls was identified the seventeen-year-old daughter of a wealthy Latvian businessman, a client of his. Spraggs would be rewarded for his work - and handsomely.

Chapter 9

A Box Of Air

Paz was relieved to return to the office after a long meeting at Fran Owens' office in London about a case. During it Fran had informed him there was plenty of new work to come but even more if he 'joined forces', by which he meant: sold out to him. Paz declined to even think about it.

Mack came to see him in his private office, smiling. 'I don't know what you'll make of this,' she said. She proceeded to tell him about an unusual matter concerning a dispute between two artists regarding a 'box of air'.

'Yeah?' He couldn't resist a smile himself. 'So who's our client?'

'Rafe Lasche. He's a conceptual artist. The dispute concerns an empty cardboard box.'

'You're kidding. A box? How big are we talking?'

'Um... twelve inches by nine by seven. But he says the artwork is the air inside the box, rather than the box itself.'

'Eh? Say again.'

'It's a standard, plain, ordinary-looking brown cardboard box, but the art is the air inside.'

'I see, I guess. It sounds vaguely weird. OK. I'm fancying something lighthearted, not entirely serious.'

'Oh, this is serious, alright.' She went on to describe the situation. Lasche had made the artwork, but another artist Rebel Riches was so enraged at seeing it in a gallery that he arranged for it to be stolen, returning it to Lasche three days later. Lasche was furious, not finding it funny at all. He felt his property had been violated and accused Rebel of seeking to devalue his art and thereby devalue him.

'So who is this Rebel character and why was he so upset?'

'He sees himself as an iconoclast. He cannot stand pretension, so he says, and cannot stomach the idea of people being conned into thinking a plain cardboard box, or the air in it, is somehow a work of art. He wants to pop the great ego of Rafe Lasche. Of course, he probably has a big ego too.'

'Well, what does the great man want us to do? It sounds like he needs a lawyer rather than us.'

'He already has a lawyer. He wants us to find his artwork. He maintains that the box he got back is a different one, even though it looks exactly the same.'

'Oh Christ!' Paz slapped his forehead.

'So he wants his own one back,' she said. 'He doesn't want us to take possession of it, just find it. Then the lawyers, and the police if necessary, will sort it out.'

'OK.' He could see the obvious problem: He'd locate the famous box, but by the time anyone showed up to take possession, it would have been spirited away or replaced by another 'fake' one. It was no more bizarre than listening to Fran Owens, though.

He arranged to visit Lasche's studio which was on the west side of the city in an old warehouse he shared with several other artists. When he arrived, he found Lasche, a tall thin angular-faced man dressed entirely in black leather, standing over a large sheet of paper on a table, scribbling with a thick felt tip pen. Though aware of Paz approaching, he did not acknowledge him and instead scribbled harder. Looking dissatisfied and about to scrunch the paper up to throw away, joining the rest of the discards on the floor, he handed it to Paz without looking at him. It bore what looked like a signature.

'This is a disappointment,' Lasche said, turning abruptly towards Paz. 'I was expecting your colleague. You must be her assistant. I suppose you know what you're about. I'm all for retirees being brought back to the workforce. I even employ a couple of over-sixties myself.' He started on another sheet of paper, suddenly stopped, looked at him, and said, 'Sorry. I'm being an arse, aren't I? She is nice, though. On the phone, I mean. That voice! I felt I was slowly drowning in spiced mulled claret - or Bordeaux. And so sexy I almost dropped my bowl of Wheaties in my lap, darling. I clean forgot what I was going to say, but she helped me along. I swear I'll have erotic dreams over it for the next fortnight. It's like golden syrup sliding off a beautiful young model's tongue onto the naked back of another, don't you think?'

'Well—'

'Exactly. But what's she doing working with an old dog like you? With that voice she could be doing something more glamorous like, well, pretty much anything really. I'd employ her just to talk to me first thing in the morning and last thing at night. Of course, people are so different when you meet them to what they sound like on the phone. Is that why she sends you out? Tell me, is she a bit of an old crow?'

'No indeed.'

'There's hope for humanity then. And, pray, is she married, perchance?'

'No, again.'

'How exciting! Tell her she can expect a proposal from Rafe Lasche. Or more precisely, her voice can.' He then asked Paz to excuse him while he found another chair.

Paz sat down on the rickety wooden one already there and waited for his host to return, shaking his head and grinning as he thought about what Lasche had said about Mack. He looked around at the various objects, mainly boxes not unlike the one that had caused all the trouble, except they all had different markings. He took out his phone and checked emails.

Twenty minutes later, Lasche returned with the second chair. He said, 'I know what you're thinking: All these boxes - what's the point?'

Paz hadn't been thinking about them at all, but the artist was going to explain anyway. He then told Paz what Mack had already relayed to him.

Paz thought the dispute ridiculous and decided to provoke the artist. 'What's the problem with the box you got back?' he asked. 'It's just an ordinary cardboard box, after all.'

Lasche looked on him with contempt, but he sensed Paz was merely winding him up. 'It's not the same at all.' He passed Paz the replacement box with disdain. Paz looked at it and then at him with mystification. Lasche took the box and shook it. There was something inside. 'My box is empty,' he insisted. 'This one is fake.'

Paz said nothing. He could already tell there was no point arguing and so, after a few questions about Rebel Riches, he left.

If he'd imagined dealing with Riches would be straightforward in comparison, Paz quickly learnt otherwise. Instead of being able to visit him, Paz was informed by voicemail he had to speak to his agent, by name of Russell. From attempting to phone Russell he learned that he could not meet him in person but only make contact via email. Paz tried to circumvent this by telling him immediately what he was calling about, but Russell would have none of it. It was obvious that neither Riches nor his agent had any incentive whatsoever to talk to him and could not give a damn about Lasche and his stupid box. Eventually, however, with persistence Paz was able to persuade Russell to engage with him. Russell said that Lasche had stolen his client's idea and passed it off as his own, which had caused his client distress, and damage to his reputation. He said the matter might have to be resolved in the courts. Paz thought that would be great if it kept him out of it. All clients were officially welcome but some drove you mad.

Mack was both intrigued and embarrassed by Paz telling her about the artist's infatuation with her telephone voice, although he avoided mention of the erotic dreams. She had done research on Rebel Riches and found his real name and address.

Paz went to see him. It was a dismal domestic scene that he ventured into. Riches was in the kitchen and appeared depressed at Paz finding him. He sat heavily at the big square pinewood table, in a striped purple rugby shirt, cargo shorts, and sandals. In front of him was a raw hamburger which he was picking at with a knife. When Paz told him what he was there for, Riches gave a murderous chuckle, jabbed at the red meat, and said, 'This could be him. That would look good on a gallery wall.' In the corner sat a large contemplative dog, while a fragile-looking woman fluttered around Riches. Suddenly, as if emerging from a daydream, he grabbed Paz's arm and said, 'Pleased to meet you, Mr Wheat.'

Riches proved warmer towards him than Lasche had been. He made it clear he thought the whole thing daft. 'He can't take a joke, can he?' he said. 'Too full of his own importance.' Paz could believe this but had to appear surprised. 'The thing is,' said Riches, 'he's the real joke. It's just a bloody box! Box of air, my arse!'

Paz pointed out to him that he'd stolen Lasche's artwork and replaced it with a worthless forgery.

Riches sniggered. 'How do you know it's worthless?'

'You can't deny it's a fake.'

'It's a duplicate and it's not worthless. In fact it's worth more than his. Inside it is an envelope and inside that is a five pound note. Therefore it is five pounds more valuable than the so-called original.'

This was a compelling argument but one Paz's position required him to ignore. 'So where is it now?' he said.

'I don't know. Quite literally. I gave it to someone else to honour a gambling debt. I never was good at poker.'

'And where do you think it might be now?'

'The person I owed the debt to has no interest in art. I owed him two hundred pounds. The thing you have to remember is that Lasche stole my concept, which I always meant as a joke. But of course he will say there's no copyright on ideas.'

Paz next went to the address of the person who, according to Riches, was the one he gave it to. At least Riches had some idea about art. Mr Mickelthwaite, who lived in a small semi-detached outside the city, did not. A grim-faced man in his thirties with a bald head and hooked nose, he was hard and down-to-earth. 'I have no time for arty types,' he sniffed. 'You're not one, are you?' Paz assured him he wasn't, although he was not sure Mickelthwaite would think more highly of a private investigator. 'Riches told me the box was worth thousands, but I'm not that stupid. He's hopeless at cards anyway. I gave it to my dad for a birthday present. I told him it was a valuable piece of art, and he thought I was joking and wasn't too impressed. I think he put it in his shed. It's probably got mice nesting in it by now.'

Paz next went to see Mr Mickelthwaite senior, hoping this would be his last stop. He was a slight, very gentle man, rather frail, and extremely polite until the question of the artwork came up. His son's protestations about its value had almost overnight turned him into a collector. He could see a way to make money, far more interesting and potentially lucrative than alternatives he'd tried. Instead of putting the piece in the garden shed, he'd transformed his suitably named box room into a small gallery. He had already acquired several artworks of various kinds, was delighted with his collection, and soon made it clear he was not disposed to surrender his box of air. Having developed a keen sense of what things were worth in the art market, he did not wish to lose the piece.

'But you haven't got the provenance,' Paz said. 'Don't you realise this is Rebel Riches' joke?' The old man then showed Paz two identical boxes. 'Only I know which one is genuine,' he said happily.

'But isn't it the air inside that's supposedly the art?'

'That's what my son said, but I told him I thought that was a load of bollocks.'

'Don't you think Rafe Lasche could potentially be a very important artist?' Paz teased.

'If that means self-important, yes.'

'I think his signature's worth more than his work,' Paz said. Mickelthwaite seemed intrigued by this and Paz produced the sheet of paper Lasche had given him after he'd signed it. 'This,' Paz said, pointing at the scribble, 'contains his actual work as opposed to pure concept.' Mickelthwaite clearly found this persuasive but not sufficiently so for him to want to swap.

In the end, Paz was able to negotiate a settlement. Mickelthwaite senior agreed to return the original box in exchange for a copy bearing Lasche's signature. This was not straightforward as Lasche insisted the boxes were muddled up, so it took two attempts to get right, Lasche clarifying that the correct piece had a distinctive four millimetre mark which he'd made just inside it. The artist tried to avoid Paz's fees, using the argument that he'd given him the sheet with his signature on 'worth more than if you worked this case for a year'. In response, Paz gave him the sheet back. Only reluctantly did Lasche agree to pay. But at least his cheque didn't bounce.

Rebel Riches almost prevailed in the end. Lasche put on an exhibition of his work including A Box Of Air. Worried about the possibility of a Riches-inspired stunt, he decided to take the exhibit to the gallery himself in his car. He was removing it from the back seat when a hooded figure passing by on an e-scooter made a grab for it. Lasche foiled him, but in the confusion he let the box slip, and a gust of wind picked it up and dropped it in the path of an approaching bus. The irrepressible Lasche was shocked but then inspired. The flattened box with the tyre mark on it was renamed Random Event 12 after the bus number. When someone pointed out the bus was not the 12 but the 12A, he renamed it The Frightening Tyranny of Pedantry.

As for Mack, neither she nor her voice received a marriage proposal from Lasche. She was not forgotten, however. The great artist insisted on taking her to dinner. She asked Paz if this was appropriate, which was mere politeness on her part as she intended to go anyway, and he realised this. 'Anything for a weird life,' she said. He approved, even though he had private misgivings. The venue was English's, which Lasche said was his favourite restaurant. For once she had her hair cut short and she bought a new dress specially for it, which she enjoyed showing Paz, knowing it would make him jealous. She liked to dress up, even if only for a man she despised. She need not have bothered, however, because Lasche wore a blindfold from the moment he entered the restaurant to the moment he left. He told her to order whatever she liked. His only requirement, which he insisted was 'unnegotiable', was that she read out the entire menu for him to record on his phone. He asked her to agree to do this once a year. This, he said, would show how the menu changed over the years 'and thus be an important statement on the vicissitudes of fashion and, moreover, the scarcity of edible fish species.' It made her wonder how long he anticipated she would commit to the task, but then, having completed the first such exercise, she took a gulp of Sauvignon Blanc and forgot about it. Apart from her voice he expressed no interest in her whatever. For her part, she was not attracted to his voice or anything else about him. She found him whiney and self-obsessed. And when he expounded on his artistic ideas she merely said 'Yes' at appropriate intervals, while sending Lily salacious texts, and occasionally moving his wine glass in order to confuse him.

Chapter 10

Steal Away

A young woman came to see Paz one afternoon. She'd left work early and had come about her boyfriend Tony. Her name was Mary. She was dark with a soft, oval face and long straight hair. She had a slightly haughty air that Paz suspected was artificial and intended to give her confidence. In his mind he named her Sweet Lady Mary after a Rod Stewart song he'd heard that morning on the car radio, though the analogy didn't work - they never did - because the song was about a liar, whereas he believed her sincere and liked her immediately. She said, 'I haven't heard from him for over a week except for the odd text. That's not like him.'

They went over the obvious questions. From her perspective there was no reason to believe he'd abandoned her. Tony was a singer, a solo performer, and he'd joined a tour with other musicians. She knew nothing about who they were, except they were travelling around north Scotland doing live shows in pubs and folk clubs. What puzzled her was that he was barely using his phone, and was doing nothing on Facebook. She said normally she'd expect him to update Facebook at every step on the tour, with a picture and a thank you to the audience and so on. She showed Paz his Facebook page. It had been busy until recently.

He asked her, 'What does he do for a living? I mean, apart from music.'

'He's a trained accountant, but he does whatever jobs he can get: construction, gardening, factory work. He likes to be well-rounded.'

'Is he on holiday from work, then?'

'No, he gave up his temporary accountancy job with a building firm. Work's always just a means to an end. To him his real job is playing music, and out of the blue came this invitation to join the tour so he went for it. He got the call on the Friday and was on the train to Aberdeen on the Saturday. Someone dropped out at the last minute, apparently.'

'So you're sure he didn't know these people before?'

'I am. They gave him some names, but he didn't recognise them. One of them had seen him gigging at a pub in the North Laines, picked up his card, and decided to contact him on the off chance.'

Paz wanted to believe Tony just had a problem with his phone or they'd had a tiff, but he was not persuaded. He talked to a contact named George in Aberdeen. George, a gruff man of few words, said he knew nothing about any little local tours but agreed to investigate.

When Paz rang Mary for any news she said there was none. Had she talked to the police? Yes, but they felt it too early to become involved because he was probably on a 'frolic'. They'd given her the usual stuff about adults having the right to disappear, which always riled Paz because often when they finally investigated they complained about time having been lost.

He asked Mary for details of the companies he'd worked for. On receiving these, Mack did searches. She discovered Tony's cousin worked as a manager in a local construction company, Bittens. Could it also be the firm where Tony worked? Paz checked with Mary who confirmed it was. Paz rang the cousin, Jeff, at work. Jeff said he knew nothing about Tony going on tour and was surprised to hear it. It wasn't like Tony to do things on the spur of the moment. He said it was highly embarrassing because it was he who'd got Tony the job and they'd wanted to renew his contract. All Jeff knew was that Tony had announced on Friday without explanation that he wouldn't be in the following Monday. 'It's the last time I do that for him,' he said bitterly.

He added that it was hectic in the office now because the police were in, following the discovery of an embezzlement.

Later, Paz talked to the police detective, by name of Maremount, who was handling the investigation of the embezzlement, and informed him of the missing person's case and the fact the subject, Tony Marsh, had been working at Bittens until recently. Maremount, who liked to talk down to Paz but at least listened to him, said they were seeking to interview everyone who'd worked there in the last three months and so would be interested in Tony.

Back in the office, Paz received a call from George in Aberdeen. George said there was indeed a group of touring musicians in town. He would go to that night's gig and take photographs. Paz asked him for the name of any venue they'd already played. He came back with a Facebook link a few minutes later. There were some photographs of the performers, but Paz didn't recognise Tony. Nor did Mary when Paz sent them to her. Paz couldn't resist the thought that Tony's 'tour' was really a ruse to escape to a new life. He asked George to let him know of any companies hiring accountancy staff locally. George complained at the continuing requests but agreed to do it.

Next day, George sent him photographs from the gig he'd attended. He said he'd enquired but there was no 'Tony Marsh'. Indeed, Paz didn't see Tony in the photos. Nor did Mary, although she said he didn't play every night and might be ill. Paz asked George if there were any similar tours around. He said there probably were but he wasn't going to any more gigs, thank you. It got him in trouble with his wife who thought he was having an affair, which, he declared with pride, he was. He had, however, found companies advertising vacancies in accountancy over the last few weeks. Mack then phoned the companies on his list, asking whether the vacancies were still open. All but two still were: one permanent, the other temporary. Paz rang the company which had recently filled its temporary vacancy, and asked for Tony Marsh. They had no-one of that name.

Using a spoof number and recording the call, Paz phoned the second company, the one that had just filled its permanent vacancy, and enquired there. The receptionist hesitated at the name but then said, 'Oh, you must mean the new person.' When put through, Paz posed as a headhunter. The man, who confirmed his name as Marsh, sounded puzzled. Paz said he had a client who was building a new team and might need to recruit in the next few months. He asked him to confirm the level of his experience, the aim being to record as much of him talking as possible. He ended by saying he'd check back with him in six months with more news to see if he might be interested. Marsh told Paz not to bother.

Later, Paz played the recording to Mary. She said, 'It's not him. There's obviously another accountant called Tony Marsh in Aberdeen. My Tony's on tour anyway. I got another text today saying he's had the flu.'

Paz phoned Maremount in case the police had found Tony. He said they hadn't and the person they most wished to interview was an accountant called Sharratt who'd left a fortnight before Tony. Sharratt was not on LinkedIn but Mack found him on Facebook, though he hadn't posted since his last day in the office.

Paz contacted George again and said, 'Just one more thing,' and George groaned. Paz said he needed him to visit Marsh's office and get a picture of him. Mack had worked out a scene in which George would put a box of chocolates inside a package with a note saying 'From a secret admirer'. Paz told George, 'Make sure you get a picture.' George complained even more, but the more he grumbled ('I'm a PI, not a bloody delivery boy!' 'Don't worry, George, I've every faith in you,') Paz knew the more likely he was to do it. The following day, George sent Paz the photograph his 'beautiful assistant' had obtained and said,

'She said she thought he suspected something, but he's probably vain and wants to believe he's got a secret admirer, so let's not worry.' It was not Tony's picture. Paz didn't need to show it to Mary.

He phoned Maremount and asked him to look at the photograph he was about to send. When he did, Maremount's responded with 'And?'

'Take off the beard and moustache of his picture on the Facebook link I've sent and I submit there's more than a passing resemblance to your Mr Sharratt.'

'You may be right,' came the grudging response a minute later. He knew it.

'And when you arrest this fellow you'll find he's using the real Tony's national insurance number and bank account. And his phone, if he doesn't sling it first. The whole folk tour story he created as a trap to get a new identity far away from here.' Later, Paz learned Sharratt wasn't even the man's real name; Leicester police were looking for him under 'Carlton'.

The police arrested Sharratt, aka Tony Marsh, later that day. The real Tony was still missing, as were the embezzled funds and his phone. All Sharratt would admit to was assuming Tony's identity, saying he'd obtained all the information he needed from Bittens' systems and with the agreement of Tony who wanted to be 'free of his clingy girlfriend'. He even claimed Tony set it all up because, having stolen from the company, he needed to create a new identity for himself, and Sharratt helped him achieve that. Why then was Sharratt using Tony's bank account? Because Tony wanted him to have the little that it contained for helping him get away.

The police believed otherwise, but neither Tony's blood or DNA, nor any other evidence of him were found in Sharratt's flat or car. The accused had an answer, however tortuous, to every question and, as his lawyer insisted, without a body there was no case.

Paz was anxious about his next meeting with Mary, even more so when she arrived looking so happy. But before he could say anything, she said she'd received another text from Tony days earlier; the tour was going brilliantly and next week they were headed for France. Paz thought, surely Mary realised the texts were fake and Tony's phone was stolen. He then passed on Mack's offer: That she immediately travel up to Scotland to track down Tony, combining it with a visit to her mother in Inverness. Mary was grateful but said he could close his file as she was satisfied Tony was alive and well. She said, 'Will you send me your account?'

'I'm hoping Tony's cousin can get Bittens to pay it, but, in any event, I won't charge you.' She left smiling, and Paz wondered whether she was wilfully blind, or did she recognise the truth whilst trying to ignore it? In a sense she was like Sweet Lady Mary in the song, though lying to herself rather than others. Some people didn't want to know the truth, merely validate their fantasy.

In the end, Sharratt was successfully prosecuted for embezzlement, but Tony's case remained open. Paz liked to imagine him touring endlessly around Europe, sending Mary the occasional text, and that being sufficient for her. More than that, he liked to imagine she found someone else.

Chapter 11

Eye On The Warrior

One morning, Paz had only just arrived in the office when he heard a soft American accent behind him. He turned round and saw a tall blonde woman, elegantly dressed and in her forties, smiling. 'Mr Wheat?' she asked.

'Indeed. Pleased to meet you. And you are?'

'Janis Lordeman.'

He recognised the name: 'Of The Lordeman furniture empire, by any chance?'

'Yes, that's right. How did you guess?'

'Oh, male intuition, I suppose.'

He took her into his private room. 'It's about my daughter Alicia,' she said. 'Her name is Jameson; I use my maiden name, in case you're wondering. I'm worried for her.' She explained that her daughter was at a university in London studying environmental politics. She was an activist in various groups, including Extinction Rebellion. Janis said her daughter had told her she believed she was being followed. She showed him a photograph of her daughter, a diminutive blonde with long straight hair and a round, cheeky face, carefree and happy in the picture.

'Is there a specific individual that she's seen following her, or is it a general feeling she has?'

'General feeling? She's not paranoid, if that's what you're wondering.' She frowned.

'No, I didn't mean it like that.'

'There's at least one person, possibly more - one particular photographer. She's seen him at demonstrations taking pictures, but other times as well. It's those other times that bother her... and me.'

'That's understandable.'

'And before you ask: yes, it has been reported to the university and the police.'

'Then why—'

'I want someone who reports to me only. Someone who will give my case priority. Someone who won't wait until something terrible happens.'

'I understand. Does she know you're thinking of appointing me?'

'Not yet, but I'll inform her.'

'And how will she likely react?'

'Not well, I imagine. Not because of any concern about you, obviously, but because of what your involvement means.'

'Why would anyone want to follow her? Because of her political activism?'

'Possibly.'

She showed him several more photographs of her daughter and one of the suspect.

'Could he be a stalker? Are you sure the police won't act?'

'I can assure you, stalker or no, they're not interested. He's made no attempt to get close to her or contact her.'

Paz agreed to take the case and he gave her his mobile number, saying her daughter could ring him if she ever became concerned at being followed.

The Saturday after their meeting, Paz went to a demonstration in Central London that Janis had told him Alicia would be attending. It was a march of about a thousand people, all dressed in vibrant colours, noisy, enthusiastic. When he arrived, there was a call and response taking place. Paz listened. 'What do we want?' a young man called out.

'Climate justice,' the marchers replied.

'When do we want it?'

'Now!'

Then they all declared, 'This is what democracy looks like,' twice. The young man continued: 'Whose street?'

'Our street.'

'Whose planet?'

'Our planet.'

'Whose future?'

'Our future.'

Paz saw the photographer who was the subject of the investigation and watched him closely. He was small, inconspicuous and sly-looking. An annoying middle-aged loser. He was alone, not interacting with anyone else. Paz took a couple of photographs of him and then followed the march, but he soon became bored with all the stopping and starting. While keeping one eye on the photographer, he flicked through a few business emails on his phone.

As the march broke up, Paz observed the subject leave the scene, making his way to the tube station. Paz followed him, closing up fast as the subject approached Holborn station. Paz made the same journey, taking the Piccadilly line and changing at South Ken and then the District line out west. They travelled all the way to Richmond. On arrival there, the last stop, Paz followed him out of the station into the street, hoping the subject was heading straight home and not merely going to meet a friend in a pub. Paz guessed that if the subject drank it was most likely alone. He followed him along roads he remembered from years previous when he had a couple of cases in Richmond. The subject walked on until, on a smart, quiet street, he left the pavement and approached a three-storey apartment block. Paz observed him unlock the front door and enter. He took pictures of the registration plates of the cars outside the house and checked the names on the panel by the front door. He took a photograph of the listed names.

Later, over a Chinese meal, Paz looked up freelance photographers in the Richmond area but had no joy in identifying any names amongst the flat occupants. He felt strange eating alone in a busy restaurant. He wished Mack was with him to talk to. He rang her, apologising, but she merely said, 'It's OK. You can call me anytime.' So warm and reassuring. There was danger for him in that voice, though, and he could see why the artist Rafe Lasche was so enamoured of it. 'Anytime,' she repeated, positively purring. 'Except when I'm with Lily, of course. I have to serve my goddess, you know. But she's out, hopefully back soon.' They talked briefly about the case and then she rang off to do a search on the Richmond house's occupants. She would run the names on Facebook, look at their friends, check Instagram, searching for a photo similar to one Paz had taken of the person following Alicia. Paz was still in the restaurant when she returned with the name Ed Slager. Her research showed that Slager himself was a private eye, specialising in personal surveillance.

The following morning, he phoned the client to let her know that the photographer was in fact a private investigator, even though he was puzzled by the fact. Why would a PI be watching the family? 'Excuse my asking, but do you or your husband have any enemies?' he asked.

'We are estranged. His name is William Dart. I use my maiden name.'

'What business is he in?'

'He's an industrialist.'

'Does he have any rivals?'

'Undoubtedly. But I wouldn't know them. Naturally, there's been hostile takeover bids for his firm. I know that much.'

Paz and Mack looked up the husband's company on the internet. They quickly found out it had a controversial and dirty reputation. There were environmental issues - pollution claims and government sanctions in the States, which struck Paz as ironic, given his daughter's activism, although conversely that might be her motivation.

They discussed what it all meant. Could it be that the husband had hired someone to monitor activists? But why would he bother to do surveillance on his own daughter? Maybe they were estranged too. Something further to ask Janis. Perhaps the company was doing surveillance on Alicia without her father's knowledge, or was there a power struggle within the firm and this was associated with it? There were too many possibilities.

Paz talked to an old colleague, Emilio, on the phone about it. These days he did freelance work in London and was the quiet, dependable if unimaginative kind of guy Paz sometimes found invaluable. And young enough to be a credible 'older student'. They agreed he would start following Alicia.

Janis phoned him a few days later. She said Alicia had told her someone new was following her and did he know anything about it? The description Janis gave him was not of Emilio, however. Paz asked her about the relationship between father and daughter. She described it as 'strained'.

Emilio worked fast. He had a couple of contacts who were students; he said they were like 'sponges' absorbing all the gossip. He reported back that there were rumours about Alicia and a married professor at the university, by name of Hassey. From this conversation Paz began to wonder whether they were on the wrong track and it was a matrimonial issue. He discussed it with Mack. They concluded it was Hassey's wife behind the surveillance and speculated Alicia was going to be named correspondent in a divorce case. Checking with Emilio, Paz was able to confirm that Hassey was indeed at the beginning of divorce proceedings.

Janis rang again. She was cheerful and said she was pleased to inform him the surveillance on her daughter seemed to have stopped. The man Paz knew as private eye Ed Slager hadn't been around lately. Paz asked her about the rumours concerning Alicia and Hassey. This was met by a nervous laugh. Janis told him the 'affair' ('I would hardly call it that, though,' she said coldly) had ended. In fact it had been merely one of Hassey's many flings. She described him as 'promiscuous'.

After the call, Paz realised the case was not about Hassey's divorce; rather, it was pre-marital surveillance. Hassey's future wife had wanted him checked out and now knew enough. Based on what Paz had learned, he did not expect the wedding to ever take place.

But then he wondered whether another academic might be behind the surveillance, after he heard from Emilio that a rival of Hassey's had been beaten up. Hassey had a reputation for having a violent temper.

Paz went to another demonstration. He'd become interested in the campaign, and he wanted to see if Ed Slager was still around. He caught sight of him on the edge of the crowd without his camera but clearly watching Alicia.

Walking back to the station afterwards, Paz caught up with him. Feeling there was nothing to lose, he challenged him. 'Why have you been following Alicia?' he demanded. Slager shook his head. Reluctant to speak, he slunk away. 'Tell me,' Paz demanded. He threatened him, telling him he knew everything about him, that he knew where he lived, that if he wasn't enough deterrent he had access to ruthless people who could do him serious harm if he didn't level with him. Slager told him to calm down. He offered to buy Paz a drink which was accepted.

In the pub, Slager said, 'I'm ashamed.' He confessed that he'd been asked to monitor someone else within the environmental movement but had seen Alicia and become infatuated with her. He had taken to following her around. He said he knew it was wrong and had stopped. So why was he there today?

'I was doing well but habits die hard.'

'You do know your surveillance caused her great distress?'

'Oh God, I swear I never meant to! That's the last thing I could want.' Paz merely nodded. Then Slager said, 'Perhaps I should apologise to her. Would that be the right thing to do?'

To Paz it was the same madness, just another facet of it. He told him to let go. 'Let go entirely or it will destroy you. Failing that, the police will get involved. You don't want that.'

Slager drained his drink and then fled.

Paz was well aware of how surveillance could lead to infatuation, especially given the solitary nature of the work. Slager was clearly lonely and a depressive. Paz had been harsh with him and it concerned him that Slager might, in a fit of depression, kill himself. In the following days he checked local news websites. He talked to Mack about it. She said, 'Well, would you?'

'Of course not.'

'Then why would he? After all, he's probably just as bloody boring as you are.' She'd meant it as a joke, but it stung him. She knew it but couldn't stop herself: 'At least there's a flicker of life in him, even if he is a creep.'

The words had tumbled out. She apologised. She looked him in the eyes and he sensed fear. He said nothing initially, choosing to let her suffer.

'It's alright,' he said at last, smarting. 'I always like it when you say what you mean.'

'But I didn't mean it!' she exclaimed. She knew it was too late; she could not unsay it. She had to hope he'd forgive her. Had she known him better she'd have known not to worry.

Chapter 12

Suzi

That evening, Paz couldn't help thinking about Ed Slager and what Mack had said. At least Janis had confirmed her daughter was not being stalked anymore. He remained preoccupied, however, something his dinner companion Suzi noted, although she was well used to it.

He usually saw her one weekend a month. Forty-seven years old, a petite blonde with surgically enhanced breasts, she was an escort. He had known her for many years, and not only was he a client, but they were friends. She was also an invaluable source of information about things going on in the local underworld. She liked to say he was her favourite client and sometimes even claimed he was the only one, which was nonsense because she could not possibly live off what he paid her. She also liked to hint they should get married, despite his assertions that she would find living with him too dull: 'All work, you know.'

Tonight she admonished him, 'This is my birthday dinner and I'm very grateful, but I sort of feel I'm on my own here.' He felt bad. She looked beautiful in her bright blue dress with low cut frilled top and her agate necklace.

'I'm sorry,' he said.

'So what's up?'

He told her about Slager, and what Mack had said, and how it had bothered him. She gave him a disapproving glare. 'I think you worry too much about what some impudent dimwit says to you.'

'Do I?'

'Oh come off it, Paz. All the things you've seen in your career - all the bad stuff - and you're all soft and gooey about what some silly girl says.'

'She happens to be the one I'm employing.'

'Then fire her. It'll shake her up. I thought you told me before, her contract was one where you can fire her anytime. She's not indispensable. What does she do again?'

'Mainly searches.'

'Oh, that's right, a few internet searches. I could do them for you. You need a holiday. You should have delegated hiring an assistant to Jane. It's her work this numpty's doing. Find someone who can write a decent letter, at least.' She started laughing. 'Anyway I have some important news.'

'Good news?' He suddenly felt relaxed. 'That's great. Let's get some champagne.'

She reached out, gold bracelets jangling, to lightly clutch his forearm. 'You may not want to.'

He sighed. 'Go on then.'

'Guess.'

'I don't know. The way you're building up to it, I could almost think you've got engaged.'

'Correct.'

'What!? You're kidding me! After all this time?'

'I got tired of waiting for you, Paz. I'm sorry, it was always your bloody work. And you were never interested in me. Not really; admit it. Anyway my fiancé has more money than you'll ever have. And you know how I like to be looked after.'

He became flustered. 'Right. Well, I'm very glad for you. No, I am. I guess I won't be seeing you in future then.'

'Of course you will. Not for the sex but...' She caught his eye, '... you know how fond of you I am. I just may not have the same tidbits for you. You know: This guy's up to x, that guy's doing something else.'

He felt strange about it. He was happy for her, but she'd mentioned 'waiting' for him. Certainly there'd been hints which he'd ignored, never taking them seriously. And maybe she hadn't been serious herself and it had all been a private joke. He would never have married her anyway, but tonight he desired her.

'Thirty years of sex with blokes I didn't even like. Except one or two, of course.' She smiled at him.

'That makes me sad, actually.'

'Sad? At my engagement? On my birthday?'

'So is your beau a client?'

'Once. We had sex and he asked me to marry him, and I said Yes.'

'Is he the first to ask you?'

'No. I've had a few "saviours". I knew you wouldn't ever. Too much of a snob. You didn't mind using me as an escort, but you never wanted my friendship.'

'Not true.'

'But you got it anyway!'

'Why him?'

'All the money. He throws it around. And the sex. He's great for me. Aggressive. I like that. Makes me feel desired.' She paused. 'Look at you now, so sad. Come back to mine. You know you want to. You expected it. And I feel horny. I fancy a bit of gentle.'

'Gentle? Do you mean tender?'

She ignored his response. 'So Terry's saved me. Not that I wanted saving, but now I'm glad he has. He's away, if you want me tonight.'

He affected disinterest: 'What is this you're doing - a tour of your favourite johns for a farewell shag?'

She was upset: 'I can't believe you said that! As though our relationship meant so little to you. I could slap you. I could throw this plate of food in your face if this chicken wasn't so good.'

'I'm sorry. Oh, by the way, have you seen this girl?' He passed her a couple of photographs a client had given him of a missing teenager.

'Here we go. Always the same. Always work, work, work. So boring. Even in Lanzarote. That twit in your office was right.'

'That's not fair.'

'It's true, though. "Come to Lanzarote for a break. Oh and by the way, I'm on a case."'

He was annoyed: 'Look, this girl is missing. Have some humanity.'

'Oh, sorry.' She became subdued. 'OK, I feel properly told off now.' She studied the pictures with exaggerated care. She didn't recognise the person in them.

They went to Suzi's place, a large semi-detached house she rented in a pleasant tree-lined street. He could not wait to get her upstairs. But no sooner had they arrived than it became obvious her fiancé was already there. A big slab of a man in a blue suit. 'Who are you?' the slab demanded.

'Paz Wheat's the name.'

'Really?' He turned to her and barked, 'Get yourself ready.'

She sighed, embarrassed. 'See you around, Paz.' She then said, 'Terry, Paz is an old friend,' and turned to go upstairs.

When she'd almost reached the top of the stairs, the brute said to Paz, loud enough for her to hear, 'So you're a client, then. Right, you can fuck off. And I don't expect to see you round here again if you value your health!'

In his imagination Paz knocked Terry out with a single punch, stormed upstairs and claimed his prize from the eager Suzi. But he knew they would just slug it out until he lost to the younger man and slumped away defeated, like the loser in a rutting contest with his antlers broken. Besides, Suzi would be distressed at the fight.

Paz left feeling sad, not at the denial of promised sex but at the thought of the relationship Suzi had entered into. He did not like the look of this Terry, and it depressed him that Suzi had taken the thug into her life so quickly. He wondered whether something had happened to her - some terrible incident with a client - that had frightened her into the arms of this awful man for her supposed protection. He would find out from her in due course. He felt guilty at having not been more supportive to her in the past. She had wanted more from him and he had not adequately responded. And yet it was not his place to guide her. He was hardly an expert on relationships. How could he be when he normally ran from even the chance of them? But how was it, after so many years of being her friend, of knowing her in the most intimate of ways, of long conversations, of holiday trips spent with her, he had learnt so little? She liked him because he listened to her, and yet she was almost as unknown to him now as she'd been when he first answered her ad in the Argus. She liked aggressive more than gentle. He did not even understand what that meant.

On returning home, he decided to find another escort to replace Suzi immediately. He quickly found a young woman he liked the look of, but then realised she was Mack's age. He rang the number but ended the call before it was answered. It was madness. He went to bed and read instead. But he was restless so he phoned Mack. She said, 'Why are you calling at this hour? If it's for phone sex, I think that counts as harassment. Just joking.'

'I just wanted to hear your voice.'

'Oh, so it is phone sex.'

'I thought—'

'I know you did. Lily's asleep. I can always tell when she's been unfaithful because she's randy as hell. By the way, I didn't mean what I said in the office. You surely realise that. So do you want me to come over? Just for a little while to talk. Would you send for me in a limo? I've always wanted to be collected in a limo.'

He was tempted by this, almost beyond the level he could resist, but reason took over. 'It's alright,' he said, trying to hide his despondency.

'So no limo then.'

'Some other time, yes.'

'You sound so sad.' But then, so did she. 'It's alright,' she said. 'She'll be awake about five wanting more of me, so it's best I don't come over. I have to serve my princess, you know, and I have to be fit for work. My boss allows no slacking. So how was Suzi?'

He told her about his evening. 'I guess it sounds pathetic, but I'm feeling sorry for myself.'

'Paz, can I tell you something? If I wasn't gay and you were my age, sort of, I'd want to marry you.' He didn't reply. 'In fact, just if I wasn't gay. There, does that make you feel better?'

'It might if I could believe it.'

He spent a restless night, wondering what he had done with his life. He also wondered what he was doing phoning Mack. That pompous Rafe Lasche was so right: there was something highly seductive in her voice. Addictive, even. His thinking ran wild. He imagined himself in court being berated by the judge for 'a pattern of harassment'. He would claim she'd set him up from the start. She would then sue him and win. The insurers wouldn't pay out and he'd be bankrupted. Maybe that was what he needed. He needed to be ruined to begin his life again. But if that happened, who would do all the work? Who would listen to those looking for loved ones? Who would spend the time to find them?

Next morning, he apologised to Mack. She told him there was no need. She said, 'I made sure Lily heard me talking. It made her jealous. She thought I had a secret lover. A jealous Lily doesn't get mad, she gets desperate to please. You should phone up at eleven o'clock every night. Just joking.'

Chapter 13

The Art Man

Paz received a call from a friend in New York who was investigating the disappearance of some artworks from a specialist storage warehouse in Maryland. Paz was intrigued: 'So what happened?' he said.

'I got word from an FBI contact. Apparently some dirtbag in Wilmington was facing a serious drugs rap and suddenly announced that if they went easy on him, he could tell them about a major art theft racket. A cousin of his had a job there and told him about the scam. The dirtbag described how the owners would spend time schmoozing the clients to find out who were what they called the 'real' collectors and who were the ones who didn't know a work of art from a toilet brush and bought them just to make money.'

'And these know-nothings were the ones they targeted?'

'Correct. Over time they would replace a few relatively unknown items on the inventory with worthless fakes, confident the owners wouldn't notice. Then they'd sell the original works on.'

'A pretty simple MO. So if the FBI are on it, what does that leave for you or me to do?'

'My clients are a retired businessman and his wife who have recently returned from an extended tour around the world. When they heard on the QT there was a problem with the storage facility, they contacted me because I'd worked for them before. This case began with press reports about the facility being, despite its grandiose claims, poorly run. It soon turned into a scandal. Records were not properly kept and items worth millions of dollars could not be accounted for. Caught up in this was the collection of my clients Mr and Mrs Trakes which they'd spent thirty years assembling. Mainly works by American abstract expressionists. They were not in fact know-nothings as you call it.'

'This fascinates me, but what can I do?'

The answer reminded Paz how much his friend liked to lecture: 'Lousy record-keeping is the golden path to fraud and theft. People become opportunistic and light-fingered and full of self-justification. They feel they're owed more than what life's thrown them—'

'But this is not the MO you were talking about. I can't see how a sloppily-run shop can help the warehouse owners. Surely, too much risk of bad publicity.'

'You're right. You see—'

Paz didn't need further explanation. 'OK. So, in short?'

'We think some of the Trakes' collection is over in England — illegally.'

'Any clues? I imagine there's many people who've obtained pieces, buying them in good faith believing they belonged to a bona fide seller.'

'I'll send you pictures of all the missing items.'

The real question for Paz was: who was selling them in the UK? His contact in the US had no suggestions. Paz said they needed to know about every one of the people associated with the storage facility. The contact then sent a list of names and their roles. Several on the list were already helping the FBI with their investigations. Determining whether any of them had created companies for the purpose of selling the art would take longer.

Mack's research concentrated on the UK end, highlighting dealers who focused on minor, lesser known works by famous artists, and with a particular leaning towards American abstract expressionists. She found a London-based dealership that sold these artists and which, based on social media talk, had a questionable reputation. Someone even implied the firm exported stolen artworks into Europe. They styled themselves a 'private consultancy' on their website, advertising only a few specific items for sale, none resembling works owned by Mr and Mrs Trakes.

Paz emailed the Hambrook Art Consultancy saying he was interested in the following artists: Clyfford Still, Barnett Newman, and especially Willem de Kooning. He received a warm reply by phone, advising him they had several de Koonings and a Still. A Newman, the young woman said, was expected soon. He asked her where they'd come from. She told him two of the de Koonings were from the estate of a deceased man and the other items were from a divorce settlement. Paz asked for a meeting to see the works.

Paz expected to be visiting a small gallery, but the address the woman had given him, which was not on their website, looked more like a converted warehouse in a rundown street hired for maybe a month or two. He decided, however, that Mack had made an astute choice.

In a small makeshift office, he met a young woman, possibly the person who'd phoned him, who had the glamorous dark looks, expensive clothes, and slightly coquettish manner of one who, he suspected, was primarily employed to subtly persuade older men not to worry unduly about the details of what they were agreeing to. He told her he was cautious. Did they have any testimonials? She affected puzzlement as to why he needed them. Adopting the doddery old gent act he occasionally used with younger people, he replied that he'd been deceived before because of his trusting nature and so had become what others might see as overly pedantic. She said she could provide testimonials to him if essential, but 'obviously' could not give full details for privacy reasons. He asked her to remind him what de Koonings they had. She leaned towards him and, making him almost giddy with her scent, showed him the paintings onscreen with prices. He explained he wanted one for his business partner who was a keen but secretive collector of the artist and had a special birthday approaching. Where were the paintings themselves? She replied that for 'security reasons' they were 'not available' for him to see there. Paz made a note of the titles of the artworks concerned.

Back in the office, on examining the Hambrook pictures Paz immediately realised he would need the help of an expert. He rang the consultancy to ask who they used to advise on authenticity.

On meeting their chosen specialist Rosnan at his small wood-panelled office in Chelsea, Paz found a man older than him, balding and whiskery, in a grey check suit and waistcoat. He seemed a stuffy, overly precise fellow, but Paz liked him. His genuine interest in the old gentleman's work led to the latter making the suggestion, though nothing more, that he might have future work for him one day, although Paz was unclear what that might conceivably be.

The main thing Paz was interested to know was whether the recipient of such stolen works would more likely be crooks or genuine collectors who'd been conned. 'You're presupposing they're mutually exclusive,' the man said with a glint and a smile. Paz nodded, accepting his own naivety, although in truth he was merely playing the 'ignorant' role to please Rosnan. When it came to the specifics, the expert advised that he had seen the works themselves on sale and was satisfied they were genuine. On later checking, however, Paz was disappointed to discover that none of the works Hambrook currently had were on the list of stolen paintings the American contact had sent him.

Later that day, he received a call from the consultancy advising him of some other abstract expressionist works they had located. They would like him to return. Would three o'clock the following day be acceptable?

Paz went along but, although he pretended otherwise, the meeting proved a waste of time. It occurred to him that perhaps the consultancy had an ulterior motive in asking him back.

He left the dealership to drive home. When out of London heading south, with the motorway blocked, he took to minor roads. Feeling hungry he pulled into a lay-by intending to eat the pistachio cannoli he'd bought in a street market. But first, so down was he after his visit to Hambrook, that he felt the sudden need for the reassurance of talking to Mack. On calling her, he learned she'd done further digging and found on Twitter an old page for the consultancy that did show a couple of de Koonings from the list. Paz was ecstatic. Once again, Mack had shown her value. She had established that three months ago these pictures had passed through the consultancy's hands.

Satisfied, he was putting his iPhone in his jacket pocket, when he realised a car was parked behind him. So keen had he been to talk to her that he'd not paid proper attention to his surroundings. He wondered if the consultancy suspected something and so were tailing him. He always worked on the assumption that everyone knew everything and he took precautions accordingly, but not this time.

Paz took off at speed and whoever it was followed him. They must have figured out he was trouble. He left the road for a more busy A-road and they did too. He tried to commit the registration to memory so he could have it checked later. He turned off to pull up outside a pub, and they did too. He stayed in the car and then pulled away again. A few minutes later, he stopped at another pub. He immediately left his car, went to the pub door, poked his nose in - the place was warm, inviting, busy but not crowded - and then turned round, causing the person behind him confusion. It was a woman in a black headscarf and gloves. He observed her hesitate but then step inside the pub. He followed her in. He was about to tap her on the shoulder and challenge her, when he realised it wasn't the person he'd seen in the car after all. Bemused, he left the pub, only to find there was a man standing by his vehicle. He was tall and bearded, wearing a dark suit. 'What do you want?' Paz demanded, feeling nervous.

'Information,' he said. 'I want to know who you are and what you're up to. I know you've been to see the art dealer Hambrook. I was there.'

Paz said he was merely purchasing paintings. The man shook his head. Paz said, 'I'm private and I like to keep it that way.'

The man grabbed Paz's arm. 'I want to know what you people are up to.'

'People? I'm not people.' Paz realised this person was not the physical threat he'd initially thought, although that did not make him feel any more secure.

The man said, 'They ripped me off. They said they'd get me a Picasso and they failed to deliver. I tell anyone who will listen. I saw you go in and I saw you come out. I wanted to warn you not to get involved with them. I was worried you'd be hostile. Somehow when you made it obvious you knew you were being tailed, it gave me courage.'

'We should talk privately,' Paz said. 'But who's the woman?'

'Whoever you mean, she's not with me. Maybe you're getting a little paranoid.'

Paz quietly accepted this was true and the woman was nothing to do with it.

Paz followed the man, who revealed his name was Dorling, into the pub restaurant. Paz found him genial company, although also annoying because when they were seated he kept looking away, as though searching for someone he knew, or to observe an attractive woman. He claimed to be a specialist in stolen art. Paz thought: Was this guy a crook? If so, he probably knew of any new expensive art coming onto the market, and the main crooks who brought the stuff in. He probably knew who collected what and the main collectors of American abstract expressionism.

Dorling asked Paz what he was looking for, saying he liked to 'compare notes' with fellow collectors. Paz said he was looking to buy paintings by de Kooning. Dorling said he'd come to the right place for he himself collected the artist. Paz asked what he thought of Professor Rosnan. 'Professor?' Dorling barked. 'Is that what he calls himself? He's a prize fraud. I'm not sure he knows anything much.'

'Why do the consultancy use him, then?'

'You may well ask. I don't think it's ignorance on their part, let's put it that way.'

When Paz arrived back home, he did a routine check and located a telltale rectangular box under his car - a GPS tracker. So that was what it was about. Was it Dorling's handiwork, or could it be the woman at the pub, who Paz was still determined to give a role in the proceedings to? He imagined Mack tutting at his preoccupation with the woman.

Thinking of Mack summoned her. She was phoning him. She told him she'd made an 'amazing discovery'. She said she'd discovered the expert Rosnan's daughter Deborah was the owner of the consultancy. Did she have a picture of Deborah? She sent one through. Paz concluded it could have been the woman at the pub.

He decided to challenge Dorling who he was sure knew much more than he was letting on. Accordingly, next day he went to visit his new acquaintance.

Dorling had a large, ivy-covered Victorian house. It was a long time before the door was answered, and Paz could not evade the wild thought that maybe someone had killed the host the night before - someone who'd figured out the connection between Paz and him. But then Dorling came to the door with a sprightly step and beaming. 'At last,' he said, 'someone who takes me seriously.' He took Paz to his study. It resembled a war room. He had correspondence and diagrams laid out on his desk, with photographs of various people on the wall and arrows linking them, as in a crime investigation room. 'I'm on the rampage,' he said. Paz was impressed by his determination and his apparently extensive records. 'It's lucky you stopped to talk the other day,' his host said.

'It was,' Paz agreed.

'No, you don't realise how lucky,' he said. 'I could have killed you if you hadn't.'

Paz laughed it off and asked if they could dig deeper into the material he had. Dorling, who did not join Paz in laughing, claimed he had information on all of the paintings. He said he would send Paz everything he needed for his US contact. Dorling was delighted at the attention. He said, 'I'm afraid, once I get started on something I don't let go. I'm obsessed with it. At least they know they messed with the wrong guy. We'll break these crooks.'

'Indeed,' Paz said, feeling a little concerned for his new acquaintance. Dorling then, with a disconcerting casualness, pulled out a pistol from his desk drawer. 'This is what I really like to collect,' he said. 'Don't worry, it's not loaded. Of course, it was when I saw you. And when I killed that crook who tried to swindle me.'

'Self defence,' Paz said nervously. 'Call it self defence.'

'Oh no. It was an execution. To claim anything else would be shameful. One down, four to go. Now all you have to do is keep your mouth shut. Or it will be two down.' He laughed maniacally, disconcerting Paz even more.

Dorling went on to explain the background. The woman in the pub was indeed Deborah the owner of the consultancy. He revealed they had both been tailing him and she was leading him to ensure there was no mistake. 'Not that I needed her help. But since it involved bumping you off, it had to be exactly right.' Dorling savoured being able to tell Paz this and witness his look of shock.

'Then why didn't you?'

'Didn't *yet*,' Dorling corrected, savouring it even more. He then revealed he had his own 'issues' with the consultancy. He believed Rosnan had knowingly authenticated pictures he'd bought from Deborah that were in reality fakes.

Paz was wary of Dorling's revelations. 'Why are you telling me all this?' he said.

Dorling did not answer directly and instead described what he called the 'Bailly' issue. He explained how he'd recently been induced by the consultancy into buying paintings by an artist called Bailly, which had been referred to Rosnan who maintained Bailly was an alter ego of de Kooning. This was compelling to Dorling who would otherwise not have been interested. But Dorling was now convinced these were fakes and indeed Bailly was not de Kooning. He felt aggrieved with Deborah and Rosnan over it. They had conned him into paying over the odds.

He had not challenged them, however, in case they decided to dispose of him. But when Deborah asked him to kill Paz for a fee, he decided to sabotage the hit.

'But why would Deborah want to kill me?'

'A humble, harmless PI? Give me a break. She knew the FBI would eventually become interested in Hambrook Consultancy, but by then they would have disappeared. You showing up meant the brief time they had before they had to split was gone. You were too quick for them. But no-one would care about you being out of the way. You would simply be just another missing person.'

Paz imagined Mack in tears sitting at her desk, determined to find out what had happened to him. She would piece the case together if the police could not. On the other hand, he did not believe a word of what Dorling was saying.

On the drive home, while still coming to terms with Dorling's outpourings, Paz was hit by another revelation when Mack called. He pulled over into a lay-by, this time mindful of any cars parking up behind him, but there was nothing there. She told him she'd discovered 'Your Mr Dorling' was Hambrook owner Deborah's step-father.

'Are you sure?'

'Of course. Do you not trust me now all of a sudden?'

'It's not that... It's just, oh Mamma Mia! One thing I can tell you is that Dorling's no fan of her father, Professor Rosnan.'

Late that afternoon, Paz phoned his contact in New York and gave him what he had, including what Dorling had provided him with. He also phoned the local police. He told them about Dorling's claims. A Detective Sumnar laughed and told him Dorling was a known fantasist, always making up stories about art, and guns he owned, and people he'd killed and been hired to kill. 'We're not so easily fooled,' he assured Paz.

'I'm telling you, Dorling has some stolen paintings by Willem de Kooning, or he knows who does.'

A few days later, he heard on the News that Professor Rosnan had died in a suspicious accident at home. 'A professional job,' he was told by one of his contacts. The police, perhaps now with less scepticism, had raided Dorling's place. They found seven stolen de Koonings. Dorling had a strong alibi for the night of the murder: he was showing off his gun collection to a group of retired policemen. He claimed he'd bought the paintings in good faith, but neither the police nor Paz believed him. As for the suspected murder, it turned out Dorling was not the only person impacted by the father-daughter racket. Someone else, another Hambrook customer perhaps, was sufficiently angry to want Rosnan out of the way.

In the following weeks, Paz's clients obtained confirmation they would receive some of their paintings back. Not all, because some had already been sold by customers of Hambrook. The clients decided to end his assignment, preferring to rely on the authorities to locate the rest. Based on past experience, Paz surmised they'd soon get frustrated and he'd be called back in.

Chapter 14

Money

Unusually for Paz, he was having a listless day, struggling to focus on work. He was in need of something different to perk him up. Mid-afternoon, he was enjoying a cup of Darjeeling, talking to Mack, when a man in his late thirties came to see him. He was quite shy and nervous and seemed unsure of himself. Paz warmed to him and hoped he'd have an interesting story to tell. The man said he was worried about his father. The old man had become very religious since his wife died, and he was becoming forgetful and vague and not really in control of his affairs. Paz thought he could understand how grief would have left the father disorientated and depressed and paying less attention to things that were important to him.

'I think he's being taken advantage of,' the son said. 'He's getting near the point where he may have to go into a care home. He's dead against it, and we don't like the idea either, but it may be unavoidable.'

'Does he have a carer?'

'It's just me and my sister. We both live near him and take it in turns. She's worried too. She would have come with me, but it's difficult with her work.'

'So whose influence is it you're worried about exactly?'

'The Church.'

This answer surprised Paz. The man proceeded to tell him that a local church had an investment scheme, and his father, who was spending more and more time in the church and talking to its officials, was minded to join it. So what, Paz wondered silently? Were they worried about his will? Surely it was his right to do whatever he wanted with his own money. They probably ought to put him in a care home but didn't want to see their inheritance whittle away in fees. And now they were worried about the Church. And if it wasn't the Church, it would be charities. Paz was becoming irritated, but at least he didn't feel listless anymore. He had a positive aversion to getting involved in family financial issues like this. 'So why have you come to me?' he said. 'I'm not social services or a financial adviser. If there's something I can—'

'There is.' He sensed Paz's irritation. 'I want you to investigate this church's money-making scheme. I know you can't advise on finance. I don't want a financial adviser. I want an investigator. I want to know what it's about because it's too good to be true and my dad's getting sucked into it.'

'OK.'

Paz felt admonished. The man gave him the name of the ministry, where it was and so on. Paz's attitude towards him softened again. He no longer saw him as jealous of his father's wealth but instead someone with a natural desire to protect his old man from sharks. He asked him if he went to church with his father. He said his father went with a neighbour.

Paz said, 'I think one of you should go with him, maybe both of you, and try to get a recording of the proceedings. Then if you're still worried, come back to me.'

'We'll both go, but it won't change anything. It won't reassure us. They're going to come and see dad and get him to sign up. He's excited about it. He thinks he's doing the right thing by God and us and that he's going to get his money back - double.'

In the end, Paz went along himself. He was an agnostic and would never normally go to church. It was a Victorian C of E building that had fallen into dereliction and been sold off but was now being revived. He saw the siblings with their father there but thought it better not to sit with them. There were plenty of people making him feel welcome, but he was standoffish. He could see that for some people the Church gave hope. And of course the preachers were charismatic and created a good show. But Paz was only there for the financial side of it.

Halfway through the service, a middle-aged, all-smiles, rotund male church official did an 'overview' presentation on the 'growth fund', showing how well it was doing. There was a board on an easel at the front and it had a chart showing the 'astronomic progress' of the fund. The faithful, mostly pensioners, began leaving their seats and lining up in excited anticipation. It was clear that some of them had signed up before and were confidently adding to their investment. The main preacher, a red-faced, barrel-chested man, then gave a passionate speech using Bible verses to help explain why it was blessed by God, and how God would respond by rewarding them. More people were rising from their seats and standing happily in the ever-lengthening line with chequebooks and cards out ready to make payments and sign the necessary paperwork. As the son had told Paz, there was no opportunity to ask questions about it. Instead, 'moved by the Spirit', people committed then and there with the promise of returns no normal fund could provide.

Paz could see the siblings arguing with their father who was desperate to join the queue, as rousing music from the stage - a loud, happy repeated chorus of 'Hallelujah! He's my saviour. Hallelujah! Hallelu!' - increased the frenzy. He noticed a young church official striding towards the family to intervene, and he likewise made his way over to them to provide a distraction. The official looked hellbent on getting the father into the queue, and the siblings were equally determined to prevent it. Once amongst them, Paz told the official he was the family's financial adviser and was puzzled as to how they could achieve the advertised returns. The man said the fund's director would be giving a more detailed update in a few moments, and that would remove any need for questions. In view of the siblings' hostility towards him, and all the associated embarrassment, the official then backed away. Paz figured this man was not part of the inside group when it came to the fund, but he seemed so committed that he probably thought it obvious to everyone it was a good thing, and therefore believed it was merely a matter of time before the father, and indeed the children as well, felt compelled to join.

As the music faded, one of the preachers, thin and syrupy, introduced the 'financial expert', the fund's director, a pasty-faced, bespectacled man in a suit, who explained how the fund was being invested in countries that were poor and needed help to develop, mainly through mining ventures. More people queued up while he was speaking, the main preacher then gave another stirring speech, and the father was almost fighting to get out of his seat. His children at last let him stand up, quickly rose to their feet, grabbed his arms, and marched the furious old man out of the church.

Paz joined them outside. The father was in such a cursing rage Paz was worried he'd have a heart attack. The overall situation bothered him greatly. The fact was, they couldn't watch him all day, and he'd be in touch with the church hierarchy as soon as he had the chance. He felt bad for all three of them. He had to do something.

Next morning, Mack did research online and found the church had several branches, mainly in the north of England. One was in Doncaster where Paz had a contact. He phoned this woman and asked what she knew about it. He wasn't expecting her to be familiar with it, but she told him she had family friends who'd become involved with the church and found the investment irresistible. They'd put money in and soon started receiving regular statements that on their face supported the claims made for the fund. But of course with the statements came the exhortation to put more money in 'for this world-saving work' to attain even higher returns, and so the process went on. 'Where does the profit really come from to feed the returns?' Paz asked.

'Only the fund bosses know.'

'Sounds like a scam in the making to me. I bet there's no real business going on. They're just recycling money, taking out commissions as they go. Marvellous. So the new church in Brighton is to get new investors in to pay for the interest payments of those who wish to cash out. It's a Ponzi scheme masquerading as religion.'

By leaving church early with his client's family he'd missed the main excitement. There had been an altercation. An 'undesirable' had been forcibly removed from the church, according to an account in the Argus. It had led to the police being called by an associate of the man involved. It had all begun when he shouted that the church and investment fund were all a scam. Paz wondered whether perversely this had been staged to gain publicity for the church.

It turned out that Paz had been recognised there. 'Didn't know you were born again,' said the caller on the phone, 'or born yesterday.'

'Charlie Kibbs. How did I miss you? What were you doing there?'

'Same thing as you, by the look of it. Help the aged. Keeping the sheep away from the wolf. My old mum is obsessed with it. She wants to put all her money in. Thinks it will be a nice nest egg for her dear son. She's already put twenty grand in. And guess what?'

'Go on.'

'It's not an investment at all, it's a gift. So taking your money out is claiming a gift back.'

'But I heard them say it's an investment.'

'Very astute. But not as astute as you think. If you listened properly, you'd have heard them say it was an investment in the people of Africa and harmony between peoples. No investment in the sense of pure money. Like I say, "You make us a gift and if you're lucky we'll give you a bigger gift in return."'

'Will you get her money out?'

'They'd better give it back if they want to stay in business.' He hoped Charlie was right but feared he was deluded. Charlie seemed to believe he only had to whistle and the MPs would be all over it, worried lest their own aged parents got caught up in it.

It turned out that the 'undesirable' they'd turfed out of church was an undercover operative employed by the Newcastle police. Paz's guess was the church had a list of 'troublemakers' to be on the lookout for. He fully expected to be added to the list. The following Sunday, he stood outside, merely watching all the people going in. He did not see the old man and the siblings. He wondered if he'd had the heart attack Paz had feared for him. This week's 'undesirable' thrown out was a journalist with the Guardian. Paz spoke to him as he was dusting himself off. He said he was investigating after a local parishioner had changed his will to give everything to the church. The parishioner had died of a fall three weeks later. He said this was the third parishioner at the various churches this had happened to.

Paz phoned his client to let him know of these developments. To his amazement, the man said his father had experienced an epiphany and no longer craved the returns the church promised. He said someone who spoke to him on the phone had persuaded him it was not the thing to invest in. No, he was convinced he should invest in a green future for his grandchildren. Thus, he'd put his money into Indonesian rainforests instead. No paperwork to worry about either. No worries over gift versus investment. The man on the phone had set it up for him automatically. All hundred thousand pounds of it. 'Just like magic,' his dad had said.

'How do you feel about that?' Paz asked, seriously concerned for the family.

'Oh, I've given up. We can't police him day and night. He's so trusting. What do you do with someone who won't be told?'

'These people on the phone never give up, do they? They're so damned clever.'

'That's certainly true,' the client said. 'It does take skill. But with practice I was able to disguise my voice sufficiently. I soon discovered I can sound quite convincing.'

Chapter 15

The Shadow Yacht

One morning, Paz was in the office early when he received a call from a lawyer based in London. The lawyer, a Ms Hayes, said that he had been chosen to investigate a case on behalf of a well-known 'international businessman' Mr van Dent. Paz asked what it was about, but she said for confidentiality reasons she would only discuss it in person. Could he attend their offices for a meeting at 10 a.m. that morning?

Paz took the train to London Bridge and a cab to St Katharine Docks. Previously all he knew about van Dent was that he'd married a Russian model thirty years his junior and recently enjoyed a reverse vasectomy - clearly not an exponent of the simple life. By the time Paz arrived he'd figured out the case was probably connected with a lawsuit launched by a female celebrity model / actress / singer called The Sexy Solution, that was trending on social media. He was intrigued at the prospect, even though it would likely be a ridiculous squabble amongst people he couldn't care less about. But it was work, and if he didn't do it someone else would, and if they did a half-decent job it would mean that someone else receiving more work from van Dent and the law firm that he could have had himself. It looked like a 'drop everything' case and he imagined his speech to Mack about its importance to the firm and she grinning at his earnestness.

The lawyer Ms Hayes was a stocky blonde in her late forties, feisty-looking, and cynical. With her was a tall, shy, young female associate with long brown hair, whom she introduced as Ann. Hayes told him she knew van Dent personally and was proud to be acting for him. She made it clear, without saying so, that this was work he couldn't refuse, and there was no doubt he would take it on. He wasn't going to argue. She then explained what the case was about. He'd been correct: it concerned the woman calling herself The Sexy Solution, real name Debra Buchan. She'd been on van Dent's superyacht off the Florida coast, unwelcome photographs of her there had appeared days later in the press, in particular a notorious scandal sheet, and this had triggered a number of claims and accusations. Sexy / Debra had sued the scandal sheet which had rather more than implied a relationship between her and the businessman. Worse, the photographs made clear that she was fit and well, whereas according to her record company, a movie production firm, and the TV channel for whom she featured in a soap opera, she was variously suffering from a broken leg, a bad back, and a serious illness requiring her to be out of sunlight. These entities had all sued her, or were threatening to, for breach of contract, and she in turn had sued van Dent. Worse for him, there was speculation his wife would seek a divorce. 'Your job,' the lawyer Hayes said, 'is to find out who took these pictures, and how, and why. Obviously we will subpoena the scandal sheet for their source, but it is unlikely the source is the person who took them.'

'You mean, they will have passed through a number of hands?'

'Correct. Like most successful people, Mr van Dent has many enemies. It could be the press, it could be his already estranged wife—'

'Six months, isn't it? That's quick.'

'—or it could be a business rival seeking to damage his reputation or scupper a hostile takeover. The current theory is that the photographs were taken by a member of the crew of the shadow yacht.'

'Shadow yacht? I'm not familiar with that term.'

'It's a support boat for the superyacht. It carries all the toys like dinghies, jet skis, diving gear, even a small sub, as well as the essentials: food supplies, freezer, wine cellar, a laundry, even a small hospital.'

'OK. And a small armoury, I shouldn't wonder.'

She ignored this comment. 'We have the crew list for the shadow yacht.'

'And the main yacht?'

'Yes, and we will provide you with lists of everyone onboard. With photographs of the crew and their work history.'

'Great. I'll need pictures of both boats and detailed specifications. And, of course, the photographs that have caused all the trouble.'

She produced an envelope from her briefcase and took out seven large prints. The woman at the centre of the dispute featured in all of them, not apparently in discomfort or an abundance of clothing. Mr van Dent appeared in several with her. The photographs looked genuine. One picture was clearly taken from a position away from the superyacht, but others could have been taken on it. Paz said, 'Were these pictures all taken with the same camera?'

'As far as we know, yes.' Ms Hayes stood up. 'Now if you'll excuse me, I have to be elsewhere. You will be reporting in the main to Ann. By the way, we customarily insist on weekly updates from investigators.' She shook his hand. 'Thank you for taking this assignment.'

She left him with Ann. They chatted and he immediately liked the young associate. She conveyed a cool manner, but what he appreciated was that she seemed, at least outwardly, respectful of what he did. He found most young lawyers ignorant about investigators, thinking them little more than rats rooting about in dustbins for dirt - a job anyone could do - whereas lawyers were professionals after years of hard study, and exams, and sparring with the finest minds. In their conversation Ann exhibited an awareness that investigators maybe had their own skills built up from experience.

He said, 'Can I ask a silly question: Why is there such urgency? Why not wait for the result of the subpoena and see where that leads to?'

'Because this may be merely part of a campaign. Photographs today, a home invasion tomorrow, stolen secrets, who knows?'

He said, 'I guess being wealthy makes you a little paranoid. But then at this point we don't know who is the real target - her or him.' She nodded and then revealed that from initial investigations the question mark was over a crew member of the shadow yacht who went by the name of Jake Maltman, a Canadian. He was the least known amongst the crew.

Paz knew from experience it was a false assumption that the most mysterious party was also the most suspicious, but it was a good place to start. 'I see from this document his role was that of deckhand.' He flicked through the photos. 'I'm strictly a landlubber, but even I can see that some of these pictures were probably not taken from the shadow yacht. By the way, as I understand it, they have CCTV on these boats. And security staff.'

'Yes. That will all need to be looked into.'

They loaded all the relevant non-sensitive information onto his laptop, and after discussing it, he asked her for the opportunity to call his office. She left the room. On opening up his phone he found there were two voicemails from Mack. The first call was about an insurer chasing up a surveillance job. This was with a freelancer who was proving unresponsive. The second voicemail was about the same freelancer who'd phoned to say he was ill with a virus. Paz hated using freelancers because too often they were sloppy and unreliable, but the difficulty was that the surveillance work often came in tranches and freelancers picked up the excess of cases he couldn't handle himself. It reminded him of the campaign Jane used to bug him with - to hire more staff so she could do more surveillance work and thus obviate the need to recruit freelancers.

He rang Mack, saying he needed her help to do some 'internet magic'. She was keen to investigate a new case. He briefly explained the situation to her and sent her the information on the shadow yacht crew member Maltman including his photograph, address, and phone number. She was intrigued.

A few hours later, he was back in his office and Mack told him what she'd done: First, a search on Maltman with the Canadian address, which had produced nothing. She had then done a search on the phone number. It came back with the name Henning and an address in Paleo New Mexico. She'd done a Facebook search for this Henning. There were two possible candidates. Neither had photographs matching the man they were looking for. It began to look like they were back where they'd begun. He asked Mack how many Facebook friends the two men named Henning had. One had 137, the other 23. She checked through the friends of the Henning with 23. Amongst them she found a picture of what looked like their man on the crew list. She did an image search on that photograph, throwing up yet another person's name.

'OK, Mack, I think we need to recap a moment. What I think we're saying is that Maltman is not his real name, it's an alias, and Henning is an alias of his too, so his real name is something else again.'

'Yes. The real person we want is called Jack Daley, but we won't be the only ones looking.'

'What do you mean?'

'His girlfriend in Orange County has reported him a missing person. I should say, by the way, our Mr Daley has an extensive criminal record. Felony thefts mainly.'

'Mack, this is great.'

It was time to check the old Rolodex. He had good contacts within law enforcement in California and was confident one in particular, Jeff Malang, could assist. He set up a conference call with Jeff and Mack. It was the first of several. These two quickly established a rapport, so much so that this led to a mild falling out between Paz and her. On one of the calls Mack in jest called Paz 'irrelevant'.

After the call, her miffed boss told her that if he was so irrelevant she could set up her own shop without him. She apologised, not only for what she'd said but because she knew admonishing her, even the need to, would have upset him more than her comment itself. Whenever she knew she'd upset him, the next day she wore a lower top or shorter skirt. It irritated him that she thought him susceptible to this form of appeasement, even whilst acknowledging to himself he was. He appreciated the fact she thought some gesture necessary but was annoyed with himself for reacting to her teasing.

With Jeff's help they managed to establish a link between Jack Daley and Debra Buchan. Through searching on social media, they were able to establish that Daley's brother Fred had once been in a relationship with her. They found evidence that Fred had helped her in her early career, and they worked on the theory that on becoming famous she had abandoned him and he was sore over this. His inability to get back with her could provide an explanation for his tragic demise - a self-inflicted shot to the head. Fred's sister Avril was known to be jealous of Debra's fame and blamed her for his death.

Jeff also advised there was speculation Fred Daley had not committed suicide but had been murdered over a drug debt, prompting Avril to claim Fred must have bought the drugs for Debra, thereby giving her an alternative reason to cast blame on her. It began to look like Fred's brother Jack aka Henning aka Maltman had taken the photographs as part of Avril's relentless campaign against Debra Buchan.

While Paz was preparing his latest report about Avril and her camera-happy brother for the solicitor Ann, he received a call from her boss Ms Hayes. She gave him some disturbing news, having learnt that morning her law firm had been sacked by van Dent. 'Why?' he asked.

'His wife's divorcing him and he's hired a different firm to represent him. He's decided to give them all his other legal work too. I'm sorry, Paz. You'll be paid, don't worry.'

'But what about my report? Won't the new firm need it?'

'No, because the case has been settled. Before the new firm was appointed, Mr van Dent hired them specifically to resolve the case as a kind of test.'

'I see.'

'They did it and now van Dent no longer has any interest in the matter, legal or otherwise.'

'I'm gutted. My assistant has been working on this night and day.'

'As I said, you'll be paid. These things happen.'

'They sure do.'

To his surprise, when he told Mack about it she merely said, 'I made a new contact at least. And I learnt a lot. Might be good for my career.' He wondered what was behind these bland statements. Was she planning to set up her own operation as soon as she'd drained him of all his knowledge? He felt disappointed with himself for having such thoughts.

Another whose career benefited from the case was Debra Buchan. The settlement included the parties suing her, and all claims were dropped. Because of all the publicity, she was linked to all manner of new media deals. The only loser from it in the end was van Dent. His new law firm botched the divorce, and a shortage of funds forced him to sell the superyacht. It was put up for auction. Paz did not bid for it.

Chapter 16

Cold Case

One morning, Paz received a call from Suzi who was now married. She was in hospital, having had a fall at her new house. He went to see her at the Royal Sussex and found her heavily bruised on her face, arms, and legs. Paz was not convinced that a fall was responsible. He believed Terry had beaten her up and he told her so.

'Your fault, Paz. You could have had me when you had the chance and you didn't take it.'

'Will you press charges?'

'Against you, you mean? Maybe. Not against him.'

When he got back to the office, he learned he'd missed a visit by Jane. Mack said Jane would phone him later. Mack was subdued. She asked him, 'When she comes back to work will I have to leave?'

He was puzzled. 'Why?'

'Because I was hired as the temporary maternity cover, remember?'

How had he forgotten? To make it worse, so surprised was he by the question, being so preoccupied about Suzi, that he stumbled over his answer, rambling into incoherence. All she wanted was reassurance.

'So I might have to leave, then,' she said, and she walked out of his office.

That afternoon, she performed her work as usual but was clearly distracted. Paz wanted to tell her not to worry, but he did not know what to say that would not make it worse. The truth was, he hadn't thought about whether he could retain both her and Jane.

On the short drive home, he wondered what he should do. Mack had performed way beyond his expectations but, as she said, she was temporary. That was the arrangement. Could he even afford both of them? Would they work well together? He thought back. After the initial frostiness they'd become cordial, though with a recognition they would never be close and, he observed, now they might see each other as rivals. The reality was that Mack was indispensable, and she knew it.

That evening, Jane called. After the initial talk about the baby, she told him that, after a great deal of careful thought, she had decided to move on with her life. Accordingly, she had accepted a job with Fran Owens. 'More money. More than you could offer.'

'How do you know?'

'Because I assume you'd have paid it before if you could. But he's also offered me a new branch to run.'

'Local?'

'Yes.'

'In competition with me, then.'

'No! It's not about you.'

'I'm sorry. It's a bit of a blow. But is it definite?'

'I don't see any real alternative. I've loved working with you, but now you have Mack, and I need to move on. Not in opposition. Please don't see it that way. I would still like to work with you.'

'And I would like to work with you in future. But you won't want to do surveillance work for me, will you?'

'Maybe. But my role will be more managerial. We might be in a position to give you work.'

That word 'we' stung him. She had moved on already. 'We' now meant her and Fran. Underneath the pleasantries the raw truth felt to him like the beginning of the end. Fran would be taking him over next. Well, Fran could try, but he would fight him off. He must ensure Mack didn't lose out. But she would be the next target. Paz said, 'Leave me Mack.'

'But what if she wants—'

'Whatever she says she wants, I will do everything to keep her.' Clearly they'd thought about it, maybe even discussed it with her.

'I won't encourage her, but if—'

'I understand.'

After the call he rang Mack but there was no answer.

In the morning, he decided to update Mack on what Jane had said. 'When is she coming back?' she asked.

'She isn't. She's setting up a new office as part of the Fran Owens empire. You may be next.'

'I'm actually quite loyal by nature,' she said in an offended tone. 'Although I wonder why sometimes.'

'I phoned you last night.'

'What time?'

'About eight.'

'At eight o'clock I was having a fuck with Lily.'

'Really? No need to be crude.'

'It's what we call it. Even Lily, whose pretty straight-laced these days. I love it and I'm good at it. Maybe it's the only thing I'm good at.'

'No.'

'Poor bitch. Barely time to get her kit off before she was bundled into the shower.'

'Please stop.'

'So do you still want me?'

'Of course.'

'You could show it.'

'Why don't you take the afternoon off? You've been working especially hard lately.'

'I don't want the afternoon off. I want to work and I want to talk. Do you like my outfit? Lily bought it for me.' She looked like the escorts he looked at online occasionally but never contacted. She was wearing red fishnet tights, black ankle boots with heels, and a short black leather skirt.

'Why are you wearing it to the office. It seems more—'

'To get noticed... by you.' She gave him an appealing smile. 'Paz, I wondered if you wanted to go to lunch. I'll treat you for once.'

'That would be nice. Unfortunately, I've a report I must read.' Like most of his lies it was partially true, but he didn't have to read it at lunchtime. It was obvious to her he wasn't interested.

'I just thought maybe we could talk about the future.'

'Future?'

'My future. And yours.'

'Yes, we should.' It was too late. He'd messed up and they both knew it. He watched Mack saunter to his door to leave, but then she paused, legs akimbo with her back to him. Tossing her red hair gently from side to side, she was taunting him. Her metamorphosis was complete: she was on fire. She knew she had the power and he was too weak to fight. It occurred to him at last that the real problem might be that she was lonely at work. Apart from a young woman called Marie on the floor above, who did she ever see to talk to in person but him?

His thoughts were interrupted by the phone ringing and he forgot about Mack's emotional health. The call was from a police officer from a small town in the north-west. She said she was investigating a cold case from eight years ago. She wanted to know about a man named Parnell who, it was believed, had moved to Brighton five years prior. It was a missing person's case. It was his ex-wife that was missing and Parnell was key. Her family were convinced he was involved in her disappearance, but the police had never felt there was enough evidence. The policewoman sent Paz photographs of him. He looked vaguely familiar, but Paz never paid much heed to that because it could easily have been someone on TV or social media he was reminded of.

Mack found the name Parnell on the electoral register. From those listed she and Paz managed to form a subset of those the man might be, and in the following days he paid each one a visit. As was invariably the case, it was the last one that offered the most potential. The studious-looking woman who cautiously answered the door told Paz that 'Mr Parnell' had moved away months earlier. He wondered whether he'd been alerted about the case being reopened and had skipped town, but then the woman said the man who'd lived there had lately used the alias Spain. How did she know? Because he had business cards printed with that name on and people sometimes phoned asking for it. But although correspondence arrived for the name of Parnell, there was none for Spain. She had no forwarding address. Paz asked her what sort of correspondence it was. She left him for a few moments and then returned with a large envelope. She said, 'You may as well have this,' and she handed it to him.

Back in the office, he emptied the envelope and, wearing gloves to remove the risk of additional prints, went through the various correspondence. He found a strange postcard that read, 'Glad you've seen the light at last. See you on your return.' It was merely signed 'A'. Paz wondered whether there'd been earlier correspondence from A, but found none. Paz called the policewoman who'd contacted him. He said he would send the letters on but added that one postcard might be an oblique blackmail message. The photograph on it was of a village near Cambridge. Paz gave her the subject's new name, Spain, but said he'd rented a property in Brighton as Parnell. He took photographs of both sides of the card before carefully placing it back in the large envelope to send to the police officer.

Mack did social media searches on both names, Parnell and Spain, but only found references to the Brighton area. Paz decided to explore the Cambridge link. Mack told him to be especially careful: the subject was a potentially highly dangerous man. He laughed, saying it was merely a necessary part of the job and he would track him down 'with the zeal of a bounty hunter', using the pretext that he was looking for an old relative. But he was touched by her concern.

The place of interest was a commuter village with no traditional centre, but it had several shops, including one that served as a post office. He enquired there whether they could recognise Parnell / Spain from the picture he showed them. The red-haired assistant looked nervous. 'Do you think you've seen him around here?' said Paz. The woman blushed. 'He lives in my street, actually,' she said.

This was going too well, he thought. He asked for the address, which she gave him. Then she said, 'You won't find him in. He's gone away.'

'Did Mr Spain say where?'

'Spain? His name is Smith. George Smith. He was going abroad, so I heard. Is everything alright?'

'What's he like?'

'Very charming. We don't see him much and he doesn't engage in social events in the village. Keeps to himself. But he's very nice.'

There was a local taxi service. He thought he would use that rather than drive as he might learn something from the driver. When they'd set off, the driver asked if he was delivering something. Paz said he wasn't.

'I don't think you'll find anyone there.'

'How do you know?'

'I drove him to Stansted airport a couple of weeks ago, and I don't think he's come back yet.'

'I see. Has he been living here long?'

'No. He took over the place from his brother Alan.'

'Oh? What happened to the brother, then?'

'I don't know. I never met him. Alan had a red Triumph. Never see it around here now.'

'What does Mr Smith do?'

'Some kind of businessman. Fund management. Something to do with Spain. He tried to interest me in it, but I said I didn't have any spare money. Some people in the village have done well out of it.'

'Really?'

'To be honest, it made me suspicious.'

'Why?'

'I don't know. Guy shows up. Next thing you know he's selling investments that sound too good to be true.'

'I heard he keeps to himself.'

'He does, but he had a table at the local show. Had all this promotional stuff out. Promised a return of thirty per cent a year. What investment gives that? Some new lithium mining development in Spain, so he claimed. The world's greatest expert on lithium mines had found it. So Mr Smith bought the land it was on. He had testimonials.'

'For the mine or the investment?'

'Eh? The investment. Do you want me to wait for you?'

Paz agreed, even though he didn't really trust him. Smith was his customer too, and he could imagine the taxi driver telling Smith all about the suspicious man enquiring after him.

The house was a detached century-old building well back from the road. The garden was overgrown and the house's exterior had not been looked after. Smith's desire for clients had clearly not extended to hosting parties at home for them. A successful investment manager could afford to hire a gardener at least. In fact, the whole place, from what Paz could see, was in a state of neglect. Surely his investors would draw conclusions from that. One thing which caught his attention, however, was the surveillance system. There were multiple security cameras.

At the end of the garden he noticed a gate to another property and found it unlocked. It led to a rough vegetable garden. There was a small chicken run and he could see a few hens. To one side there was a red brick bungalow with a hint of smoke emerging from the chimney. As he approached, a slim young woman in a floral headscarf slipped out to confront him. She was smiling but in a condescending way. 'What did you want?' she asked sharply. 'There's no eggs, I'm afraid. They're not laying just now.' He explained that he was interested in the investment scheme that Mr Smith had going. He showed her the photograph the policewoman had sent.

'That's him,' she confirmed.

'Do you know where he is now?'

'No.' He sensed this was a lie. It was the way she looked at him - shyly.

'Can I ask, did you know the other Mr Smith - Alan - who lived here before?'

'No.' He asked her if she knew where he'd gone and she said she didn't. Another lie, he suspected. Then she volunteered, 'I haven't been living here long.'

In the car he mentioned to the driver he'd met the bungalow resident. This amused him. 'Rather sweet,' he said. 'I never can quite understand what the setup is there, though.'

'Are they related?'

He didn't reply, merely laughed, which Paz found odd.

He decided he needed to stick around the area and so spent the night at a B&B. In the morning, he talked to the owner, a middle-aged woman, about the investment scheme. She asked him if he was interested in joining it. For a minimum of five hundred pounds he could sign up. He asked her whether he'd need to see Mr Smith for that. She said, no, he wasn't the main person running it. She said it was managed by a Mr Allen. He'd lived at the house before Smith but then went abroad on business and stayed there. It was he that did the initial presentations. After Mr Allen left, Smith did them.

Paz thought about his conversation with the taxi driver. 'Do you mean Alan, his brother?'

'Not brother. People thought they were because they were similar in looks and because Allen is a common Christian name.' She said she had a form about it if he was interested, but it was all done online. Paz said he'd defer his decision about joining the fund until one of them returned, but he took the form, which looked professionally done. There was no contact information on it, only a website.

Back in Brighton later that day, Paz phoned his police contact. He told her he'd found the trail for Parnell aka Spain aka Smith. He told her about the lithium mine investment scheme, saying it sounded like a scam. He said 'Spain' was probably a fake role he played as an 'independent financial adviser' to steer investors to himself as 'Smith' as fund manager. He told her she might also want to look into Allen who was apparently the mastermind behind the scheme.

The policewoman rang Paz back the following day, saying she'd learned Allen had died in a house fire in Corfu, and she confirmed he was connected to Parnell through business. When he told Mack about this she teased him about whether he would 'need' to travel round the Greek islands to track down Parnell. No, the case had become a police matter again.

They continued to follow it. The Spanish lithium mine investment scheme showed up in British ex-pat communities in Corfu, Tenerife, and Cyprus. The young woman he'd met in the garden was Parnell's stepdaughter who'd moved to the bungalow to be close to him in hope of learning the fate of her mother. Press reports advised Parnell's wife's remains had at last been found. She'd been strangled, and this was established as Allen's cause of death also. The house fire had been set to destroy the evidence. Allen had a life insurance for the benefit of the business, which was now owned by the suspect.

Parnell was eventually arrested and jailed for fraud and then tried for the murders of his wife and Allen. He got a life sentence on Allen but was cleared on his wife's death due to lack of evidence. That case went cold again.

Chapter 17

The Chagall Lithograph

It was a quiet afternoon at the office when a Mrs Clark came to see Paz. She was about fifty, quite neat and prim, with small delicate hands and a shy manner. She appeared embarrassed, with the look of someone feeling foolish for something they'd done - his favourite kind of client. But he noticed her hands were almost trembling as she clutched her cup of water, and he'd rather she were more relaxed. She placed the cup down on the desk with exaggerated care and began her story about an auction she'd attended. 'It was quite busy that day,' she said.

'Take your time,' he said gently to calm her. 'So, where are we talking — London or more local?'

'London, but not one of the big houses. It's not there now, unfortunately. Out East. I went along because I'd been before with my sister who lives near it, and she and I own a small gallery around there. I went on this occasion because they were auctioning a Chagall lithograph *Nuit des Oiseaux,* and I fancied it as he's a favourite artist of mine but I've never owned one of his. Anyway, this lithograph came up with a reserve price of forty thousand pounds. Very rare. Very small print run. Hand signed. And above all, those blues and yellows I love so much — warm and joyful. I was so keen, I was sure I'd be able to secure it. There was quite a bit of interest, but in the end it came down to me and another bidder. I got up to seventy-three thousand, but then I suddenly got that feeling — you know it, I'm sure — when you just realise it's a lost cause, and the only way to win is to put up silly money.

So I just stopped. You've always got to be prepared to withdraw. So I let it go to the other bidder.'

'I know exactly what you mean,' he said, 'although auctions are not really my scene.'

'Nothing else that day interested me much, but I stayed until the end just to see how the rest of the proceedings went. As I was leaving, something very odd happened. A woman approached me, saying it was her husband that had successfully bid for the Chagall, intending it as a gift for her because of her love of the artist. She said, "I've talked to my husband, and seeing how much it means to you — you seemed so disappointed at missing out, and I can't blame you because it's so lovely — we thought we should offer it to you. Not at what we paid for it, obviously, but at your highest bid." I found this all rather strange.'

The visitor paused, waiting for some response, so Paz said, 'Yes, I can understand that.'

She continued, 'She seemed sincere but I was cautious. When I said I'd feel compelled to pay the same as her husband, she waved the suggestion aside. Then she confided, "I will confess to you we have an ulterior motive. Well, to be honest..." — she was almost whispering at this point — "...the truth is, we can't afford it. I mean, we could at the time — my husband bid in good faith — but less than an hour ago we learned that the stockbroking firm my father built up — in fact, my husband worked there — has gone bust. We'd intended to sell most of our shares in it to expand our organic food shop, but those shares are worth nothing now." She looked so downcast as she said, "Therefore purchasing the Chagall was a mistake, and actually it would assist us if you were to buy it."

'At that point, a woman came in — maybe a sister or sister-in-law — and she thrust her arms around the first woman and said, "Oh, Diane, I'm so sorry!" which only added to my embarrassment. So they are both in this mournful state, which only makes me want to get away as soon as possible, and then the husband appears, smiling, relaxed, and seeing his wife so upset he takes me to one side and apologises for her theatricality, explaining that she tends to exaggerate, and that, although they really were going to have to sell it, there was a ready market (which is true, there is), and a dealer in Paris had offered to buy it from him even before the auction, knowing he'd be successful because he always was. He said, "I must say, though, you gave me a tough fight. I felt like a fisherman reeling in one of those big marlins. But forget what my wife said, she gets very stressed out." I said, "OK, I didn't understand it anyway because of the buyer's premium you'd lose." He said that was true but they'd make a good profit from up-and-coming British artists at the same auction (which I remembered), so they'd still be ahead. He said, "I can put it up for auction again or sell it direct. It's no problem."

'At this I said I'd buy it off him for the seventy-three thousand I'd bid at auction but, to my surprise, he politely declined, saying he was confident of selling it for a higher price. At that point, I was determined not to pay more, especially as his wife had said it would be accepted. We argued in a friendly way, and in the end he said with exasperation that I was tenacious and so he would sell it to me if he hadn't sold it in a week's time and if I was still interested. We exchanged business cards. I was excited at the possibility; it was a good price for a genuine, rare lithograph with a certificate of authentication, and I'd realise my long-held ambition of owning a Chagall.'

'Hmm,' said Paz. He was fascinated by her story but wanted the opportunity to mull it over for a moment.

He thought she might want coffee but she declined, so keen was she to continue. It was as though she were unburdening herself of a guilt she felt to herself: 'Anyway, I didn't hear for three weeks and had given up on it, but then received an email asking if I was still interested to let him know by the end of that day as someone else was keen. I left it. I didn't care anymore. But then next day he turned up at the gallery with the picture. I wasn't there so he went away again. My assistant gave me his message: "Let me know today as Paris pressing." I couldn't be bothered so didn't phone until the following day. I had decided to let it go, so it was merely a courtesy call. When I rang, he sounded stressed. He said I was too late and he was compelled to sell it to Paris for ninety thousand. He then talked to someone else out of my hearing, before telling me with a huge sigh that he would come out to the gallery one final time. So he brought the picture and I confess I fell in love with it all over again. He said he'd felt duty-bound to me, but he was clearly out of sorts because he kept saying, "Paris will be so upset". I felt guilty and in the end offered eighty thousand which he rejected, saying he knew his wife had promised me they'd accept seventy-three, but I insisted and eventually he agreed to take eighty.

'Thus, delighted, I put it in our gallery — not to sell, but it seemed the best place with the security system we have — and it attracted quite a bit of interest and favourable comment, even offers to buy it which I declined. Then one day, months later, a man came into the gallery, quite professorial, claiming to have a passion for Chagall's work, and he asked me what I wanted for it. I said it wasn't for sale. I didn't like him anyway, pompous ass. Then he said he'd offer me three hundred pounds. I was furious with him. I said I wasn't so easily conned and told him to leave. So he told me it was a fake, a poor quality copy, and he could show me how I could tell, and I literally chased him out.' At this point, Paz looked her over, thinking he could not imagine her as a great threat, physically at least, although maybe she might be when justifiably riled as she obviously had been. She continued, 'I talked to my sister about it and we agreed to consult an expert, to be on the safe side. We found one, and my fear was that it would turn out to be the man I'd thrown out of the gallery, but to my relief it wasn't.'

'Did you not consider taking it to the Chagall Committee?'

She smiled. 'I thought about it. The ultimate authority, in Paris. I might never have got it back.'

'Indeed, if they deem it a forgery they hold the right to destroy it in front of a magistrate. I would love to see that, though not in this instance, obviously.'

'Anyway, the expert we saw agreed everything the other chap had said and told us I should have accepted the three hundred pounds. I said, "What about the certificate of authentication?" and he roared with laughter. "Fantasy,' he said. He even told me a genuine print wasn't rare and could be bought for under forty thousand, the reserve price at auction. I asked about the dealer. He said he must be a joke, someone who knew nothing except buying and selling. It was pictures this week, it could be tinned peaches next. He said that me and the dealer were an auctioneer's dream: Two ignoramuses bidding like crazy. I asked about the Paris dealer and he said, "A turnip may show up in Paris but it's still a turnip." He apologised for being harsh but said if I ever wanted a genuine Chagall print he could find one for me. So after this I knew I'd been scammed, especially as the couple had disappeared off the scene, and through the bank I've learned that the account I paid into is closed.'

'Do you have a photo of the lithograph?' She produced one from her handbag. 'Fake or not, it's beautiful,' he said. He found it almost mystical. 'Tell me, have you informed the police?'

'Yes. But with all the fraud going on these days I'm not expecting them to do anything. Plus, it seems less of a crime, more stupidity. Chagall lithographs are notorious for fakes. I knew that, but not the extent of it. My enthusiasm got the better of me. A fan without the necessary knowledge is always at risk.'

'So my guess is that you want us to track down these people with their fancy sob story, with a view to bringing the police back in if necessary when we've done it.'

'Yes. I already took the liberty of informing the police I'd be hiring you. I'm sorry if I was a bit presumptuous there.'

'No worries. I have always cultivated good relations with them — not being ex-police, I'm not tempted to try telling them their job — and I look forward to being in a position to hand over what we get on these crooks. Of course, the advantage with the police is that they're a free service.'

'I just hope these people haven't tried this game on others.'

'Whereas I hope they have. With you they might claim you swapped their genuine lithograph for a fake, but they can't keep saying that with everyone.'

He handed her a paper showing his fees. He said, 'As a practical matter, I don't bill for all my time and expense. I usually cap it at a figure we can discuss when I have a better handle on the case. Plus, I have my assistant do as much as possible, and her rate is obviously cheaper.'

Afterwards, Paz and Mack did some checking and found a major stockbroker had gone bust on the day of the auction. Mack looked up the names the client had provided and found the couple's website. She also checked Facebook and Twitter and looked for other auctions of Chagall's works. They discussed the case and concluded it was the crooks who, through a circuitous route, had put the fake print up for auction in the first place, bidding it up to inflate the price, and then homing in on the losing bidder if they thought them gullible enough.

Mack searched for upcoming art auctions and, ten days later, Paz travelled north to one she'd located in Harrogate featuring various artists including Chagall.

As soon as he arrived at the hall, he saw a middle-aged couple having a fierce argument in the car park. He became transfixed by the beautiful cobalt blue dress the woman was wearing. He then noticed another couple who, based on photographs he and Mack had found online, could be the fraudsters. Inside the auction room he saw the woman in the blue dress again, this time alone. A Chagall lithograph was lot 19. When it came up there were several bidders. Paz even put in a bid himself in an act of bravado. He then sweated, waiting for someone else to bid. This alone was enough to put him off doing so again. One thing he could not afford was a piece of artwork by Chagall, genuine or fake. In the end, however, it was the woman in blue and the suspects battling it out. The suspects prevailed after a tough fight. Paz kept an eye on them and hung around until the close of the day's proceedings. He was hoping to witness a scene similar to that which his client had described. Sure enough, in the car park he saw the female suspect talking to the woman in blue.

Paz decided to get as close as possible to secretly record the conversation. The suspect's partner then arrived. The conversation didn't last much longer, before it was interrupted by the partner of the woman in blue. Red in the face he shouted at her, telling her to let the piece go; he didn't want it and whatever it was they couldn't afford it, and this was the reason he hadn't wanted to go to the auction in the first place. She argued back at him and the suspects looked embarrassed and began to walk way. But the man then seized upon them. He accused them of being crooks conning people with fakes and claimed they owned the company that put fake lithographs up for auction.

He made as if to grab the male suspect by the lapel, but the latter pushed him away forcefully. The angry man lost his footing and fell back towards the bonnet of a car, hitting his head on it. The woman in blue then started berating the couple, accusing them of causing her partner to have a heart attack. The suspects tried to leave but Paz strode towards them and ordered them to stay. He'd witnessed what looked like an assault and now they'd have to wait for the police. The male tried to knock him out of the way but Paz grabbed his arm tight. Others arrived and surrounded the couple. The woman in blue told the crowd the man had beaten up her husband. The police and an ambulance then arrived. Paz rang the police contact his client had provided and informed him the suspects had been apprehended. He then rang his client.

As it transpired, the injured man had not suffered a heart attack. Like much of the case this was fake. He and his 'partner' were not even a couple but actors employed by a private detective. As for the suspects, they'd worked their auction scam several times and this was their first failure.

Time would show the fraudsters, once prosecuted, had enough in assets to pay off their victims. Paz's grateful client would get the bulk of her money back. 'That's less your fees and my stupidity discount,' she told him happily.

Chapter 18

The Biggest Mistake

One evening, Paz sat down with his old friend Jack, a homicide detective visiting from the US, in the Bristol Arms. He'd chosen a table from which they they could look out at the sea and the starling murmurations, and from his chair Jack could see the Palace Pier. They were sharing war stories and Paz told him of his worst day which was when he ran over his client who'd hired him to watch his wife. 'I ended up paying his medicals. That was pretty tragic,' he said drily. 'But he ended up running a successful car sales business, and he even gave me another case when he was checking up on his second wife.' Jack told him about what he believed was his biggest mistake. 'The case I kick myself over the most concerned the so-called celebrity Shakes Slocombe.'

'I don't remember him.'

'Yeah, you do. He was a comedian, sleazy TV personality type, always schmoozing with the rich and famous. Short and slight. All grease and no grit.' He paused. 'You know what, this is a longish story but a good one, so before I start I'll get some fresh beers in.' He stood up and went to the bar. As soon as he'd sat down again he began, 'Well, it all starts with a couple of free spirit kids getting it into their idiotic heads to drive out to the desert.'

'Where we talking?'

'Nevada. Esmeralda County.'

'OK.'

'They were going to an all-night party in an old ghost town.'

'Lucky them.'

'Maybe. On the way, to get in the mood, they start drinking and popping pills. Sure enough, they leave the main highway and manage to get themselves lost. They start to worry about gas. They find a derelict old shack off the road, and they proceed to get drunk on the beer and wine they brought with them. When they've achieved that, they start taking more drugs. Quite a selection they had, by the sound of it. They are soon completely intoxicated. Then the penny drops, but slowly like it's sliding through thick treacle, that they're too stoned stupid to drive on. They're stuck out there in this dilapidated old place with whatever creatures are sleeping there waiting to emerge. It's going to be a cold night. They decide to look for stuff they can use to keep warm. They find some blankets and shake them out.'

'Snakes?'

'No doubt. Scorpions and God knows what else. Don't forget they're dumb and stoned. Then they open an old wardrobe and quite casually out slips a dead body.'

'No way!'

'And they start screaming. There they are at the beginning of the night, completely out of it, and now they've got a corpse on their hands. They think of walking out onto the highway but soon give up on that idea. Besides, they're too intoxicated to walk more than a few yards. So they go out and sit in the car and hope for sleep which doesn't come. They stay there raving until they pass out. By late morning, one of them's just about able to drive. Before they leave they go inside and cover the body with the blankets.'

'I wonder what state it was in. And the smell! Anyway, then what?'

'They make it to the nearest gas station, then to the nearest police station. One of the boys says, "It looked just like Shakes Slocombe." And when the police down there go out and investigate they find it not only looks like him, it pretty sure *is* Shakes Slocombe. A sad end. His career had been in a steep dive and, like most people in the public eye, he'd picked up a few enemies along the way. Now he'd been killed.'

'We in homicide had no leads. Nothing. We were satisfied with the boys' story. They were just a couple of idiots. We could have busted them for the drugs in their car, but we let them off. Of course, the press were soon all over it with their crazy theories, but the investigation went cold almost immediately. Four weeks went by, but then we got a tip. A drug dealer in jail came out with a story that he was offered thirty thousand dollars to arrange the death of Shakes but had turned it down. This jerk was a pure fantasist. A few questions soon showed he was lying. But then he said another inmate, name of Simons, told him *he'd* been offered it. We managed to verify this was true from a third inmate who also heard it. The only trouble was that the real person of interest—'

'The second inmate, Simons?'

'Yes — was now out of jail, and what's more, as we soon discovered, he was dead too.'

'Oh boy!'

'We checked out his place and found a gun with bullets in it beside his body. And we got a break: The bullets in the gun matched those found in Shakes' body. So prima facie he had killed Shakes, unless the gun was planted. The problem was: Why had he done it? Was he hired by someone or did he have his own issues with Shakes? We could find no evidence of a link between the two. Therefore we decided to pursue the angle that someone paid him to do it, as he'd claimed.

'So we looked at Shakes' dealings. We found in his heyday he'd been a promoter of various rackets and most recently an investment scheme. We figured maybe an angry investor had hired the killer after being ripped off. We checked the correspondence and found early investors were happy but later ones were not. They'd paid in but got nothing out. We interviewed a few of them but got nowhere, so we looked further into what had made them so unhappy. The investment was in an oil business, the JBR company. They had a few small leases and were now bidding for bigger ones. We went to see the company. We learned that JBR had hired Shakes to bring clients in. They were wanting to buy these leases but didn't know what they were doing and underestimated how much it costs to drill a well. Minimum ten million for one well. And they needed to raise about eighty million in all, but the money wasn't there. One of the partners knew Shakes and approached him about it. Shakes was down on his luck and thought it could help him get back on TV, so was enthusiastic. He began doing adverts encouraging people to invest. But he overstated his influence and it soon became clear he couldn't bring in the backing he claimed. Time was running out and the initial investment would have been lost. Next, as we know, Shakes was gone.'

'What about JBR?'

'I'm getting to it. So we visited JBR's business premises. The owner was a lay preacher. We also met his wife there. She kept the books for the company. We searched the place and found nothing incriminating. The preacher was solid. Once again the search went cold. Still we didn't know why Shakes was killed. There was no connection we could trace between him and his killer, and no easy way to find out since the killer was dead too.' Jack suddenly became pensive: 'Detectives like to strut and make out how clever they are, but a lot of it's luck, as you know.'

'So at this point you needed another break.'

'Right. And we got it. We got a call from JBR to remove a woman from the car park who was screaming abuse. Because it was JBR we took a particular interest. We interviewed her. It turned out she went there every day shouting abuse directed at the preacher. She'd been in a relationship with him and he broke it off. She said she'd seen us visiting and knew why, but thought we must be looking in the wrong place. We were confused because JBR's place was clean as whisky. We asked the woman to elaborate but she refused. She said we should look again.' At this point Jack paused to take a breath and a long swig of beer.

He continued, 'So we did. We checked the books. We found payments out. It wasn't clear who the payees were. The wife said they were service companies — truckers and the like. This proved correct. Still we were getting nowhere. So we did some digging and we found all of these service companies were owned by a holding company and that company was owned by the wife.'

'OK. Odd, but so what?'

'Right. Strange maybe, but not illegal. But it got us looking harder at the wife and her business dealings. We discovered that she had a collectibles business, so we visited her store. Again we found nothing. But then we discovered that the wife was not the preacher's wife at all, but his sister. She'd been married but divorced and reverted to her maiden name. People thought she and the preacher were married and that suited both of them fine.'

'So her business was under her maiden name?'

'Correct. And knowing her married name opened up another door. She had another business under that name. A pretty small business. A business selling guns.'

'Ah-ha!'

'Including stolen guns. We interviewed her and got nothing. She denied any connection with the killer Simons. We believed different. We knew she had a daughter in her late teens, so we hauled the daughter in on some pretext. She opened up. She knew Simons. She owed him money for drugs. She couldn't pay and Simons had his own debts. So her mother persuaded a reluctant Simons to kill Shakes in return for her daughter's debt plus another twenty thousand.'

'I see.'

Jack laughed. 'You think you do but you don't; he reneged on it. He took the ten grand down payment, which more than covered the debt, and took off. The woman threatened him over it, and he threatened her in turn with exposure to the police.'

'Huh! So who did kill Shakes?'

'Her lover named Fenton who happened to be a potential investor in the oil lease.'

'Wow. OK, but why did Shakes have to die?'

'The lover / investor said Shakes was out of control, that he'd taken money from people who wanted to invest and kept it instead.'

'Shakes was stealing money meant for JBR.'

'Yes. And Fenton said they had to get Shakes out of the way before he would invest. There was more: Fenton held a grudge against Shakes. Shakes had made a pass at his son once when his boy was a teenager.'

'And Simons?'

'He had to die because of what he knew and because he was unstable.'

'And because he'd ripped her off.'

'Right. So the idea was to frame Simons and then make it look like he'd committed suicide.'

'Oh boy! But why was it your biggest mistake? After all, no-one was harmed by what you did or didn't do.'

'My biggest mistake was, and still is, to make assumptions. I made so many on this case: I assumed the woman was the preacher's wife, I assumed any guns would be owned by the husband, and I assumed that when it comes to an investment, if it goes wrong the biggest threat will come from an unhappy investor and not a potential one.'

'OK. But how did Shakes wind up in that shack?'

'Ah, that's another story.'

'Yeah!? If I didn't know you, I'd think you made it all up.' A gulp of pale ale emboldened Paz. 'In fact, I think you did make it up. There was no desert shack. There was no wardrobe. Who has a wardrobe in the middle of the desert? What were you watching on the flight over — a Halloween movie? You made this shit up. There was no Shakes Slocombe.'

'Look it up.' Jack was rattled. 'Look it up, if you don't believe me. Or if you're too lazy, get your assistant to look it up.'

'Lazy?' Now Paz was irritated. 'I'll tell you what's lazy: your story. More holes than your grandpa's old string vest. Your biggest mistake is trying to sell me a load of BS!' He drained his glass, and soon afterwards they left the pub. Disgruntled, Paz headed home by taxi.

Chapter 19

The Fugitive

Next day, a bleary-eyed Paz asked Mack to look into the Slocombe case. He wanted it done right away. Mack pointed out he'd asked her to make the new Wessman case the priority and agreed she could have the afternoon off as Lily was treating her to afternoon tea. Was Slocombe really more important than Wessman? He did not reply but admitted to himself it wasn't. He explained to her about Jack's 'biggest mistake' story. 'I think he made it up,' he said.

'Why would he do that?'

'Oneupmanship.'

Resigned to the fact that her boss was not going to let the matter drop and that her afternoon off was in jeopardy, she complied, quickly gathering all the information she could find. She sent it to him. Paz was delighted. He went through the reports - police, court, newspaper, social media - looking for errors to confront Jack with. His search was successful as he found multiple discrepancies between the reports and what he remembered of what Jack had said. He also found out how Shakes Slocombe had ended up in the desert shack. Fenwick (Jack's "Fenton") was a film producer and hated Slocombe, as Jack said, believing he'd abused his son when he'd been a child actor. Fenwick conned Slocombe with a story about a role for him in a comedy western where the shack would be one of the key locations. After luring him out there, they shot him and, for reasons unclear, stuffed him into a trunk.

A trunk! Paz was so pleased, he told Mack she could have the following day off as well. She looked at him, puzzled - and worried: Was he still feeling the effects of the alcohol? She knew he was a 'lightweight' when it came to drink. 'I'm going to phone him right now,' he said, 'pointing out all his errors.'

'Do they matter?' she asked.

'Matter!?' He told her of all the discrepancies he'd found. She was bemused; none of them seemed to matter objectively. 'I'm going to tell him his biggest mistake is his frigging memory,' he insisted, picking up his phone.

'Based on this? Really? Surely not.'

'What do you mean?' He was not overly pleased at her trying to pop his bubble.

'Did you know he's not even a police officer anymore?'

'Not homicide, I know.'

'Not anything. He was thrown out for tampering with evidence and bribing witnesses.'

'Really!?'

'Only his connections stopped him going to jail. I rather think that might be bigger, don't you?'

He paused, staring into her eyes. He had not known any of it. 'OK,' he said, slowly placing the phone down onto the desk. 'You're right.' He sighed heavily. 'OK, you can carry on with the Wessman case.'

The Wessman case had begun with a call Paz received from an FBI contact. They were looking for someone they thought was in England - a suspect who'd been granted bail and made a run for it via Canada.

It was an interesting case involving a wealthy married couple who were initially considered victims of an attempted carjacking in a rundown part of Los Angeles; Jenna Wessman was killed and husband Sam was shot but survived. A few local suspects with relevant criminal records were interviewed, but they all had alibis, including two suspects in jail at the time. But it struck investigators as odd that she was shot in the head execution-style, whereas none of the three shots he received caused serious injury. After months without tangible leads, police charged Sam with murder. His lawyers argued it was lazy police investigation; they could find no viable suspects so it had to be the person closest. Sam had argued unsuccessfully that his wife, as a lawyer handling high profile cases, was a target and that it was a professional hit job. Influential friends maintained he was not a flight risk because he was so devoted to his young children. Bail was set at two million dollars. Grateful to his connections and the judge, Sam Wessman immediately went on the lam.

Paz would be one of many people looking for the fugitive, including bounty hunters seeking to earn their reward, and websleuths. He ignored this 'noise', but part of Mack's role would be to monitor any new social media chat and theories. He discussed it with her and she was excited by the case. The first step would be to look at everything they could find on the man. In reality, Mack would find and Paz would speculate.

Sam Wessman once had a successful business, shipping French wine to the rich and famous. He cultivated relationships with influential people, not only through his business but by his calculated support for their philanthropic ventures. He particularly liked the theatre and sponsoring productions. But the arc of his life was already levelling off when he met Jenna Myerdale, the daughter of a jewellery tycoon, in a Broadway bar. She had recently received an inheritance and did not need to work for financial reasons. But 'homemaker' would never be enough for her and, blessed or cursed with a high moral conscience, she had graduated as a lawyer to pursue a career in human rights work. Despite the twelve year age gap, she was smitten; Sam still had the charm that had enabled him to schmooze amongst high society, and he ensured they were soon married. His business was waning, then poor French grape harvests and the continuing rise of New World wines sent it into freefall. He lacked the drive and imagination to diversify into other ventures and instead became morose; having a wife who earned more than him did not sit well with his alpha male personality. From his once wide social circle only a few of the wealthy remained, a remainder that preferred cocaine, gambling, and sex parties to fine dining and the theatre. His outgoings far exceeded his income, Jenna realised his spending was out of control, and the twelve year gap began to matter. With other potential suitors waiting on her with varying degrees of patience, she filed for divorce.

Paz thought it likely the subject would want to continue the life he had before as much as possible. If he liked cities it was probable he would gravitate to a city now. It was a tough ask to find Wessman, though. If he had any sense he wouldn't be advertising online where he was. He might not even be in the UK. He could have moved on to Paris or Berlin or Rome. Assuming he was in the UK, Paz had a team of contacts he could call on to also be on the lookout. It meant sharing the gravy but he didn't care about that. He couldn't do it all himself, and he just wanted to find the subject. He was idealistic in that way. And he told himself he was dumb enough to believe in Karma and that good gestures would bring rewards.

Paz wanted to learn as much as possible about Wessman. Mack began with his Facebook page. She looked for contacts in the UK and reviewed his work career, interests, and passions. As for motive, to Paz it looked like good old greed. In other words, from the fugitive's perspective it was necessity. The man had to kill the woman he no longer loved to get at her life insurance, using a plan the insurers and police could not see through. The man still behaved like a high roller whilst living well beyond his means. He liked fast cars, luxury travel, and expensive restaurants. Rich fugitives often either felt invincible or, conversely, felt a certain inevitability that they would be caught. Either way, they were reckless in their actions. Then when they were caught they relied on lawyers to fight extradition and suddenly developed medical conditions that made it perilous for them to travel.

Paz and Mack concluded London would be his base. That was the punt. But who knew what alias he might be under? Paz went to see his main London contact, Marla. She had good inroads into Scotland Yard who believed the fugitive was in France. Marla disagreed with this. She suspected he'd gone to France under one alias and returned to England under another. One thing Paz gathered from Mack's social media research was that Wessman was a showman. He would have to reveal himself. He could not help it.

Marla had a friend who liked to go to the theatre, and because she thought the fugitive would be attracted by a new American production opening, she took her friend to see if he'd be there. Of course, he wasn't; but then she realised she didn't need to go to shows, all she needed was to watch people going in and coming out at the end. She and Paz had a laugh about it. It was a particular kind of madness that made them do this kind of work. They loved coming up with theories and trying out ideas. Marla was a joy to work with and she made him feel good. She was a decade younger than him, attractive, and enthusiastic.

They divided the work, covering as many theatres as possible, watching who went in and who came out. The former was easier because people tended to mill around waiting to go in by the main entrance and they went in slowly, whereas at the end they left through different exits and were rushing for taxis or trains. It was a fun game but no more than that. Paz even tried matinées as well. On the other hand, he couldn't help thinking it was a ridiculously indulgent waste of time and effort. He had too much other work to do, as Mack's frequent updates and pointed questions reminded him.

Notwithstanding Paz's concern at it being a wasted effort, there was a major development when another friend of Marla's, whom she'd brought in on an unofficial basis, claimed to have seen the fugitive in a restaurant in the Strand, and had managed to obtain a photograph of him - and the person he was with. Despite the momentary humiliation of a complete amateur getting a break denied the pair of them, they were delighted.

Paz reported back to the FBI to seek their confirmation on the identity of the man in the photograph, but to his surprise it was not forthcoming. They weren't convinced it was Wessman.

Paz and Marla felt deflated at this. But there was a twist: when they looked closely at the woman the fugitive was with they realised she looked like the deceased wife - same shade of blonde hair and style, same makeup, same earrings and pearl necklace, same blue jacket, all based on a photograph of Jenna on Twitter. They were intrigued. The man had adjusted his appearance with a new beard, presumably to fool the FBI, but had persuaded the woman to look like his wife. Marla thought that in some weird way he was trying to reclaim his innocence, for why would he want to date a woman that reminded him of his crime? Paz's answer was that it didn't remind him of the crime. Instead, it reminded him of an idealised version of the woman he once loved.

Marla's friend checked with the restaurant. She knew the maitre d' there and he gave her the name Chown, traced the booking and found a phone number. She asked him whether Chown had an American accent. He said it was a 'clumsy' English accent. Paz had Mack do a search on the phone number. She found it was the contact number for Edie Sinth. Further investigation showed she was an escort based in East Croydon. Marla conferred with Paz and they decided she would call the number. An app enabled her to pretend to be calling from a delivery company. She said she was ringing for Mrs Chown. 'This is she,' came the answer.

'We have a parcel for you but there's a discrepancy on the address.'

'I'm not expecting a parcel,' came the sharp response. 'What address have you got?'

Marla gave her the number of a house in a major local street. 'It's probably flowers,' she said.

'It couldn't be mine.'

'It says for the name of Chown' said Marla.

The weary-sounding woman then surrendered her address. After this Paz and Marla bought some flowers and, posing as a deliverer, Marla went to the door while Paz discreetly took photographs.

'What's she like?' asked Paz afterwards.

'Hard. And very much not the so-called Mrs Chown though claiming to be her. It's obviously Edie's phone number, but the "restaurant woman" is someone else.'

Paz decided to do surveillance on the property, since it might be where Chown was hiding. He followed Edie's car, hoping it would unearth the fugitive and / or his restaurant friend. He had a couple of visits to a shopping mall as a result. On one occasion, Edie went to a coffee shop and there met the woman who, at least superficially, looked like the one in the restaurant photograph.

Afterwards, Paz was confused because the two went back to Edie's place. Perhaps this was where the 'restaurant woman' was hiding from the police, but it also occurred to him that maybe she was hiding in fear from Chown. Paz was impatient with mysteries such as this and was tempted to ring Edie's number. But first he needed to talk to his client. He rang his contact at the FBI and told him he'd found the woman in the photograph taken at the restaurant. Did they want him to pursue it, or did they still think 'Chown' was not Wessman? The contact was unsure and told him to proceed.

On seeing her emerge from Edie's place, Paz approached the 'restaurant woman' and, although it was rash, simply asked her straight out if she knew Chown. She said she didn't. She continued walking while he tried to show her the photograph. Again she denied knowledge. She walked faster. Paz called out that he was seeking a fugitive in connection with a brutal murder and he was sure she knew the suspect. She demurred in a colourfully blunt manner, but he insisted that if she was hiding a fugitive she was breaking the law, and he was working with the police.

She slowly stopped walking and turned towards him. 'You're not going to go away, are you?' she said.

'Call the police if you want to.'

After further terse discussion, she agreed to meet him at a local café.

Over coffee Paz was able to obtain from her confirmation she had met Chown, though without knowing his real background. She said Chown told her 'fake agents' would come after him making enquiries and spurious allegations. He claimed to be a theatre impresario and philanthropist who'd recently inherited a villa in Provence. She found this hard to believe, but when she started questioning Chown about it he became abusive, blaming her for being 'stupid'. She told Paz that Chown was staying at the Savoy.

'Is he likely to still be there?' he asked.

'He said he was heading for the south of France.' Paz thought she was lying. He then told her of his belief that Chown had chosen her for her physical similarity to his wife. She said she'd encountered that before but not with a killer. 'Suspected killer,' she corrected herself, which almost sounded worse. She said he bought her jewellery and clothes to wear when with him and was exacting about her hair. 'It was tiresome,' she said and then opened up, telling him all she knew. She said, with Chown she had to pay for everything and he would reimburse her with cash. 'That was *super* tiresome,' she complained. It was always him phoning her, usually from a different phone. She had no number for Chown and would have deleted it anyway. She said she only kept numbers of 'regulars'. She said any time Paz was 'at a loose end...' He nodded.

Paz updated the FBI and they liaised with Marla's main contact at Scotland Yard. By the time the police arrived at the Savoy, Chown had flown, but from the hotel's phone records they found a contact he had in France. French police raided his hideout but he had already moved on again. He was finally caught in Ireland, but the authorities there would not extradite him to a jurisdiction with the death penalty, so that had to be waived. They threw him in jail anyway, so he agreed to return to the US.

After this case Marla and Paz explored a mutual interest in the theatre. Whenever Paz was in London he would take Marla to one of the shows that had been running when they were investigating Chown. She even came to Brighton for an opening night at the Theatre Royal. When Mack heard about this she became jealous and so he had to take her there as well. She bought a new dress for the occasion. As she took her seat in the Dress Circle she asked, 'Do I look elegant? I've always wanted to be called elegant.'

She wasn't his idea of 'elegant', but it was a lie worth telling. She did look pretty, however, and she enjoyed herself which was all he cared about that evening.

Eventually, Sam Wessman faced court proceedings. The first trial was halted due to non-disclosure of evidence by the prosecution. In the second, even with his high-profile defence team, his acquittal was still a shock. Wessman walked free and within weeks he was married again. With the proceeds of his first wife's life insurance, and his new wife's not insubstantial wealth, he was able to retire to a mansion in Palm Beach, Florida.

Marla wept at the outcome. She said she felt guilty. Paz tried to console her, adding that he was well-acquainted with this feeling that maybe he could have found more evidence. Nevertheless, they'd done what they were required to do, and they could have hardly been expected to record a confession by him. And, as the defence attorney put it: being a fugitive did not make a man guilty.

Chapter 20

The Client

Paz sometimes felt he chose clients more than they chose him. All private investigators wanted work, but some he did not wish to do. There were some detectives who wanted, in some small way, to do good in the world, and there were others who would rather dig dirt. Then there were those for whom digging dirt was not enough; it had to be planted first. In his preferred way of thinking about himself he fell into the first category: seeking to do good, or at least not do harm. In reality, digging dirt could not be avoided; planting it, however, he balked at.

Sometimes a person would call round with the offer of work and Paz immediately looked for a reason to decline it, though having too much to do was only infrequently a reason. Sometimes people came in looking like what they really sought was a good row. One such was Oliver. Paz was unsure whether that was his first name or surname. He was a big man with threatening eyes who said he was looking for his sister. He told Paz she kept moving and he was tired of following her around. Paz said, 'So you want someone else to do the following? OK, but why does she move around so much? Is she hiding from someone?'

'Yes. She has a stalker.'

It didn't add up for Paz. Why did she not tell her brother where she was? When Paz asked him questions, he became impatient. He just wanted Paz to find her and that was that. Here were the details, here was a photograph. More questions from Paz, more impatience from Oliver. In the end, the latter grabbed back his documents, stood up and snapped, 'If you didn't want the case why didn't you make that clear at the outset instead of wasting my time — and yours!? You people are the scum of the earth!'

Afterwards, Paz told Mack about it. 'Always good to have a satisfied client,' he said, failing to hide the fact the man had got under his skin.

'What was up with him?'

'He objected to me asking questions. I knew he was a problem when he came in. Oh well, most clients are not like that. It's good to know now and then what we're missing. He'll easily find someone else to do his bidding.'

Over the following fortnight, Paz saw the man around town a few times. To his surprise Oliver made a point of saying Hello, which Paz found odd in the circumstances, but he always responded in kind. Perhaps the nearly client realised what a jerk he'd been, but more likely he mixed Paz up with someone else. It brought his name to mind - Oliver - but Paz still did not know, much less care, what his other name was.

A couple of weeks after Oliver's visit, another man came to see Paz. Smaller, reminiscent of a fox, he told Paz a similar story to the other fellow. Except in his case he wanted not to hire a PI but find out information about one. The name Oliver came up again. The new man said his sister was called Lena Adams and she had a stalker by name of Oliver. Of course Paz speculated it was perhaps the other so-called 'brother' who'd visited him. He told the new man he knew of someone of that name who'd been concerned about his sister and wanted to know where she was. This information triggered the visitor into a tirade: 'You people will take on anyone for a client! You're the dregs! What you do should be illegal.' He put on quite a show and Paz found it entertaining, feeling almost sad when forced to explain, 'I didn't take the case.'

He seemed disappointed at Paz removing his justification for haranguing him. 'Do you know who did?'

'Why do you suppose it was anyone? He was even more disparaging than you about my profession.'

Paz could see the visitor was tempted to make some remark about 'profession' but stopped himself. 'Someone's tailing her,' he said. 'I want to know who. She already has a stalker. Now there's someone else — must be a PI.'

"He told me he just wanted to find her.'

'Anyone she wants to hear from knows her address already. Surely that's obvious.'

'I don't speculate,' said Paz.

'I have to protect my sister,' the man said in a tone approaching histrionic. 'Tell whoever's doing this job to back off.' Paz could have pointed out this was not within his gift, but he had work to do and was not interested in a prolonged discussion with him that would arrive at no conclusion, however conciliatory he might contrive to be.

The following day, the latest visitor, the fox-like man, sent Paz a photograph of a car. He wrote 'Who's this creep?' The car was a red Vauxhall. Paz's guess was that it was Chippy Norton's. Chippy was a PI but didn't do much these days. He wanted to retire but couldn't afford to since his divorce. He was cantankerous, bitter, and didn't give a damn about anyone. Nothing was outside the perimeters of his contempt. Paz phoned him. 'What do you want?' was Chippy's greeting. Paz said he'd received a visit from someone claiming to be the brother of Lena Adams. 'Never heard of them,' he snarled. 'Is that all you got?'

'Are you acting for a man called Oliver?'

'What if I am? None of your business.'

'I thought it would be useful to have a chat.'

'Chat? Why would I want a chat with you?' They were both silent until he sighed and said, 'Alright. Six o'clock in the Barley Mow. You're buying.'

When meeting Chippy it was hard not to feel a sense of the absurd. For a man who so cultivated a grouchy, mean-spirited manner, he was surprisingly flamboyant in his appearance. Eyepatch, large round glasses, flourishing moustache, military jacket, and a cape. When Paz had got him his Bacardi and coke, he explained about the two visitors: Oliver and the fox-like man. Chippy made it clear his disdain for Paz's enquiry about his 'private affairs' was undiluted. When Paz told him he always respected what he did, Chippy said, 'Go easy on the toffee. It's bad for my blood sugar.' He took a sip of his drink. 'Look, this Oliver bloke, he asked me to find his sister. I did that. Not exactly difficult. Then he asked me to keep an eye on her. So that's what I do.'

'But what if he's not the brother but a stalker?'

'I've seen no evidence he's a stalker. Mind you, I've seen no evidence he's her brother either, but he might be a half-brother, I suppose.'

'But then you don't want to know, do you?'

'It's a job. I need the money. It's alright for you. You get the classy work.'

'Classy?'

'You know what I mean. American work. You are a Yank, after all.'

'Only to you Brits. To the Yanks I'm a limey bastard.'

'And a phoney to the lot of them!' Chippy's face struggled to contain his pleasure at being able to say this. 'Well, unlike you, I have to pick up scraps. Look, am I committing a crime in your eyes?'

'Aiding a stalker? Is that a crime? I don't know. It must be pretty close.'

'Aiding—' He was furious. 'If anything, I'm helping *prevent* stalking. Everything I get goes back to him. He's no reason to stalk because everything he gets from me means he doesn't need to. So, indirectly I'm protecting her. I don't expect any problems with the cops. If I do, I'll remind them of the work I did for them in the past. A few drug dealers are doing time...' He looked around the room to see if anyone was eavesdropping, and lowered his voice: '...because of my background work. A few big names too. I don't think you ever did that.' He then announced that, 'Unless there's anything else' he needed to get back to work. 'And get rid of this garb,' he added.

Paz never went back to the fox-like man who'd seen Chippy Norton's car. A few days later, Chippy rang, extremely upset. 'Your friend's a madman!' he barked. 'I'm doing my job and he tries to assault me. I can assure you I can look after myself. So you might want to warn him of that. Plus, if I don't fix him I know plenty of people who'll do it for me.'

'I don't know anything about it,' Paz said, and Chippy rang off.

Paz was fed up with the whole situation. All the aggravation associated with it had earned him nothing in fees. He had no desire to become a public relations officer and felt most unsuited to such a role anyway. But he was prevented from forgetting all about it when his eye caught an Argus headline about a violent assault involving a stalker. All manner of ideas ran through his head. He was sure there were other stalkers in the town, but he naturally thought of the one he knew of: Chippy Norton's client Oliver. But he also knew from previous experience that nothing ever turned out the way he expected.

He'd barely begun reading the piece when Chippy was on the phone. Paz wondered what spin the old cuss was going to use in trying to protect his client. Once he had a client he was tenacious in his defence of them. 'Well?' Chippy said in a challenging manner.

'Well what?'

'What do you make of it? I'll accept your apology now.'

'Apology? I don't know—'

'You obviously haven't read it. Read the Argus. Read it and weep — but not for me. I'm sick of this game, Paz. No integrity anymore.'

He rang off and Paz went into his private office, determined to shut out the world. Chippy's client Oliver and the second man who'd come to see Paz had got into a fight outside Lena Adams' apartment. Blood had been spilt. That didn't surprise him particularly, but the rest of the piece did. Neither of them was Lena's 'brother'. Both were former boyfriends, and it was pretty clear she wanted nothing to do with either of them. The stalker turned out to be the fox-like man who visited Paz second, and not Oliver. When Chippy told Paz he was protecting Lena he was technically correct.

Chapter 21

The Everything Man

One Monday morning, Paz was going through a sudden rash of new assignments, wondering how they'd get them all done, when like a genie, a stocky man in his early thirties, all smiles and dressed in a smart pale grey suit, appeared in his office. When Paz asked him what his business was there he said, 'Wondering if you needed help.'

'Help?'

'Yes. I've heard people like you — that is, professionals like yourself — often employ freelance people. Well I'm free and my name is Lance — Lance Jasonby aka Lanky. I'm pretty sure I could fit into your team. I'm very much a team player.'

'Really?' Paz felt decidedly cold towards this proposal.

'Let me tell you about myself. And excuse me for being a bit chipper but I scored 132 not out yesterday to win a match.'

'Who do you play for?' Cricket fascinated Paz, even though he didn't fully understand it despite his frequent visits to Hove.

'On this occasion it was my old school team. Playing out Ringmer way.'

'So you helped win the match?'

'Pretty much single-handed, to be honest. When I went it at 25 for 4 it was all doom and gloom — "We're gonna lose, we're gonna lose" — and I said, "We will if we take that attitude," and I showed 'em. We needed another 189, the rest scraped together 52 with ones and twos, there were a few no balls, and I got the rest.'

'Remarkable.'

'Not really. Just a pretty average afternoon. I'm a great believer in, well, belief. It's limitless what you can achieve if you set your mind to it.'

'Indeed.'

'And I thought with my contacts I could assist you in your work.'

'Thank you. We are always looking for freelancers we can work with — it's difficult to find suitable people — so if you send me your CV—'

'I have it right here. And some references from people I've worked for. I can start anytime. Today if you like. I'll try my hand at anything.'

Paz pondered for a moment before answering, 'Most of the work is routine: checking up on injury claimants, that kind of thing. Pretty unexciting.'

The visitor was unflappable. 'Meat and drink to me,' he said with pride. 'I have a nose for fraudsters. So if you'd skim through that document, tell me the terms, then we can discuss starting date.'

Paz couldn't stand any more of his patter. He told him he'd get back to him by email. He was already thinking of the best way to say No.

Afterwards, he asked Mack what she thought. She was unimpressed, perhaps worried it might somehow impact her. Mind you, he observed, if his work achievements were anything like his sporting ones he would be a definite Yes: cricket at highest club level (career best 206 not out, bowling 8 for 15, 7 catches in an innings), played in Wimbledon juniors finals three years running, top-level croquet champion, played for several leading non-league football clubs, Formula 3 racing driver. Then there were the jobs: company director (various), investment analyst & expert, insurance broker and consultant, charity trustee, private investigator; prior to that: policeman, jeweller, accountant, and events manager. For academic achievements Lance cited a First in Psychology at Durham University and various work-related qualifications. Paz wondered if he could give him a one-off surveillance job that was the closest possible to a mere formality and therefore low risk.

In the end, Paz thought of trying him on the Smithson case, which involved routine surveillance including video. Accordingly, he sent him a version of the contract showing the lowest rates, still half-hoping he would find them unsatisfactory. Instead, Lance responded immediately with an acceptance, stating that he could not wait for his first assignment.

Paz still had nagging doubts, so called him in for another chat. It was a similar performance from Lance, this time enthusing about all the fancy surveillance equipment he had. Paz reminded him that they had to have the right balance - if they were too heavy-handed, which he suspected might be the case with him, it could backfire on them, with the insurers they worked for being portrayed as the kind that tried to make criminals of the merely unfortunate. Lance said he knew all this and followed best practice 'to the very last letter and full stop'. Paz then gave him Smithson to investigate.

After the meeting, Paz turned to his own cases, in particular an inheritance matter he couldn't wait to get started on. A wealthy man had been pressured by one of his offspring into giving a living will. Another son he didn't even know he had was now on the scene to challenge it. Paz's job would be to investigate this newcomer's background.

When he left for the day, he noticed the bookseller / landlord was clearing out a room at the back. Paz asked him what this signified and he indicated he had a new tenant: 'It's that chap you've got working for you now. He offered me good money, too. He said he just needs room for a desk, phone, and filing cabinet.' Paz mulled the situation over and decided it was not a bad idea for Lance to be based downstairs, although there was a potential risk of confusion for clients. Besides, he'd only given him one case and might not give him any more.

Lance's report on Smithson, although quirky in some respects, which Paz put down to inexperience on his part, appeared adequate, while the video he took clearly showed Smithson was completely able-bodied and not incapable of walking, lifting or 'performing work of any kind'. Thus, he could in theory edit Lance's report, put it under the firm's banner, and send it to the insurers. However, out of caution he sent it on to Mack for her to look over, given her reservations regarding Lance.

That night, he took a flight to Germany on a missing person's matter. The business partner of the subject maintained the latter had passed away in an air crash, but a suspected sighting had been made in Dortmund and Paz was to meet a contact there and see what could be established, if anything.

His trip by its nature was of indeterminate length and he fell ill during it. As a result, he was out of the office for over a week. This in itself was not a major problem because he could work remotely while Mack dealt with routine matters, except for the second day of illness when he was too incapacitated to even look at the computer screen or conduct a sensible conversation.

One of the emails he initially missed was from Mack on Smithson. She said it was not merely Lance's prose that was shoddy but his video was suspect, and she questioned whether it was really Smithson. The insurers would be unhappy, she said, and she suggested the surveillance be redone, and by Paz himself. He thought perhaps she was being harsh on the new freelancer, maybe because she'd taken a personal dislike, possibly out of a misplaced sense of rivalry. Nevertheless, if she thought the insurers might be unhappy, he could not ignore her concerns.

Mack also complained that Lance was becoming a 'nuisance', constantly bothering her with questions about the business. This Paz did not understand. After all, they had only given him one case. Quickly installed in his new office downstairs, Lance was now calling himself Lance Investigations, despite there already existing a firm of that name. Indeed, he was obtaining work under it. Mack said in her pithy email that she believed Lance was trying to steal Paz's business by ambushing people heading to the office, claiming Pascal Wheat was away and therefore the best person to help was himself. Not only that, but he'd also put Wheat Investigations on his business card.

All this was very weird and troubling. He suspected that Mack was jaundiced against the newcomer, but she had a good 'sixth sense' and he did not like what he saw in Lance Jasonby aka Lanky. He decided a showdown - something he hated - was inevitable. He was always prepared to give a person the benefit of the doubt, but there were too many questions surrounding this man for him to feel comfortable having him around, and certainly having him do work in the company's name. Paz had a good reputation, which had been earned with difficulty and hard work, but it could all crumble if he put out bad advice or a client thought he'd done a poor quality piece of work.

When Paz returned from Germany one morning the following week, feeling refreshed if still a little jaded, he walked straight to what was now Lance's office. 'Your new tenant not in today?' he asked the bookseller. 'Is he a late riser?'

'He's not been in since last Thursday. He phoned me Friday to say he wouldn't be in for a few days. He had a case come up in the south of France he had to give absolute priority to, but hoped to be in later this week.'

Paz looked at the old lush who'd already had his first drink of the day by the time most of the working world were still at the gym. 'Do you believe that?' Paz asked him. 'Seriously?'

'What do you mean?'

'Did he pay you any rent yet for that converted broom cupboard he calls his office?'

'No, he asked if he could defer it until the end of the month when his first 'revenues' as he called it came in.' He stared at Paz with his bloodshot eyes like a dog seeking clemency. 'I thought with the connection he had with you, it would be alright. Seeing as how he's doing work for you and all.'

'Connection? There is no connection. I gave him one piece of work, and by all accounts he did a lousy job of it. Mack tells me he's even taken to putting Wheat Investigations on his business card.'

'I believe that's so, yes.' Paz looked at Mr Cairns, the bookseller who sold maybe one book a day, who probably drank more bottles of wine than he sold books, whose marriage was as much a wreck as his drink-ruined face, who shook and stank with it, cowering in front of him like an addled courtier before Henry VIII, and he felt like screaming out loud at the sheer pity of humanity and its chaotic affairs, but instead he said in a calm, quiet voice, 'I'm afraid, he's done a runner. You have always been kind to me; I fear you will not see any rent from Mr Lance Whatever-His-Name-Is, and if that is the case I will pay you what he owed, in view of the fact you were under the unfortunate but understandable misapprehension that he was in some way "connected" as you put it with Wheat Investigations.'

Paz did not observe or wait for any response from him and instead went straight upstairs and announced to Mack that he was taking her to a 'celebratory brunch' there and then. He did not explain what was behind it until they were in the restaurant. He began with an apology for bewildering her, followed by another apology for inflicting Lance upon her. 'I fear he may have bugged the place,' he said. 'I also fear he may have attempted to steal clients from us by any means he could devise. Having said that, I do not believe that investigation is really his thing. Not enough money in it. Too much hard work for not much reward. My guess is that what he's after is inheritance cases. Somehow he wants to inveigle himself in them in order to make claims against estates, and it may be he mistakenly believes our files can help his plans. I think it best to fear the worst and be pleasantly surprised if it doesn't happen.'

Mack said, 'My guess is that this is not new. I've checked and I think he may be what you'd call a "seasoned fraud". I bet he's got a shedload of aliases and a ton of people who would love to find him.'

'So why don't we find him?' said Paz, and at that moment he had a great desire to hug her, even though he'd never do so for fear of 'inappropriateness'. 'The first thing,' he said, 'is to assess our own damage, if any, and then go after him.'

Assessing their own damage took a little time but his fears were realised: Lance had pirated the firm. When Paz hired his old friend Zeke to urgently redo Lance's investigation, he quickly established that Smithson was indeed a fraud. But the person in Lance's video was an entirely different party. Unfortunately, by the time Zeke had done this investigation the insurers had already acknowledged receipt of the report with thanks and confirmed the fees would be paid into 'the new bank account as directed'. Paz also received acknowledgements for reports on cases he hadn't even heard of. Lance had taken the assignments, sent videos of innocent people, and collected the fees. Mack, with heavy assistance from Paz, wrote to all of their existing clients advising them that the firm had been the subject of fraud. This in itself was deeply humiliating - a firm involved in investigating fraudsters caught out by one itself. It would give the clients he'd known for years something to joke about; the newer ones might be less kind.

A thorough search of the premises revealed Lance had placed bugs both in their own office and downstairs. Paz contacted the police. He found them sympathetic. He told them he'd like to track down Lance himself, and they were fine with that. There were already umpteen police forces on the search for him, but so far he had eluded them at every turn. As Paz suspected, inheritance was a particular interest of this fraudster, having been able to steer a couple of estates his own way, either directly as a long lost son, or through investment ripoffs of the proceeds.

Naturally, as with any wounded animal in the bush, the firm's predicament brought out the hyenas of the business world. Mack received job offers which fortunately she declined and, at least ostensibly, without hesitation. Paz was grateful, but there was a warning there that he'd have to give her a good pay rise when circumstances allowed. And not surprisingly, a rival firm started enquiring about a possible merger, by which of course they meant a takeover. Paz was gracious about it - after all, if Lance's activities reached their logical conclusion, his business would fold, so he did not take the other firm's approach as essentially hostile, even though he knew it was. In addition to this, there was a parade of consultants all there to advise on how to prevent it happening again, and amongst these smartly dressed people with their fix-it-all certainties and plain brass neck, there was no doubt the odd Lance-in-the-making, and possibly even the man himself in a new guise, like a beast returning to the well with the sweetest water, for con artists had no mercy. And there was the press coverage about it. All of it, the whole saga, was deeply and enduringly embarrassing, so much so that the depression this led to made Paz think of giving up on the firm. But, although tempted, he believed that him giving up investigating would be like, say, Danielle Steel giving up writing.

They talked about attacking Lance's firm, about 'sinking it like a ship', but they concluded it was best to let it run on so that they could watch it for clues. Besides, if Lance closed his investigation firm, he'd probably already have two dozen other company names lined up. Paz felt the best place to start was close to home. He thought about luring him with a fake investigation job, but he was sure Lance would never return to the office and would merely send in one of his standard reports with a video of some innocent person, and nothing useful would be learned. Paz phoned the number Lance had given him. The line was, as expected, dead. The next thing was to visit what was supposedly his Brighton address on the east side of town. At this dismally grey building, Paz had more luck. Listed on the panel by the door, amongst what read like the names of prostitutes, was Lanceby Investments. Paz rang and to his surprise it was answered. A young woman's voice. He figured it was another prostitute. The woman said, 'He's not here. Are you a client?'

'Yes,' he said. 'I would like to invest money with him.'

'So you've invested with the company before?'

Sensing a possible trap, he replied, 'No. Not yet, but I would like to.'

'Come up then,' she said. 'Third floor.'

The building was as shabby inside as its appearance on the outside. By the office door of Lanceby Investments, there were an additional six companies listed. A furtive woman answered the door. She was not how he'd imagined her from her voice. She was older. 'You'd better not be the press. He's not here,' she said again.

'I know that. You said I could come in.'

'That was my colleague. OK, you want to wait for him? I make you coffee?'

'With milk, no sugar. Thanks.' He went in. There was a reception area that looked untidy with cardboard boxes in the corner, but was basically clean. The woman, who he decided was Spanish, gave him a coffee that was obviously from a machine but surprisingly good. As he waited, he prepared for the showdown with Lance. Mostly he prepared his fists, even threw a couple of pretend punches, but stopped himself lest the woman see him. He noticed there was a brochure promising 'stellar returns year on year'. It was standard financial huckster fare. He became absorbed for a few moments and was then surprised by a voice he recognised but could not place. He was sure Lance had many voices. But when he looked up it wasn't him but a man called Michael Ray, handsome and smiling in one of the pale blue seersucker suits he always wore. Paz had known him for years and almost admired him. But whilst he could never be accused of respectability, Ray always stayed a step away from criminality. 'Paz,' he said with a fine imitation of warmth, 'this is a pleasure. What brings you here?'

'Lance Jasonby,'

'Another of his names. He has enough for a full deck.'

'Is he working with you? Or against you.'

'Neither, I'm afraid. He's dead.'

'Come off it, Michael, you know I can't accept that. You'll be saying you bumped him off next.'

'Well, in a way I did. I sent someone down to Spain, where he lives, to shake some money out of him - he ripped me off same as you - there was an unfortunate incident and poor old Lance is no more.'

'Michael, I don't believe you.'

'So you think I'm lying. Charming. I wish we hadn't made you that cup of coffee. Fancy saying that to your host.'

'Look, I'm prepared to accept you believe it, but I don't accept it's true. What was the someone you sent's name?'

'Joseph Nutt. He came with glowing recommendations.'

Paz felt he was getting nowhere with him, so he left for something to eat. He decided to walk for a while. The sun was glinting on the sea. He stood and gazed, taking it in. Then he went to a bar for lunch to think about it all. He phoned Mack to ask her to check Joseph Nutt online. After finishing his quick meal of whitebait and chips he returned to Michael Ray.

'Paz, once was a pleasure. A second time, I'm not so sure.'

'Never mind that. Did you speak to Joseph Nutt after the incident you spoke of?'

'No, but my assistant did.'

'It's my bet that it's not Lance who died but Nutt. Where is he? I'll fly out there and see for myself.'

'No need for that, old boy. Mr Nutt is right here in town. Want to meet him?'

'OK then, we'll meet here. Give me a call when he's arrived and I'll come straight over. Tomorrow, if possible.'

Paz returned to the office, by which time Mack had preliminary results. Paz quickly formed the view, unfair or not, that Nutt was of a similar ilk to Ray - not criminal but not exactly straight either.

Ray set up the meeting. Nutt was a sour, ruddy-faced man with thick long hair and a big face. He didn't strike Paz as particularly intelligent, but as a threat he was strong. Nutt told him in his gruff voice that it was Lance who landed a blow to Nutt's chest. It had been unprovoked, out in the street outside Lance's place in Marbella. Nutt put his arms up to protect his face - Paz stopped himself from saying it wasn't much to protect - and Lance landed a second blow hitting Nutt in the arm and then fell back, convulsed as if in seizure, writhing on the ground.

'Quite a performance,' said Paz.

'He was rushed to hospital. The police came. A witness confirmed everything I just told you. When I phoned up the hospital, they told me he'd discharged himself, had another seizure, and passed away. Some kind of brain condition. The police did not press charges against me.'

'Was there an autopsy?' Paz said.

At this point, Ray interjected, 'Paz, you're clutching at straws.'

'I just have an inkling.'

'Save your inklings for something else. You're just sore he got the better of you. I have to say, I'm not thrilled about it either, but I chalk it up and move on. Get the show back on the road, I say.'

'Give it a rest,' said Paz, unable to hide his irritation. 'Nothing like this has happened to me before, and it's hard to deal with.'

'Of course it is, Paz.'

'But unlike you I can't accept someone as crooked as he obviously is getting away with faking his own death.'

Later, he talked with Zeke and Mack about it. They were as sceptical as him. Paz said, 'I wonder if the answer's in his apparent obsession with sports. I'm interested in exploring the croquet aspect. There are not many places of a good standard to play croquet and one of them is near here.'

Next morning, he drove out to the croquet ground. He found someone working there, a middle-aged, forbidding-looking man. Any optimism that had taken Paz there all but disappeared. When he had at last been able to convince the curmudgeon that he wasn't leaving without the opportunity of talking to him, Paz asked if he knew many of the players there. When the man confirmed he knew some, Paz asked if he recognised the name Lance Jasonby. He said he didn't, although Paz suspected he'd have said that whatever name he gave him. When Paz showed him a photograph, he said he recognised him, saying he was indeed a player of a 'reasonable' standard, but he had not seen him there recently. The man suggested he call round on Sunday when there'd probably be players there who knew Lance. On reflection, Paz thought a better option might be Lance's cricket team, but he was growing ever more impatient to confirm whether Lance was still alive and decided on a direct approach.

Returning to the office, Paz declared there was nothing for it but to go to Spain. This made Mack laugh since poor weather was forecast for England, but she admitted it made sense. He thought Joseph Nutt would be useful, given his prior involvement. Nutt, however, had a funeral to attend up north and would be unavailable for a few days, so Paz decided he'd wait.

A couple of days later, a darkly-dressed woman with a careworn expression visited the office. She asked Paz if she could have a private word. Thinking her a potential new client, he took her into his room and offered her a drink. She asked for water. After taking a couple of sips, she told him she was Lance Jasonby's mother. He was sceptical but even more sceptical about the tale she told him. She firstly confirmed what Michael Ray and Joseph Nutt had said: Lance had passed away. She also confirmed Nutt's version of the incident in which Lance lashed out at him but had some kind of seizure.

Around the time Lance was in Brighton, his mother had received word from his solicitors, who'd lost contact with him, that he had, after years of legal wrangling, received a settlement in the amount of approximately eight hundred thousand pounds for an injury sustained in a motor accident.

He asked her, 'Can you tell me when this accident occurred?'

'It was in Spain five years ago. The exact date I don't remember offhand, but obviously it's in the paperwork. The accident was a very serious one. He suffered a brain injury. It changed his personality. He could no longer tell right from wrong, or even truth from fantasy.' She then produced her birth certificate and passport, as well as Lance's death certificate in Spanish. The name on her passport was not Jasonby. This was either a rather basic error by a fraud or she'd married again. He queried it and she merely said she'd reverted to her maiden name after divorce. He decided not to pursue it.

'Can you please clarify something: are any of the stories in his CV true?' Her brief perusal of the document induced a combination of tears and knowing smiles. He wondered for a moment whether showing her was a mistake, but it was too late. 'Was he really that good at sports?' he said. 'I know that's less important than his work career, but it intrigued me.'

'He really did take seven catches in an innings once. That was before his accident.'

'And the 206 not out?'

She laughed. 'I doubt it. More like 26.'

'When he came to see me he said he scored a century the day before.'

'He did love his cricket. It's possible but rather unlikely.'

'I believe your son discharged himself from hospital, is that right?'

'He did and, fearing another seizure - very presciently, as it transpired - he went to see a lawyer with Roldos y Montgomery who'd handled the settlement. He told them to pay you a hundred thousand pounds for all the damage he caused you.'

'I'm sorry?'

'He was determined to pay you.'

'Did you say pay a hundred thousand pounds? If so, why? Why me? Is it because I was his latest victim and so I was most on his mind? I find it all rather difficult to believe. I repeat: Why would he want to give me money?'

'He said it was because you were the only one to give him a chance. All the others said No to him.'

He thought about how he'd felt a little sympathy for Lance and in a moment of weakness had offered him an easy job at the lowest rate, how Lance had accepted it without hesitation and done the job in a fraudulent manner, and from then on he'd caused him all manner of problems and almost destroyed his business. 'But I nearly said No,' Paz replied at last. 'I damned well should have said No. Afterwards, I wished I had said No.'

'But you didn't say No and he respected that and was grateful. Now you will need to sign a confidentiality agreement.'

'Woo, wait a minute. I can't accept money. That would be unethical. Besides, should not this money go into your son's estate?'

'Apparently not.'

'Or a pot to pay all the victims of his activities?'

'And if the money went into such a pot — and no such pot currently exists and might never do so — fees and all the issues with allocating the monies, and every kind of potential dispute amongst lawyers and everyone else would mean that you would gain little from it, and not for a very long time. What would be the point of that? This money was not gained through illegal means. It was compensation for the accident that was the source of all his problems. Besides, that would go against my son's wishes. He has never been charged with any crime. He was not a criminal. He was ill, and he knew he was ill.'

Paz had listened carefully to everything she'd said. It sounded both fantastical and, as it affected him, sentimental. That the death might be fake, and that she either was or was not aware of such deception, added another layer of the bizarre. It also gave him a dilemma over what to do. He asked her for the opportunity to think about it because the situation was so unusual. She was clearly disappointed but said she would return next morning. He would have liked more time and she sensed this. 'Any dilemma you feel will not change, whether you wait one day or a thousand,' she said. She was correct, of course, although in a thousand days he might have better information. He might at least know if Lance really had died. It occurred to him that this was actually a buy-off; Lance was concerned Paz would track him down and wanted him to give up the hunt.

Rather than merely wait for the woman's return, Paz and Mack researched online for major motor accidents in Spain of five years previous, and particularly any that might have resulted in major settlements. It was depressing work and they found nothing that made them think they'd found the accident in question.

Next morning, the woman arrived as arranged. Paz asked her why they could not find Lance's 'very serious' accident online. She frowned and said that, although Lance received a blow to the head, the circumstances of the accident were not dramatic, no-one else was seriously hurt, and the true extent of his injuries were not immediately evident.

Paz was annoyed, after a poor night's sleep from trying to decide what to do. He flared: 'Either you are in on the con or he has deceived you.'

She was also impatient, perhaps from the same cause. 'Have I wasted my time coming here? Everyone in the world except a few billionaires want money, and most would do anything to get it, but you don't even seem to want it. Sign the damned confidentiality agreement and I can give you the cheque and then get on with something else. Do you not think I have enough to deal with? And that's without the fallout from whatever my son did or didn't do.'

This mollified him. 'I'm sorry,' he said, 'I truly am. You must excuse my being suspicious. It would help if I could defer signing the agreement until after the cheque clears.'

'That's nonsense. If the cheque doesn't clear the agreement will be of no effect anyway.'

He signed the agreement and she gave him the cheque payable to Wheat Investigations. He thanked her and apologised for his hesitation. She said she understood, and with that she left. Paz talked to Mack about what had happened. She said he'd done the right thing. He stressed the need to keep the payment quiet.

The cheque cleared. The finality of this was not matched by his conflicting thoughts on the matter as a whole. He still worried whether Lance had bought him off in the belief that not to would cost him far more in the end. He'd conned Paz once and could do so again. Or was everything the woman who claimed to be his mother told him true? Mack looked for her profile online but could find nothing. Paz reminded her this in itself did not mean they should ascribe evil motive.

Paz showed the police a copy of Lance's death certificate and said he had no reason to believe it wasn't genuine. He revealed nothing of the settlement. It was not his responsibility. The matter was closed as far as he was concerned.

He never heard any more rumours about Lance's activities. Maybe he was out there somewhere, having pulled off the biggest coup of all, but he doubted it. He did, however, caution his friend Zeke that, as a Sunday cricketer, if he ever scored a century he'd rather he kept it to himself.

Chapter 22

Stud Fire

One morning, Paz received a call from a loss adjuster he vaguely knew but had never worked with. Rick Terman was investigating a recent fire and was checking on a case Paz had years earlier at a stud farm. Paz recalled it had been upsetting with several horses killed in the blaze, though most escaped, which was good except one was later run over on the motorway. What intrigued Terman was the fact the latest fire was the same owner.

'Do you know if your case was paid out?' he asked Paz.

'I think it was, yes. I'll check.'

His memory was correct. It was paid out. But there had been a lot of concern on the bloodstock insurers' part. They believed the fire was set by the insured. The star horse had failed to perform at stud and the business was ailing. The adjuster on that case hired Paz to pose as a potential buyer of the remaining business. That ruse had worked well, but there was not enough evidence of arson by the insured, and with the threat of a lawsuit looming, the insurers reluctantly paid up. Then the insured had sold off the rest of the horses, bought a boat, rented the house out to a famous model down on her luck, and sailed around the world. The insured's name was Mrs Chilner but this new case was in the name of Maris. Had she married again?

He called Terman and said, 'How do you know it's the same person?'

'We did a background check. She remarried. She didn't declare any previous fires, but we had someone do a search on the name, and one of my Underwriter contacts told me they thought you'd been involved in a case with her that had been somewhat fractious.'

'"Fractious" would be an understatement. I got along OK with her but wouldn't trust that woman to say her own name. So what happened to her first husband?'

'First husband? If you mean Chilner by "first", he was actually her third. I want you to find out what you can about Mrs Maris as she now is. And by the way, I'd be willing to bet at least one family is investigating what happened to a loved one and would be keen to know what you find.'

Mack worked on putting together the 'unfortunate' woman's past history. In fact, Mr Maris was her fifth husband. It would be brave to predict a happy future for the couple; of her four previous husbands none were surviving. Indeed, only one of them had survived marriage to her, but he'd later died in an accident. On examination of reports, however, Mack established that his body had never been found. Paz held the hope, however slim, that he'd escaped - faked his own death or survived a murder attempt. Paz decided this man, by name of Snipe, would be the focus of their initial investigation.

Mack did further internet exploration and managed to locate a photograph of Snipe. She tried a reverse image search that located him in another's Facebook photos. This other person, a young woman, had the married name Samedi. Paz wondered whether she might be Snipe's daughter. Mack found her address in the Leicester area and a phone number which Paz rang. The woman answered, but he found her hostile. He asked if he could meet her but she declined. He realised his enthusiasm for interviewing her had got the better of him. He'd anticipated she would want to talk - always a foolish assumption.

In the end, he went to visit Mrs Samedi on the off chance. It was a small terraced house in a smart street in the suburbs. She and her husband, both lean and rather gaunt, answered the door together. They appeared nervous and hesitant but after a few conciliatory words from Paz, allowed him in. They invited him to sit down but did not offer him a drink. Paz was right: Mrs Samedi confirmed she was Mr Snipe's daughter. He said that he'd been asked to investigate her stepmother.

To his dismay, however, she announced she'd changed her mind and did not want to talk to him and would only deal with the police. 'That is obviously your right,' he said. 'I won't pursue it with you if you don't want me to, but please believe me when I say I'm on your side.'

It was awkward. He was getting nowhere and the couple clearly wanted him gone. Fortunately, at that moment they heard heavy hailstones on the windows from a cloud burst, and he could hardly be expected to leave.

'OK,' she sighed after half a minute of the noise. 'What exactly is it you want?' Before he could reply, she left the room to attend to a crying baby. On her return she said, 'If you're after money, I'm afraid you'll be unlucky.'

'That might be an interesting assignment, but my clients are not seeking money. Not from you anyway. How do you feel about the woman who became your stepmother?'

'I don't feel anything because I try not to think about her. If you're acting for her you can go to Hell.'

'No, I'm not acting for her. I'm looking into her background. It concerns a fire, and I've been asked to assist the investigation. We know that she's been married several times, and your father—'

'He's in hiding. Even now.' She relaxed and opened up: 'Her plan was for two hired thugs to kill him because he knew too much about her dubious history. They beat him up one night and threw him off a bridge to drown, but he survived.'

'My God! But how do you know she was behind it?'

'It's what he believed, and that's good enough for me. He was afraid they'd keep after him if they knew he was alive, so he laid low after that. She claimed on the life insurance which was the reason she married him in the first place, but the insurers wouldn't pay out because there was no body found. She was furious. She threatened to sue them but they wouldn't budge. She would have to wait seven years for a legal declaration of death. Then he began phoning us up from time to time. Always on the run. My brother and I told him to stop running. It was no way to live. In the end, he relented. He would not go to the police, but he did phone up the life insurance company to tell them he was very much alive. Of course, she found out about that. They tracked him down, had another attempt at bumping him off, and then he fled abroad.'

'Who's the "they" tracking him — the thugs?'

'She and her boyfriend Maris. Because Dad was still alive, she had to take on a fake identity and in that guise she and Maris had their wedding in the States. I haven't seen Dad for years. I talk to him on the phone now and then. But it's frustrating and so bloody unfair. He's a kind man. Wouldn't harm anyone. She should be locked up.'

Paz phoned Rick Terman with his findings but omitting contact information for the Samedis. He said he predicted Mrs Maris would soon be Mrs Someone-Else.

'Why do you say that?' said the adjuster.

'Three dead husbands and a fourth who would be dead if she'd had her way. I'm sure the fifth won't be around long. The previous fire you asked about was paid out under duress. The insurers didn't want to go to court. So that's their client for you. I guess they never know the true risk they're taking.'

Terman seemed to find it hard to believe, and Paz wondered for a moment whether he had fallen under the woman's charms. Certainly from what Terman told him, he was not finding much to support denying the latest claim, but that was not Paz's business.

Paz forgot about Mrs Maris until he read one day that she'd disappeared. He wondered whether he'd get the missing person case but he didn't. Perversely he began to feel sorry for her. Perhaps no-one cared. It made him wonder whether that was her problem in the first place: No-one cared about her. People who did bad things usually got a bad start in life. She became his private cause célèbre and he told himself this had nothing to do with him finding her physically attractive. He even looked forward to hearing that her fifth husband had died and she had remarried.

But then he received a call from someone saying they knew the latest claim, which Terman had investigated and subsequently recommended for payment, was fraudulent; the fire was set. The caller, who had a distorted voice that could be of any gender, said that Terman began an affair with Mrs Maris during the investigation. It was common gossip in his office that they were an item. How did the caller know? Because they'd been working there at the time. They were ringing Paz because they knew Terman had contacted him for information. Terman had been checking up on Mrs Maris to see if he could trust her. Paz asked what they meant by that. The caller explained Terman wanted to get the latest claim paid in order to split the proceeds with Mrs Maris but needed something he could use as leverage with her if she wouldn't agree to the split. If she'd been paid out on an earlier fraudulent claim, that would be leverage enough. Paz was intrigued and asked to meet the caller but they refused, saying they'd ring back to discuss what to do.

The call put Paz in a quandary, but he was especially busy at the time and so left it. After a week the caller rang again and asked Paz what he'd done about it. He said he'd done nothing. The caller was appalled. Paz retorted, 'So who did *you* speak to at the insurer?'

'No-one.'

'Why not?'

'I didn't think anyone would believe me. Or want to. Besides, I don't work for the adjuster now and it has nothing to do with me. I rang you because of your prior involvement on a case involving her.'

Paz wondered why they thought he'd have success and they wouldn't. They said they'd ring back in a week to find out what he'd done. He told them not to bother because he probably wouldn't do anything. Their tone made clear their displeasure at this.

Paz relented and rang the insurer. He spoke to the manager of the claims department that handled the latest fire. They did not sound pleased to hear from him. He told them of the strange calls he'd received and his role on the case and they softened a little. He asked what they thought and they said they'd heard the rumour about Mrs Maris and Terman being in cahoots but there was no evidence, only hearsay. Paz thought he'd wasted his time, but something he'd said had caught the claims manager like a raspberry pip between his teeth and he said, 'There is one thing.'

'Yes?'

'We'd never used Terman before and we found him extremely expensive. He was the claim handler's choice and he's left now. Any evidence of overbilling would be handy.'

The next time the strange person with the distorted voice rang, Paz asked them about overbilling and how Terman got assigned the case in the first place. The caller laughed, which with the distortion was most disconcerting. They said Terman had worked with that particular claim handler before and bribed him to get cases, so they paid him back in inflated fees.

Paz reported back to the insurers but was aware there was still something missing. The opportunity to find that came when Paz heard from his former colleague Jane that Fran Owens had been approached by someone wanting to join his firm. 'Doesn't everyone?' sighed a frustrated Paz. This man, called Tupp, had once owned half of Terman's adjusting company but the two had fallen out. Paz rang Tupp and, at the man's suggestion, went to see him.

They met at Tupp's rambling old house which now contained his makeshift office.

The calm, quietly-spoken, studious-looking host said there was a simple explanation. Paz said he liked those. Tupp explained that Mrs Maris preyed upon Terman's greed and gullibility. Paz asked him to clarify. Tupp said that Terman realised the claim was arson by Mrs Maris and tried to cash in by asking for fifty percent. She turned it around by claiming he'd blackmailed her by using the first claim, the one Paz had been involved with, as leverage. Mrs Maris had nothing to lose. She could always find someone with access to money to look after her. She claimed to know nothing about insurance so she relied on Terman as an expert. He, meanwhile, stood to lose everything. It would have destroyed his career. Yes, they'd had an affair but there was no love in it. Terman was just a cash machine that would need to go on paying. 'I don't understand it,' said Tupp. 'I don't see the attraction. She does nothing for me. You?'

'No,' Paz lied.

On the drive home, he thought back to the couple of meetings he'd had with her, when he'd posed as a buyer. In truth, he'd found her bewitching and seductive - her pretty face, her bright blue eyes and that flirty look he read as 'Come on, if you're man enough,' and her comment, 'I've nothing to sell but when I do you'll be first to know.' Ever the professional, he'd put his feelings aside. He suspected the loss adjuster he'd reported to on that case was of a different stripe. Paz had seen her with him in a restaurant a week after he'd sent him his report. And again a week after that. But that was the last time because the case was then closed. Paz heard a rumour the man took up a job offer in the States, but he was never heard of again.

Chapter 23

Mr Relationship Counsellor

One morning, unexpectedly, Paz's escort friend Suzi turned up at the office. She was a terrible sight. Her face was red and heavily bruised, she had a black eye, and looked like she'd been beaten up. He was immediately concerned. What had happened?

She sat down awkwardly in his private room. In their conversation she revealed that husband Terry had turned out to be a monster. He was a total control freak. He wanted to know where she was every minute of the day, and if she didn't comply he believed the worst and assaulted her. She said she thought Terry might be a bigamist. She believed he'd been married in the US before he met her and had never divorced. How she'd arrived at this conclusion she did not elucidate.

She asked if she could stay with Paz at his place. She said she felt too unsafe at home. He asked her about finding a women's refuge, but she shook her head and said she wanted to stay with him for 'just a few nights'. He wanted to help, but was not comfortable with having her at the flat because Mack was staying over at the time.

'You can rescue me,' Suzi said. 'I've always wanted the feeling of being rescued by you.'

'It's not in my gift. I could shield you, even hide you, but I can't rescue you, as you put it.'

She was unmoved, and eventually he reluctantly agreed to let her stay at his flat for one night. The only snag was Mack's likely reaction. He did not want her to leave the flat and so said nothing to her about it.

But Mack was quick and suspicious. 'Who's that?' she queried when Suzi had hobbled out of the office.

'A friend,' he said. 'A friend on hard times.' He did not elaborate. He immediately knew he should have done.

That evening, Suzi appeared at the flat with a suitcase. Mack, alarmed, asked Paz for a private word. They went into the room Mack slept in. She was nervous and upset. She said, 'Is she staying?'

'Just for now. One night only.'

'Do you want me to go then?'

'No.'

'Why didn't you tell me she was staying? I suppose I should have guessed when I saw her in the office.'

'I don't want you to go. I didn't want to upset you.'

'Well, that worked, didn't it?' She was struggling to restrain her anger. 'There's only two bedrooms. Am I expected to listen to you two making out? I'll have to put on loud music or something. Or maybe I could watch. I've always wanted to see an old slapper get a good pounding — not!' She began preparing her bag for leaving.

He asked her not to. 'I'm sorry,' he said. 'I messed up. You deserve better.'

'You're not wrong there. Does she know about me?'

'Yes.'

'What happened to her anyway?'

'She was beaten up... by her husband.'

'Now I feel bad.' She became pensive. 'Maybe she should have married you.'

He did not respond, merely smiled weakly. She stopped packing her bag and returned to the lounge. Suzi had turned up the TV, which made conversation difficult. Mack made an effort, but it was obvious Suzi resented her being there. Mack sensed Suzi was jealous of her closeness to Paz but also suspected some of her disapproval arose from Mack's sexuality.

Later, Paz faced more uncomfortable questions in bed with Suzi. 'What is she, your plaything?'

'No.'

'Do you love her?'

'She's gay.'

'I know. That's not what I asked you. You're going that way yourself anyway. You can't even do it tonight. Are you nervous because of her? Or is it because of how I look?'

'No.'

'I mean, you were always boring, but you used to have a bit of fire in you. It hurts you, doesn't it, me talking like this? I can tell. Then fuck it out of me, Paz. Do it.'

For Suzi, to be found sexually arousing to her man mattered more than anything. It was part of her identity. That the man she was with, whichever man, might be indifferent to her was devastating. But she'd always had special feelings for Paz. It wasn't so much that she loved him romantically, but he was the least unacceptable of the men she knew.

Of course, suggesting her lover was turning gay achieved the desired effect. It was true he lacked the energy and vigour of his younger days, but he could still make her feel beautiful and desired.

Once satisfied, she returned her attention to Mack. 'Why is she even here?'

'She likes to spend time when her girlfriend's away. She doesn't like to be alone.'

'Come off it, Paz. I wasn't born last week. If it's not about sex, you must be exploiting her: getting her to work all hours.'

'Not so.'

'Then the little dyke's exploiting you. You indulge her. I think you're a little bit — maybe more than that — in love with her.' He said nothing and she began rambling: 'I see the way you look at her. I can see how much you dote on her. Not sexual, but love nevertheless. Fatherly, that's it. She's the daughter you never had, Paz. The daughter you never had with me. I always wanted a daughter by you. A beautiful daughter. More beautiful than me. And kinder. No, on second thoughts, I prefer to think it really is about sex. I find it hilarious that you hired some tart thinking you could get her in the sack and she turned out to be gay.'

'Stop it. That's not how it was.'

Next morning, Paz decided he would ask Mack, who'd left his flat early that morning, to research Terry. He suspected that Suzi was right in thinking him a bigamist. First, though, she could look up women's refuges. But when he passed her the request, he found her resistant. In fact, she refused.

'Don't you feel some sympathy for her?'

'Yes, that she got beaten up. But I heard what she said about me. It was hurtful and homophobic.'

'She's not homophobic.'

'I'm used to it but it still hurts. No I won't help her.' He looked hard into her eyes. She was determined. They were both tired and both already on the edge of a ridiculous row that could quickly slide out of control. He would order her; she would refuse. Either he would sack her or she would resign. There would be upset and tears. Even he might have tears.

'If you try and force me, I'll quit.'

'OK,' he said.

'OK what?'

She was being foolish, completely out of order. She deserved to be punished and she knew it. But he relented; it wasn't worth an argument. He would do the work himself. He'd thought about giving her a permanent contract but changed his mind. 'OK, you don't have to do it. Forget I asked.'

This deflated her. She was up for a row and he'd denied her. Paz was not Lily. With Lily, Mack was used to a passionate fight followed by a passionate reconciliation. Paz, on the other hand, did not like conflict and did not admire it in others.

Mack did the search for refuges. At the earliest opportunity, however, still intent on a row, she marched into his office and threw the sheet of paper on his desk. 'Here's what you fucking asked for.' He caught her eye. There was fear there. 'I mean, here's what you asked for about refuges.' She turned away.

'Mack.'

'Yeah, what?'

'Thank you.'

'You're welcome.'

They avoided each other for most of the day. Then she came to see him and apologised: 'I felt she was getting between us. I was jealous and it was wrong of me. Lily's back tonight anyway.' It sounded like a carefully prepared little speech.

'You have nothing to worry about,' he said.

Before she left for the day, he relented again and told her he would put her on a permanent contract. She merely shrugged as she left his office.

The problem Paz knew he had was that he could not escape relationships. He'd tried to ignore them but doing so left him naive, inexperienced, and clumsy. For all her temperament, to lose Mack would be a disaster, yet he felt his actions or inaction were making it more likely all the time.

Chapter 24

Surveillance

Mack researched Terry and quickly established he was indeed a bigamist. It took a while to uncover because he used different aliases. He was already married twice with both wives living and neither of them divorced. His second wife was trying to locate him and the Minnesota police were also interested. Suzi was thus not legally married. Mack, embarrassed at her initial reaction to being asked, had researched it partly in her own time. The case, like most others, fascinated her.

By now, Suzi had found a refuge centre in Leicester. She'd been staying at a cheap hotel at Paz's expense, which she resented. On her last night at the hotel, Paz told her what Mack had discovered about Terry. She was thankful, expressing her gratitude in her customary carnal way, but he said she needed to thank Mack. She was reluctant but Paz insisted. Accordingly, she wrote Mack a personal letter.

When Paz gave Mack the letter unopened, he informed her that he would be giving her a pay rise, although he did not elaborate. She queried whether he could afford it, but he said he didn't care.

It was at this point that a client arrived in his office for an appointment.

Paz had known Alf for many years. He tried to be neutral about clients generally but didn't particularly like him. Alf was always having problems with his wife and wanted her watched. He was now on his fourth wife, but the previous marriages had all ended the same way. Sometimes the surveillance had been to assist him pursuing his divorce, sometimes it was a defence mechanism in case she divorced him. Sometimes the pretext was her love life, other times it was her spending habits. He told Paz every time he got married he was immediately thinking of his strategy in the divorce. Marriages were never final, merely stepping stones, albeit not stones that led anywhere except to the next one. He'd been married to his current wife Elwyn for a year and it was time for surveillance to start. He liked to spread the work around so the wife did not get used to seeing the same car and start wondering why. Traditionally, Paz and Jane had alternated their shifts to help this effort.

Elwyn was from a wealthy family and it had been thought likely, in the eyes of those unlucky enough to know Alf well, that for this reason it would be a longer relationship. But lately he was spending more time away from home 'on business', which was usually an unspoken invitation for the wife to explore other avenues for amorous adventures.

Paz didn't envy his client. It was true of most of them, but in Alf's case, he couldn't help thinking he brought trouble upon himself, whereas others were plain unlucky. He couldn't understand the drive to get married while all the time knowing it would end in tears, or at least dispute. Paz had little capacity for aggravation in his personal life because he knew it would affect his whole existence. Others seemed to be able to tolerate trouble and even relish it, and that was probably why they were business big shots, whereas he was just a solitary dog scratching a living out of other people's dirt.

In divorce cases he often felt more sympathy for the subject than the client. Alf was unreasonable, a bit mad, impetuous, narcissistic. Elwyn was an ostensibly pleasant person who just wanted the wealthy, glamorous life she'd been led to expect from an early age. When Paz watched the marital home, he hoped the man in his forties she'd welcomed at the door would make her happy. He made Paz happy, for there was nothing worse than doing surveillance and finding nothing. At least she was faithful to one lover which made surveillance less interesting but easier.

The ways of love, however, never followed straightforward paths, and Paz began to notice a falling off of visits by the lover, and an end to trysts between them at hotels and elsewhere. He talked about this to a freelancer he'd employed to work with him on the case. The freelancer had noted the same thing. Paz felt there was something they were missing. Something they couldn't get at. Something unsaid. He wondered if she sensed danger. He reported back to Alf their conclusions. 'Not your role to speculate,' he reminded Paz. He wanted him to carry on watching. 'She must be seeing someone else,' he said. Had Paz possessed any doubts about it, it was now obvious that Alf had no reason to be away from his wife; he just wanted her to fall into the trap.

Paz soon became aware of other cars outside Alf and Elwyn's house that might contain people doing the same job as himself. One day, as the lover left after one of his increasingly rare visits, an Audi that had been parked fifty yards along the street edged forward and then pulled up for the lover to enter on the passenger side, leaving behind the Peugeot he'd arrived in earlier. The lover looked surprised, harassed even. Paz wondered what was going on. Had the man entered the car because he was afraid? Paz was completely confused; this wasn't part of the script. Perhaps Alf had changed his mind and now wanted to destroy his rival. Or scare him, at least. Paz wondered whether he'd just seen the prelude to a grisly crime. It was one of those moments he regretted his job, down amongst the most tawdry aspects of life. He was tempted to try to follow the Audi to see what happened next. But Alf had stressed to Paz that would not be his job. He was employed to watch the wife, not follow her lovers. So he waited for something else to happen, confident nothing would. But soon another car arrived and the driver got out and called in on Elwyn. Paz liked to think it was her lawyer there to talk about divorce. She would be better off without Alf.

He wondered whether Charlie Kibbs might be able to confirm who the lover was. Paz knew he was in Brighton and so called him in. Charlie took one look at the photograph Paz showed him and said, 'That's Richard Manowar. Is that all you wanted? Didn't you know who it was? Not very good. I should do this PI lark.'

'Believe me, Charlie, you're best as my consultant. I don't need the competition and, besides, all the waiting around would give you restless legs.'

'Any more people you don't recognise?'

'Just an odd situation this last time that bothers me. He came out of Alf's house and a car pulled up and he entered it. He left his hire car—'

'How do you know it's a hire?'

'We always get the plates checked. Sometimes he uses cabs. He never came back for it, all the time I was there.'

'He's left it there to be stolen,' he said.

'Why would he do that?'

'So the others in the gang will sell it and give half the proceeds to him. You're not very bright, Paz. I know what you thought. You thought he got into the car under duress with someone pointing a gun at him. You watch too many films.'

It transpired that Paz was right to be bothered. Manowar never did reappear and the Peugeot remained where it was until the council towed it away. So much for it being intended for stealing. He watched Elwyn. The man he'd decided was her lawyer, although that didn't prevent him being more than that, visited her again. He left soon afterwards.

Over the following days, it became quite boring. She did not go out and no-one visited her. Paz sent his regular reports to Alf, but he did not respond.

The period of ennui ended dramatically when Richard Manowar was discovered dead at the foot of Beachy Head. The police believed it was suicide, according to the Argus. But why had he jumped? Paz did not believe for a moment that it was suicide. The question was: Who had murdered him? It could have been Alf or whoever it was in the Audi that picked him up that time, which may have been someone employed by Alf. He phoned Charlie about it.

'Just because you're right for once,' said Charlie.

'I would rather be wrong.'

'That's what they always say. Now you want to know who I think done it?'

'I was sure you'd have an opinion.'

'I don't think it was your mate Alf. Manowar had a business partner, by name of Dolman. Ostensibly all very amicable. Some would say not. The business was going to pieces so they were falling out. Dolman blamed Manowar for overextending the business and quit. But there's more: Dolman had started working for Alf, and Manowar didn't like it.'

Paz was still wondering whether Alf had arranged for Manowar to be taken out, when the man himself arrived in his office to pay the bill. But Alf had a big surprise for him. He revealed he'd had a fundamental change of heart. He said all along he'd encouraged his wife to have affairs, calling it an open marriage, even though he had no affairs himself. But he now realised how 'special' Elwyn was, and he was having second thoughts about divorce. Paz thought Alf must be going soft in the head. There'd be no more surveillance work from him, which would be a relief. Or so he thought until Alf told him he wanted Dolman watched. 'I don't trust him,' he said. 'Especially after Manowar. He wants to go into business with me, but I don't know what he brings to any deal other than insatiable greed. Since he joined me at the body shop, cars we work on keep disappearing from the yard. He knows some pretty unsavoury characters.' Alf's tone was growing harsher. For once in his life he was feeling under threat. 'I let him work with me at the body shop, which he was happy with, but now he wants to take over. I think he's setting up a rival business on the side.'

'Has he talked about buying you out?'

'Yes. I told him emphatically that I was not interested. Since then he's trying subterfuge. And he was screwing my wife, 'cept I've got no proof. He stopped when I instructed you. Funny that, don't you think?'

'I hope you're not implying anything.'

'As if I would. I'm a bit paranoid perhaps, but I don't believe in coincidences, Paz. You can prove me wrong by following him now. I'm joking. I've known you for years. You're too boring to try anything cute.'

'Thanks. So a new assignment, then. Great.'

Alf paused. 'No. It's a continuation of the old one.'

He gave all the details to Paz who did not relish the idea of watching Dolman, given his violent reputation.

On the first surveillance at Dolman's place, he realised the subject was the man he'd imagined as her lawyer visiting Elwyn after Manowar had disappeared. Alf had said he thought Dolman had stopped seeing her and so either he was mistaken or lying. Paz watched Dolman's car leave his drive and then observed another car follow him up the street. In Paz's growing uncertainty he wondered whether the second car was another PI. He assured himself that it must be a coincidence.

Surveillance proved difficult because Dolman used three different addresses, and he always drove fast with little apparent concern for speed limits or red lights. Fortunately for Paz, he didn't need to worry for long: the assignment suddenly ended.

Dolman was working under a car one day at Alf's shop when the jack slipped and the vehicle landed on his chest, killing him. Paz saw it in the Argus.

He phoned Alf, 'What happened?'

Alf naturally sounded subdued. 'I let him work on his own car at the shop. His jack gave way. Tragic.'

'Weird.'

'These things happen, Paz. Accidents happen, as you know.'

'It seems odd, though.'

'Sure. Anyway, your file's closed now. Send me your fees.'

'What if the police—'

'There'll be no police.'

'You asked me—'

'To watch my wife, and you did that. Don't worry, you'll be paid for the extra work, Paz. We have to learn the lesson from these things.'

'Lesson?'

'Accidents, Paz. Things happen. It could be me. Or you—'

'But even so—'

'Or that pretty redhead who works in your office.'

'Eh?'

'You know: Walking home after work.'

'What?'

'Walking alone in the dark to that luxury flat she shares with her girlfriend.'

'You're kidding!'

'Lovely part of town, Paz, but you never know who's round the corner. No street's completely safe.'

'Alright.'

'Or when she's on her way to yours.'

'OK. I see.'

'I think you do, Paz. I think you do see. A sensitive soul as you are who cares about his young staff.'

Paz did not reply immediately and merely took a deep breath. Finally, he said, 'Yes. I see it all very clearly now.'

Chapter 25

Undercover

Paz received a call from his former colleague Jane. It was his immediate naive hope that perhaps she wanted her old job back, that maybe working for Fran Owens hadn't been so wonderful after all. But instead, she was seeking help of a different kind. At the retirement flats, where her father lived, there was a strange young man who was supposedly a policeman and was always there despite not being resident or working there. What was particularly strange was that every time a major local crime occurred in the area he claimed to have been on the scene. He never tired of talking about such things. That incident on the beach under the pier - he was there. That robbery in Portslade last week - he was there.

'Why is he at the flats?' Paz asked her.

'He claims he's related to one of the residents, but the resident won't acknowledge him.'

'I see. So he likes to talk about his work. And maybe he glosses it up a bit so that he's always playing a key role. But what's the problem with that?'

'Don't you think it's strange he's always involved? I mean, always. Racing to the scene, making the key arrest.'

'A fantasist.'

'More sinister than that. Imagine if he's not legitimate. He could be using his policeman role as a ruse to find out the secrets of the residents. To find out who has money.'

'Does your dad have money, then?'

'No. But the so-called policeman gravitates to the really old folks as opposed to the younger ones. The old ones who'll soon be in a care home. He makes time for them, makes out he cares for them.'

'And?'

'He gives them financial advice. He plays the role of the holder of secret knowledge he wants to share with his new friends there.'

'OK, so who's the client here?'

'I'm asking as a favour, Paz.'

'Forgive me asking, but why don't you do it yourself? Would old Fran not allow it?'

There was a noticeable pause. 'That's a cheap shot, Paz. My father simply wouldn't believe me. He's condescending, still sees me as his little girl. He doesn't think me careful enough, thinks I'd be too easily fobbed off. I honestly don't think it would be much work.'

Paz agreed to Jane's request. He was fascinated by fakes of all kinds, especially people. He also felt maintaining good relations with Jane might make it less likely Mack would be enticed away by Fran Owens.

So was the 'policeman' a fake? His name was Brown which was not helpful to investigation. Paz soon established that Brown was not with the local constabulary. When he arrived at the smart four-storey building that housed the flats, he encountered Mr Skadee, a red-faced man with a large head who wheezed a lot. Other residents called him The Professor. Skadee invited Paz to his flat, advised him he was a big supporter of Brown, and told him with a hushed voice that the young man was with a London-based unit working undercover and investigating corruption in the Sussex Police. Skadee revealed he himself was keen on this subject because he'd long been convinced that such corruption existed throughout the British police and, indeed, throughout all British institutions. It was for this reason that he believed Brown's life, and for that matter his own, were in great danger.

When Skadee began launching a tirade against 'the elites', Paz told him he needed to leave for another appointment. His host was disappointed but brightened when the phone rang. 'That'll be the Home Office,' he said confidently.

Paz went next to the man whom Brown claimed was his father. Mr Ebury was a shy but friendly man with a furtive air reminiscent of a nocturnal forest mammal. His speech was likewise cautious. It soon became clear to Paz that Ebury was puzzled by Brown. He said it was 'possible but unlikely' that Brown was his son, but he had no recollection of this ever arising before. After divorcing his wife forty years prior, he'd lived a 'hedonistic' lifestyle and couldn't recall the names of most of his partners. He found looking back painful and so did not like to be reminded of the past. Brown was therefore an irritant to him. Moreover, he had delegated all his affairs, financial and otherwise, to his eldest daughter, and she was adamant her father would never do a paternity test. He said, 'She and her sister obviously have their own interests — they think I have money.' He laughed, although in a way that convinced Paz the daughters were correct; they didn't want the old man's estate to have an additional appetite to fill. Consequently, they had complained about Brown to the residents' board of directors who ran the flats, urging them to warn Brown off.

Despite his protestations of good faith, Brown suddenly found himself barred from the flats. Paz wanted to meet him and approached Skadee for contact information. Skadee, however, had decided Paz was 'working for the elites, consciously or unconsciously', and so could not assist him. 'If you persist,' Skadee said without elucidation, 'two phone calls and I can have you arrested by special forces.'

Fortunately, the building's on-site manager, a short, bustling middle-aged woman with a lazy left eye, had contact details, and so Paz was able to pressure a reluctant Brown into meeting up.

They met in Brown's 'office' which was a small bedroom in his untidy apartments a few streets from the retirement flats. He had local press reports pinned to a board on the wall. Paz had a look at a couple of them. 'What's with all the scene-of-crime stuff?' he asked the sallow, smooth-skinned man with an arrogant demeanour. 'I hear you're everywhere, wherever there's a crime.'

'So what?' he said nonchalantly.

'Why are you deceiving people?'

He grinned. 'It's an inroad, that's all,' he said.

'I don't think people are that stupid. Old people are smarter than you seem to think. You're not on the scene of these crimes. You're not some undercover policeman. Look, I'm not the police, but I was asked to check you out — I won't say by whom. Someone connected to one of the residents, is all I'll say. So what's your real game?'

'Is it Mr Ebury's family?'

'No, but what's that about anyway? I don't believe you're his son, are you?'

He merely shrugged. Paz was satisfied Brown, which probably wasn't his real name, had no interest in the truth. He was just an annoying joker who liked the attention and so made stuff up. Paz rose from his chair. He would tell Jane her father had nothing to worry about. Brown was just an idiot.

As Paz was leaving, Brown asked, 'Don't you want to know the real reason I was there?'

'Not really. I might if I could believe a word of it.'

'It was about money,' he said. 'But not the way you think.' Paz sat back down on the edge of the chair, prepared to stand up as soon as the nonsense started again.

Brown said his real purpose had been to make enquiries about a man called McIntyre who'd left the flats a few months earlier. He said he was hired to trace McIntyre because he'd been left money in a will and no-one knew where he was.

'Is this another one of your stories,' said Paz.

'Entirely legit,' Brown insisted. Paz decided to just listen, however bizarre the story was.

As Brown described it, McIntyre was an intriguing character. He often used the name Crabtree which had been his mother's maiden name. He did this because he had so many creditors after him. Due to mental health problems, McIntyre had never held down a job for any length of time, and he scraped by on the generosity of others. He'd lived with his male partner who owned the flat. The partner died but had never put McIntyre in his will or on the deeds of the property, which had a small mortgage on it. McIntyre had no assets of his own. Ownership of the flat fell to his partner's children, but they were too young to live there and allowed him to continue, provided he paid the service charges. He didn't pay them and so they were contacted by a lawyer acting for the residents' board of directors. One of the directors had a dispute with McIntyre, claiming that he'd stolen from him. This was never resolved, but the director used his influence to get McIntyre thrown out. It was believed the man was now homeless, living on the streets under an alias, possibly as Crabtree, but Brown had been unable to trace him.

'You say your search was because of a will. How much is he due?'

'Over two hundred thousand.'

'My God!'

'Exactly. And he may never get it.'

A few weeks later, two down-and-outs were arrested for fighting on the beach under the pier. A resident at the flats had seen the incident and reported back to the directors that one of the pair was Brown. The house manager informed Paz who checked with the police. They told him Brown's real name was Baker. He was a small-time crook who thought he could hit the big time with a variety of rackets. The police persona was merely a ruse to catch vulnerable people, especially pension age folks about to enter care homes. As regards McIntyre, it was a scam Baker had worked before. He would track down the victim claiming they had a large inheritance coming their way, extract a fee from them, then disappear, there being no inheritance.

Paz went to see Brown / Baker again. Expecting him to be in poor shape, he was surprised to see him upbeat and dapper. Over strong filtered coffee, the defensive Brown stressed his business dealings were entirely legitimate and showed his card referring to himself as an 'agent' of a major life assurance company, under the name Baker. In further questioning, he maintained he really was hired to track down McIntyre and insisted there was no scam involved. The subject had been left the money in the estate of an opera singer he'd once helped by getting her an audition through contacts he had. Brown had only posed as a policeman to gain trust.

'So how did you end up in a fight with a down-and-out?'

'I was trying to find out information about McIntyre's whereabouts. The rumour was that he was homeless, so I spent time amongst these people to try to find him.'

'OK, but why the fight?'

'Because in my attempt to locate McIntyre, I had to ask lots of questions. They thought I genuinely was a policeman. They were not overly impressed by that. And, by the way, I still have no clue where McIntyre is.'

'Kind of ironic,' said Paz, grinning. He was still sceptical. Why all the stories and aliases and so on? Brown said it was necessary to use subterfuge to achieve results. Paz agreed it was occasionally necessary but nowhere near to the extent Brown did it. All it achieved was distrust and disbelief and, as in the recent example, violence. He demanded to see correspondence from the solicitors instructing him. Brown produced a crumpled letter and Paz took a photo of it. The letter was addressed to 'Mr Brown'. Paz told him to avoid all contact with anyone at the flats. He told him that he would inform the residents' board of their conversation, and if he heard Brown was still in contact with residents he would tell the solicitors they'd put the McIntyre matter in the hands of a fraudster; moreover, Paz would offer to take over the work himself for a nominal fixed fee. Brown tried to 'explain' but Paz left, having heard enough.

Back in the office, Paz sent an email to the residents' board updating them, then rang Jane to inform her. She was pleased to hear from him, not least because she was going through a difficult time with boss Fran Owens. Her brusque style was falling foul of one or two of the staff. Paz sensed her discontent and joked, 'Well, when you come back...' knowing that would never happen. They ended the call and Paz glanced up to see Mack standing there frowning. She had returned with a piece of research he'd asked her to redo, something the sensitive Mack did not appreciate.

'Is she coming back, then?' Mack asked. She sounded hurt.

'No, I just—'

'Coz she can have her bloody job back.' Paz stared at her. She was prepared for an argument. He was not. 'What was wrong with the research anyway?'

He began to explain where he felt more work was needed, but she appeared more stressed with every word and suddenly exploded into rage. 'I've had enough!' Over the next couple of minutes it was as though all the hurt she'd ever felt since working for him came to the surface through her words. He began to argue but she left his office while he was mid-sentence. She returned a moment later and threw her office keys on his desk, saying, 'There you are. I quit. It's what you want so Jane can come back. And don't try and dissuade me because you can't. For the record, I think you're an evil, manipulative sod...' She waited for a response. There was none. His eyes were cast down, staring at the keys. He was hurt already, but she wanted him to suffer more: '...and a dirty bastard ...and a misogynist twat.' She then told him she was going to work for Fran Owens 'who knows how to treat people.'

He was stunned. He raised his head but all he could manage to say was that he wanted her resignation in writing. Why? Because it was the professional thing to do. She snatched back the keys. When he stood up and tried to give her a conciliatory hug she told him to fuck off and walked out, only pausing to pick up her things from her desk.

So shocked was Paz that he cancelled his remaining appointments for the day, went for a long walk along the seafront, had a few drinks alone at the Colonnade bar next to the theatre, and took a cab home. He was in two minds. He didn't want to lose her, but nor did he want her there unhappy. She was out of order with her comments about him. He was disillusioned for he had encouraged her in every way he could. She had flourished. And yet he was reminded of something Suzi had said: He was exploiting Mack or she was exploiting him. He had the power, so it was his fault. The excellent work she'd done for him hadn't been matched by rewards. He had let her down. He was getting what he deserved.

That evening, he expected her to turn up at the flat to say it was all a big mistake and she wanted her job back. She didn't. He couldn't stop thinking about her. Her outburst was brutal but she was indispensable. Out of desperation he phoned her. 'What do you want?' she said.

'I wondered if you'd had time to think, maybe had second thoughts.'

'No. Why would I?'

'Well, I just thought maybe, you know... So you have nothing further to say?' He felt helpless.

'Correct.'

'Well, if you...'

'I won't... Paz?'

'Yes.'

'Thanks for phoning.'

After the call he wondered why she'd added those last three words. It gave him hope, even if false. But if nothing else, phoning had at least shown he cared.

Next morning, he was in early and waited for her to arrive. She was late. He tried to engross himself in reading about a new fraud case but could not concentrate. Suddenly he became aware of her presence in the room.

'Here you are,' she said. It was the voice that caught him. After this day he might never hear it again. 'You believed I couldn't write a letter but I've written this one at least.'

'I never said you couldn't.'

'I said you *believed* it.' He sighed and opened it. It read, '*Dear Mr Wheat, Confirming our conversation, I resign. Alison.*' He was disappointed. There was no thanks for the opportunity, no recognition that she'd enjoyed the work, no sadness at leaving. 'OK then,' he said and he returned to his fraud case.

'Is that it?' she said after a pause.

'What do you mean?'

'Aren't you going to reject it? Aren't you going to tear it up?'

'No. Why should I?'

'I thought, because you wanted me to stay. Clearly I was mistaken because you don't.'

'What's it all about, Mack? Why?'

She paused. 'Alright,' she said. 'This is very difficult for me.' Another pause, then the words came quickly: 'I think you underestimate me. You often don't tell me how cases work out. You rarely introduce me to clients.'

'I don't have to.'

'And when you do it feels like, "Here's my sexy assistant".'

'I've never said anything like that.'

'It's true; I think you just see me as a sex object. I've known from the start that you were attracted to me, but I never really thought about it until I heard that dog Suzi taunting you and then being forced to listen to you having sex. That disgusted me. You should not have put me in that situation. But admit it, you only employed me because you fancied me.'

'That's so not true.' He was becoming annoyed.

'You coerced me into getting half-naked to save my job, coerced me to dress exactly the way you like: short skirts and all, coerced me into staying at the flat to work extra hours. All for a pittance. And now you want me out.'

'No!'

'You don't appreciate me. I want to feel wanted for what I do.'

'I do appreciate you.'

'And face it, our relationship's... inappropriate.'

It took him a moment to collect himself. He tried to speak and failed - twice - then he said defiantly, 'OK, perhaps you're right. So what? It doesn't matter now because you're leaving.' He was tempted to launch into a tirade of his own. Since Suzi's visit the quality of Mack's work, although still high, had declined, as though she'd lost interest. But he did not want a fight. He said nothing further until, with apparent reluctance, she left the room. He returned to his reading but couldn't focus on it. His heart was pounding, or at least he imagined it was.

Mack lingered in the main office, frustrated. Finally, she re-entered his room. 'You don't get it, do you? I've been fighting my feelings. That's why I said what I did.'

'What do you mean?'

'I mean, I love you, Paz. Maybe I shouldn't, but I do.' She began crying, 'Don't get me wrong, I love Lily to distraction, and she will always be my first love, but I have another kind of love for you. I know it's real. And it's crazy. I've been fighting it but I can't anymore.' She paused to see if he'd respond. He didn't. 'So there, I've told you now, and I feel like a complete and utter idiot. A total fool. I'm an emotional mess. I wish I could be like Jane — dispassionate and dry. I can't help it; I put everything I've got into everything I do. It makes me wild and volatile, it gets me into trouble. I need reassurance that it's OK to be who I am. Sometimes I want to leave Lily and come and live with you. It's madness. And I know my love is unrequited and will always be.' She looked into his eyes. 'Please say something.'

He was as bewildered by what she'd just said as what she'd said the day before. He had feelings for her, but he suppressed them and would continue to do so. He could not stand emotionalism getting in the way of work. He took a deep breath. He would make a spontaneous speech to which he would give every last bit of the power of persuasion he had. He was determined not to lose her. He could not look at her. 'OK. I never realised you were so unhappy. I should have done. Everything you've said — every criticism of me, at least — I accept as true. I have the frailties of any man. Further, I will say this to you: I acknowledge I have failed you in at least three ways. Firstly, I should have dissuaded you from staying at the flat. I didn't because I like it.' She was about to interject but he raised his hand. 'I love your company. I love talking to you.' He took a sip of water.

'I love your company as well,' she said through tears.

'Second, I should have made your contract permanent after all this time. This is a serious lapse on my part. Third, I should have given you a pay rise. I will correct these last two things immediately. Your work is bringing in more cases. That I very much appreciate.' He did now look her in the face, even though it hurt him to. 'Listen, you must never diss me in front of a client or third party because that could be detrimental to the business. In private, however, you can say whatever you want to me, even though some of what you say may be hurtful. I will still admire everything about you. Now, for Heaven's sake, dry your eyes. You know I can't stand tears in the office. I suggest you take a break — a week on full pay — and when you come back we will continue as before but with the two things I mentioned corrected. If what I've said is not enough, then I'm sorry.'

She gently took back her resignation letter and put it in her bag. After quickly updating him on a couple of cases, she left. She felt relieved that the morning's proceedings were over, and walking home in the sunshine she even skipped for a moment or two. After that she felt ashamed. She had lost control. She had let herself down. Once before, when conned by Jude, now with Paz. Paz of all people! How shaming was that!? But then, he had let her down. He hadn't appreciated her. He had taken her for granted. Fran Owens would not have been so inept, but it was Paz who gave her the chance in the first place, and she would never forget that.

Meanwhile, in his office Paz sighed, 'Oh dear!' about emotions getting in the way of business, as he struggled through the ritual of editing a report for Fran Owens' clients.

Chapter 26

An Unfortunate Family

When Mack returned to the office after her week off, Paz noticed she seemed subdued, perhaps worried he'd decided she was more trouble than she was worth and so would dispense with her. Nothing was further from his intentions and he would seek to reassure her over it. Although he'd forgotten about the commitments he'd made to her, her return prompted him into action. That morning, he gave her a letter informing her she would receive a fifteen per cent pay increase, backdated for six months, and making her a permanent employee. He told her he'd missed her, and to make up for it he would take her out to dinner. Where would she like to go? 'Not English's, please,' she said, thinking about her visit there with the blindfolded artist Rafe Lasche. 'No, on second thoughts, English's would be great, to create new memories there.'

She asked for the same table as on that previous occasion, and she had the same meal. She told Paz more about that earlier visit and he, thinking Lasche ridiculous, delighted in being able to mock him. 'Fancy taking you out just to listen to your voice!' he exclaimed.

'It was nice to feel appreciated, though,' she said. 'And not to be ogled. He didn't look at me once the whole time.' She laughed. Paz was silent, detecting admonishment, hopefully playful. 'I'm sorry,' she said. 'After this can you take me for a drink? And can we walk along the front for a bit?'

Paz had hoped for a quick meal so he could spend the rest of the evening reading a report, but then he was reminded of Suzi's complaint about him being boring about work.

'I wanted to talk about my week off,' Mack said. 'I was hoping you would be interested.'

'OK,' he said, trying to sound convincing. 'Let's do that.'

He took her to the Druid's Head pub which was one of her favourites. Mack told him how her week had started with a call from her friend Nicola, whom she called Nikks. Nikks was worried about her father. 'She told me he wanted to reinvest his pension and she was worried he didn't know what he was doing. He'd been looking at websites and talking to people on the phone and suddenly decided he was some sort of financial hotshot. She was worried he would get scammed and wondered whether Lily knew about all that stuff.'

'And does she?' asked Paz.

'Not really. But because she works in finance — private equity — the idea was that she might impress upon Nikks' father — Giff is what people call him, short for Gifford — that he was getting himself involved in something he shouldn't.'

'OK.'

'Besides, Lily has been a bit down lately. Worried about business, and her business partner's dad who's ill, and a bit worried about me, I guess, after you know—'

He took this to mean, her recent outburst. 'OK. So was Lily receptive to the idea?'

'Well, I kind of screwed that up. I guess I'm not doing well on that score lately.' She gave a rueful laugh which Paz pretended to ignore. 'I sold it to her as a day out. Something different to get her out of herself. Lily is such a city girl these days, but she loves nature, and Nikks and her dad live off the beaten track. And Nikks has young kids and Lily loves kids. And animals.'

'I get the picture. So how did it go?'

She frowned. 'Not well. It started off OK except Lily was driving way too fast, scaring the shit out of me, which is maybe a bit rich coming from me who can't even drive.'

'You should learn. You need it in this game.'

'I know. I know. Anyway, Lily was a bit spooked by the narrow country roads, but instead of easing up she went faster — she's like that — and I was relieved when we got there. Anyway, so Nikks lives in a caravan on Giff's land, and the kids are there, and cats everywhere, and an old dog, and larks singing overhead when we arrive, and Lily's beaming with joy.'

'So what went wrong?'

'The TV's on and there's a true crime show set in Los Angeles, and Nikks drops the comment, 'I lived there once,' and Lily's fascinated because her friend Gloria's in Orange County, and she wants to know everything about it. She loves any excuse to mention Gloria, supposedly living this perfect life in her mansion, and she started asking how big the swimming pool was and such trivia as that, knowing it annoys me. She loves ostentatious wealth and she's so vain herself, dressing like a million dollars just to go to the shops—'

'Gloria or Lily?'

'Lily.'

'Stop dissing the woman you love.'

'Trust you to speak up for her.'

'So what was Nicola doing in California?'

'Living with Stu, her financier boyfriend in a beautiful villa with two expensive cars, an infinity pool, palm trees, sea views and everything. She doesn't like talking about it much because it's painful for her. It was all fake, you see.'

'The boyfriend?'

'The boyfriend, the job he didn't even have, the house was rented (and he wasn't even paying for it), the cars were leased. It's embarrassing for Nikks, and she must have wished she hadn't said anything, because Lily, who's a little slow in social situations sometimes, doesn't realise and keeps asking questions, thinking she's being friendly.'

'OK, but why was it so embarrassing? I'd be a bit like Lily, I think. Inquisitive.'

'You would be. The thing is, Stu made Nikks his guarantor. And then he took off.'

'Oh no!' he sighed.

'So Nikks' dad Giff then comes in, and Nikks raises the subject of his pension and says Lily deals with investments and is very successful (which, of course, embarrasses her), and he asks if he could buy shares in her business. Lily says it's a private company and so he can't. "So you're in private equity then?" he says, clearly ticked. She nods and then he launches into a speech about private equity vultures "savaging" a local shop. Lily responds, saying she's used to it — a whole menagerie of hyenas, and sharks, and fat cats, and all the accusations about asset stripping, and redundancies, and whatnot.'

'Good for her! I'm liking your Lily.'

'You would. So Giff realises he's been rude and gets off his high horse and asks her about some foreign exchange fund he's interested in that offers 25% a year or something ridiculous like that, and she says she can't advise him on it but she herself wouldn't be interested. He says he's also tempted by a fund to support "surefire" litigation wins — court cases that can bring in millions. "Betting, in other words," says Lily who adds that lawfirms are notorious for breakups, with all the complications they cause, and anyway what if the cases turn out to be losers?'

'Quite right too.'

'And he's miffed at this and asks about cryptocurrency, and Lily gives the same answer as before: Can't advise but wouldn't herself as not her cup of tea. Green investment funds? Same answer again. Bored, Nikks then changes the subject to her sister Emmy who'd been for a job interview for a "holiday event" business. It was done via video. Quite clever. Then she was told she'd got the job. Nikks told her, any decent job would never be got as easily as that.' Paz coughed at this, reminded of his 'interview' of Mack - she smiled in recognition. 'Then they told her she needed to pay for background checks.'

'Oh dear!'

'Then they directed her to a website where she had to give her bank details.'

'And did she do it?'

'No. She realised what was going on after Googling about it and finding people complaining. They'd paid their fees and then never heard anything.'

'Emmy sounds a smart one,' said Paz.

'She gets herself in scrapes but usually gets out of them. She says she's like a magnet drawing in scammers. She was going to buy herself a holiday on Instagram, but then realised that was a scam. The place doesn't even exist. Or it does, but not in the same town, or even same country. Out of curiosity, I checked the same image online and found it appearing in several different holiday destinations.'

'OK,' said Paz. 'So what did Lily say about all this afterwards?'

'On the drive home she complained to me that it was supposed to be a relaxing day in the country, and she felt she'd been browbeaten about things she didn't know about. "And all that sermonising!" she said. So I told her the real purpose behind the visit was to dissuade Giff from his foolish investments, and she was mortified. The thing is, although Lily is socially awkward (though less so than she used to be), she's kindness personified. "We must do something then," she said. But when I phoned Nikks next day to see if we could arrange another chat with Giff, she said it was too late. He'd been to the bank and made the transfers already into some fund he'd heard about.'

'God!'

'Nikks is resigned to it. Her father's incorrigible. Apparently he's got his own relationship manager. That was the deciding factor.'

'Really?'

'Someone on Facebook.'

Paz chuckled. 'Pretty safe then.'

'And the person who put him up to it in the first place is his bloody barber!'

'It sounds like Scam City alright.'

'Lily was bemused by it all. She said, "They do seem a rather unfortunate family," and that sums it up pretty well: Giff and his pension, Nikks and her boyfriend, and Emmy with all her problems. But I felt such a jerk. I felt I'd let them all down and should have explained to Lily in the first place. What an idiot!'

This enabled him to give her a 'Don't be hard on yourself' speech. His words mollified her, as did the mere fact of him wanting to say them.

Mack then told him how, later during her week off, she'd received another call from Nikks. She had a new boyfriend by name of Robert, a policeman she'd first met when he was investigating a report that she and Giff were growing cannabis. She thought it was a joke, but Giff said it was no surprise because of what he'd been saying about local hobby farmers, even though, as far as Nikks knew, he'd only been saying it to friends and family. Giff used the opportunity to inform Robert and the other policeman who called round that he'd seen drones in the area and believed crooks were checking out his property to steal his farming equipment. On a second visit, Nikks asked Robert about her father's investments, and he declared unequivocally that Giff had been ripped off. This, plus Lily's guarded scepticism about the fund, had led to a change of heart. He tried to get his money out but was told early withdrawal required a hefty penalty payment and tax. Any doubts Nikks had about it being a fraud were now extinguished.

Mack said Nikks' call was sufficient prompt for her to put her 'investigating boots' on. She started with the website of the fund, looking for the names of anyone connected with it. For every name she found, she went searching on social media for connections. She could not resist the thought that maybe her old lover / adversary Jude was somehow involved with it. She found one name kept coming up and found a YouTube video in which this person was being challenged by an investigative reporter. Mack tracked the reporter down and gave him a call. He told her the person he'd challenged reported to someone in the Bahamas but didn't think that was where the trail ended.

Mack told Paz she'd dreamt of having a conversation with him in which she broached the subject of her going to the Bahamas to investigate further. She said she thought he'd think her a pisstaker. He said that he would. What he didn't say, however, was that if she pushed hard enough he'd probably agree to it, such was his paramount desire not to lose her.

Afterwards, Paz walked her back to Lily's place. The top-floor light was on. Her face brightened. It was the face of someone deeply in love. She glowed with it. 'Early night,' she said, clearly cherishing it in anticipation. Her joy at this moment reassured him, though he still did not know whether he'd lose her.

Chapter 27

The Peculiar
Death Of Quinn Clark

A few days after their chat, Mack again raised the subject of the 'Giff' case with Paz. She told him she'd done more analysis and was now of the opinion that the nexus of the case was in the US.

He smiled. 'I see how this is going,' he said. For a moment, he wondered whether the whole 'resignation saga' had been set up for this: Bahamas to soften him up, then 'compromise' on the US instead. He'd worked with people's mischief and cunning long enough not to miss this. 'OK, I know what you want,' he said.

'You mean, a trip to the States?' she countered. 'But we have no client to pay for it.'

She was learning, he mused. 'So what's the answer?' he said, trying to avoid sounding like a schoolmaster.

She'd clearly thought it through whilst pretending not to have. 'Find some clients, I guess. Find other people in the same predicament as Giff.'

He did not need to answer. He did say, however: 'I don't mind you working on it in the office.'

'Just not to the detriment of my other work, right?'

'Correct.'

It was then that Paz received a call from a young-sounding woman who requested he attend the office of a local solicitor about a new case.

Contrary to his expectations, their office was not in the kind of smart multi-storey building he was accustomed to with lawyers, but in a rickety old place with a decidedly dodgy lift. The solicitor he met looked like she could have been there since the day it was built, but people never matched Paz's initial impression, and the woman's dour demeanour was outweighed by the warmth that came from her. Paz figured maybe she didn't receive many visitors and so was glad to see him for that reason.

The woman said she was the executor of the estate of George Parker-Smith. The estate wanted him to locate someone called Quinn Clark. She said George had been an eccentric and had grown more so as he got older. However, he resisted all attempts by his family to get him to agree to a power of attorney. 'In all honesty,' she said, 'he was compos mentis — just cantankerous and irascible. He was a keen player of the markets, and in his later days this was all he did. Instead of putting his affairs into as straightforward a fashion as possible for his heirs, however, he chose to make them as complicated as he could devise because he thought them all "graspers". He also sought to reduce his assets. Consequently, every wild scheme and racket going he signed up for. I'm afraid his family upset him so much that he hated them at the end.'

'And where does this Quinn—'

'Quinn Clark. He was added to George's will shortly before he died. No-one had heard of him until the will, and no-one knew how he came to be added to it. But then he himself died — or so it was thought.'

'How did you find that out?'

'It was in the local paper. But lately someone claiming to be Quinn Clark has appeared. Not in person, I should add. Only by phone. What I would like you to do is find out if this person is an impostor. There's other things I could say, but the appropriate thing would be for you to read everything you can find on this matter — I'm sure you do that anyway—' Paz nodded '—and you will obviously appreciate the sensitivity of this matter.'

After this conversation and Mack's review of online news reports and social media commentaries, it did not take Paz long to realise why the solicitor seemed bemused by the case. It was rather weird. The three sibling heirs had been approached by an estate agent named Al Shilling who claimed to know Quinn Clark. Over the phone he said Clark was very secretive and hard to engage. He preferred to conduct all business at arm's length. Shilling offered to meet them, and when they agreed he invited them to his boat for a few drinks to talk about strategy.

When they were on board he took the boat out to a pretty spot where they could enjoy the sunset. They talked about Clark whom he described as a 'conman'. At one point, however, when the siblings, who all liked a drink, were quite inebriated they suddenly realised Shilling had disappeared. On searching the boat, they concluded he had gone overboard. One sibling had boating experience but was too drunk to navigate, and they called out the coastguards. Back on shore, the police inspected the boat and found traces of blood, leading them to believe foul play might be involved. A theory then circulated, based on a tip-off to the police, that Shilling and Clark were one and the same, and that the siblings discovered this and killed him. They had both the motive and the opportunity. If Shilling was Clark and he was dead, their father's estate would be split three ways instead of four. They claimed to have no knowledge about their host's disappearance and insisted it must have been of his own volition. The difficulty for them was that all the time they were suspected of his murder they could not inherit. The situation had also led to discord amongst them, with one son at odds with the other siblings over what had happened. Their late father would have been delighted.

The police had an open file when Paz went to see them. They were intrigued at him saying he'd heard Clark might still be alive. The detective handling the case told him he'd heard this rumour before but believed it was made up. He also thought the siblings capable of anything. Paz preferred such cases, where he did not like the clients, or the ultimate beneficiaries as in this instance. It helped him to be dispassionate.

He and Mack had difficulty finding information on Quinn Clark himself. He had no social media presence. There was nothing to go on. The only good thing was that he had a relatively unusual first name. What Paz did have was the name of the boat: *The Donna Mar*. He went back to the police. The boat was not registered in the name of Shilling or Clark but another man, Richard Hames. The police said they had looked into Hames' background but found nothing of interest.

A few days later, the client informed Paz that Clark's solicitors had written to them. This was the first time anything had been put in writing on Clark's behalf. What was odd was that the letter came from the Paris office of a Spanish lawfirm. Whoever Clark was, he was relentless in his games with the estate, although all the letter asked for was the current status of probate.

Paz reached out to the Paris lawyers. They told him they were dealing with authorised representatives of Mr Clark and not the man himself. He asked them for details of the representatives, but they were unwilling to tell him beyond saying that they were based in the Canary Islands.

Having established the lawyer had an office in Lanzarote, Paz decided he needed to have a few days over there. This enabled Mack to joke about his 'reluctance' to visit sunnier climes. He had the fear it would prove a waste of time (in which case he wouldn't bill it), but he insisted he'd found over the years there was no substitute for attending in person. There were exceptions, of course. He might not take the same stance if it meant being in, say, a Siberian winter.

He flew to Lanzarote the following week. Being on the island brought back memories of his previous trip there with Suzi, when she complained about his obsession with work. He felt melancholic at this memory.

Soon after arriving in Arrecife, he phoned the law firm. In his rough Spanish he asked if he could speak to Mr Clark. Paz said he was a representative of the Parker-Smith estate's executor and they wished him to establish contact, bearing in mind the Paris branch of the firm had already made written enquiries. He gave them the opportunity to check with Paris.

The lawyer he spoke to was initially dismissive, but Paz stressed how it was to the benefit of everyone for him to obtain answers, and in the end the lawyer agreed he would ask the client's representatives to contact him. Paz made clear he was only on the island a few days so there was urgency in terms of arranging the meeting.

The following day, Paz received a call from someone claiming to be Clark's representative. He sounded young and had an English accent. He said Clark was a very private person who was averse to meeting strangers on account of a nervous condition that had worsened. Paz realised this was nonsense but played along. He said the estate would need proof Clark was alive in order to move things forward. The caller said he understood. A little later, the man rang again to confirm the time of the meeting which was to take place next day.

They were to meet in Paz's hotel room at eleven a.m. Clark was late and there were no messages to explain the delay. Paz tried ringing the contact but without success. Frustrated, he went for a walk down by the sea. When he returned he expected to find his visitors waiting in the lobby. He enquired at the desk. Nothing. He returned to his room and lay down on the bed and stared at the slowly spinning ceiling fan. He'd fallen asleep for a few minutes when the phone rang: 'Two gentlemen' had arrived. He went downstairs. He was met by a short, rather severe-looking, clean-shaven man; stooped, he looked as though he'd emerged from being stuck inside a fold-up bed for a week. He introduced himself as Clark and was accompanied by an upright, jocular, glad-handing fellow who Paz could imagine as someone always on the lookout for a joke or a party. 'Can we be private?' Paz said.

'Mr Barth is my most trusted colleague and goes with me everywhere,' said Clark sternly.

Paz now formed a different impression of Clark's companion. He could see he would be useful in a fight and his easygoing air was deceptive. But Paz was puzzled at the need for Barth's presence, and Clark read his look: 'You may think I'm paranoid but I have to keep safe. I live in fear of those lovely siblings.'

Paz took them to the bar which was empty. As they sipped their beers at a table in the corner, a now relaxed Clark said in a quiet voice, 'I know what you were thinking. You thought I was a fraud. Please don't underestimate the danger I'm in. They threatened to kill me and would do it if they could. They probably killed their father. That's what he thought would happen. Arsenic poisoning.'

Paz asked him to explain how he'd become involved with the family. He said, 'Their father contacted me. I had known him years before, when I was a struggling artist, and we were very close for a while. One day he overheard his children plotting to get rid of him and it upset him so much he decided to sabotage his estate. He started investing in every dodgy scheme he could find and made it as complicated as possible with bank accounts all over the world. He put one investment worth a million pounds in my name exclusively, and he added me to his will to share the rest equally with them. My role after his death was to frustrate the probate process as much as possible. And I was to fake my own death but make it look like murder so that they would be accused of it. It would be a sort of payback for them killing him. Hence the episode on the boat. You heard about that, right?'

'Yes.'

'Al Shilling was me, and I left my blood in different places and made it look like a struggle had happened. Then I disappeared over the side.'

'So what now?' said Paz.

'I want it over with. I'm tired of all this fearing for my life. In fact, I'd be prepared to give up my share of the estate for a quiet life. After all, he gave me the million pound investment.' Seeing Paz's face brighten, he added, 'But they'd never agree to it.' He showed Paz his passport and gave him a certified copy. 'This is just one of them,' he said. 'Once you've gone home I'll be changing my appearance — I don't usually look so crumpled as this, by the way — and I'll use one of my other passports. I'll be moving elsewhere.' He produced correspondence from George and a photograph of himself as a young man.

After reviewing the documents, Paz said, 'I can't see disposing of you will do them any good. They're already being accused of murder. They'd be better off proving you're alive.'

'I don't think that would bother them overmuch,' he said. 'But tell them they can have the boat. That would convey a certain piquancy. Hames is another one of my aliases, in case you were wondering.'

As soon as he was back in England, Paz went to see the solicitor who'd instructed him. She queried why it had been necessary for him to go to Lanzarote, but her attitude changed when she learned of the outcome of the trip. Paz declared, 'I am satisfied that Mr Clark is alive and that he is not an impostor. I realise that is not what you wanted to hear.'

She was sanguine about it. 'So the estate, what's left of it, will be shared amongst four and not three. It's immaterial to me but disappointing for them.'

Any disappointment regarding the number of heirs did not last long. Three weeks later, the brother and sister were discovered dead on a beach in Gran Canaria, with no evidence of foul play. Paz concluded their enthusiasm to track down Quinn Clark had got the better of them, but he wondered how they'd found him, or even if they had. He told himself it was a weird coincidence.

Later he was contacted by another PI about the case. The siblings had appointed him and he'd found out about Paz's involvement for the estate and followed him. Paz had unwittingly led him to Lanzarote. He'd then followed Clark to Gran Canaria and, having established where he was, reported back to his clients. He'd anticipated they'd wish him to act for them in negotiations. Instead, they fired him and decided to deal with the matter themselves, with disastrous consequences. Whatever had exactly transpired, Quinn Clark, as always, had been a step ahead. George Parker-Smith would have been delighted.

Chapter 28

Las Vegas

Paz was in the office in the middle of reading a report on an identity fraud case when Mack phoned up from Las Vegas. She sounded anguished.

He'd had misgivings about Mack's trip to the States, which was intended as a 'rescue mission' to recover Giff's pension monies. While Paz was involved with the Quinn Clark case, she'd worked hard to obtain a handle on the scam. She and the London-based investigative reporter established that the centre of the business lay in the southwest of America. They found others in the same position as Giff in wanting their money out, but Mack said Giff was increasingly anxious about it and she presented Paz with a proposal to consider.

After discussion, Paz agreed to fund her share of the trip including an initial holiday in Las Vegas, on the basis that if the recovery action proved successful the costs for that would be reimbursed first, with the firm receiving an additional two per cent of anything left after Giff got his money back. Because Mack was not a licensed investigator he said that, if challenged, she was formally acting on a purely personal basis and not as the firm's representative. He stressed the importance of keeping costs down so that Giff got his money, or at least a 'worthwhile' part of it. He'd envisaged her working under the unofficial guidance of a private investigator he knew in San Diego, but to his dismay she went with Giff's daughter Nikks, girlfriend Lily as driver, and Nikks' new boyfriend, policeman Robert. Excited, Mack called it Giff's 'ultimate dream team'.

Mack was phoning Paz now to inform him of a huge row amongst the group. She was keen to tell him all about it, and he decided to be the good boss and listen, persuading himself his interest was not prurient, although he knew he was lying to himself.

After arriving in Las Vegas, after the initial shock of the heat, Nikks had wanted a good time and persuaded Mack to go out with her for a drink and gamble. Nikks wanted to get away from Robert, saying he was too obsessed with the case. After a few drinks Mack began to feel unwell, and so they returned to the hotel. Arriving at the room she was shocked to find Robert with Lily, both looking dishevelled and embarrassed. 'This is a nice surprise,' she said but it wasn't. Robert left and Mack demanded to know whether they'd had sex. Lily denied it but confessed they were going to. She then revealed Robert had been pursuing her in Brighton and she had not wanted him on the trip. He'd found her on Facebook which Lily picked up because she received notification of him as someone she 'might know'.

Mack got mad and, inspired by drink, slapped her hard around the face. Lily, feeling guilty, asked her to do it again, only harder. 'Go on, beat me up. I know you want to,' she said but Mack refused, even though in her heart she wanted to trash her pretty face and scratch all the beauty out of it. She told her she wanted to punch her so hard her fist would go right through her. She then locked herself in the bathroom and wept. She shouted insults at Lily but soon gave up. Later, Lily told her she loved only her and was 'a hundred per cent committed', so Mack tested her by asking her to marry her. Lily said she couldn't.

Mack said she then gave Lily 'sex that would blow every last cell of her stupid brain', and when Lily was at her most tender and vulnerable she told her in the harshest way she could muster that she was dumping her, and for good. Feeling 'like utter shit' she then walked out and went to Nikks' room; Nikks had thrown Robert out after Mack phoned her from the bathroom to tell her what had happened.

'Does Nikks drive?' said Paz.

'No.'

'Brilliant. So you've expelled the two drivers amongst you. How are you two geniuses going to get around? Look, this is not a fucking college break you're on!'

'What!?' She was shocked at his tone, as was he.

'This firm's paying for you to be there. And what about Nikks' father? Don't you owe him? I suggest you use a little humility and get back with Lily.'

She rang off, disgruntled.

For Paz this was a reminder of why he couldn't stand personal issues getting mixed up with professional ones. Mack was immature. How could he expect her to be other than that?

Three hours later, there was another call from her. He was aggravated and found it hard to conceal it. She described going downstairs alone to the hotel casino and feeling uncomfortable there, sensing she was being watched and half expecting security to come over and ask her to turn out her bag.

At this Paz sighed, imagining the Argus story: 'PI girl seized in Vegas vice swoop'. He was tempted to ask what she was wearing.

To make matters worse, a man at a slot machine started talking to her. He didn't resemble her impression of what a hooker's john would look like, but she wondered for a moment if he might have a saviour complex. He said he was waiting for his wife and told Mack she looked upset, and she blurted it all out. He seemed to draw it out of her, listening attentively, giving words of comfort.

At this point, Mack began crying down the phone. Paz put the receiver down. He could not listen to it.

She apologised and described how the man revealed that 'Lily' (Liliane) had been his late first wife's name. At that point his current wife Candi - blonde, suntanned and athletic - arrived.

'What was the fellow's name?' asked Paz.

'Alitmeyer. Harry Alitmeyer. He asked me if I wanted to join them for breakfast, and to invite a friend. So Nikks joined us. Then he said, "It's a sad day for us. It's our daughter's twentieth birthday but she's no longer with us." I thought he meant she was dead, but he clarified that she was missing. He said they'd put out fliers and notified the police but there'd been no sightings. Molly's her name. Someone in Vegas claimed to have information about her disappearance, but they hadn't shown up. Nikks then told them I was a private investigator, which embarrassed me. Harry said, "We had a bad experience with a private investigator." Candi added they'd heard of a possible sighting of Molly in Houston and there was a story she was being held by a drugs gang. The PI they hired said he needed to recruit some muscle to raid the place where she was at—'

'Where she was at?' Paz queried. 'You're turning more American with every minute.'

'So anyway they paid the money up front for the muscle, but the operation was a complete failure. The gang had already hightailed it—'

Paz decided her odd turn of phrase was endearing.

'So they heard from someone in the know that this so-called PI was merely a conman. They never heard from him again. Harry said they had all sorts putting themselves forward. Some well-meaning, others just out for a quick buck at their expense. You get all the mediums and psychics out, and people claiming inside knowledge.'

Paz said. 'This is good education.' He could see the trip was proving useful in unexpected ways. 'What about the police?'

'They just said there was no evidence of foul play, she's an adult and has the right to disappear if she wants to.'

'That figures. That's another thing you've learned.'

Alitmeyer then gave her his business card so she could write her details on it, and another one for her to keep. Mack asked them to let her know about their daughter, and they confirmed they would.

Mack told Paz, 'I resolved privately to see what I could do to help.'

'But only if you really want to,' he said. 'You can't help everyone. We're not signed up by them and can't presume we will be. If you're interested, there's no harm on an unofficial basis. You know where to look. But remember: Giff's money is the number one priority.'

'I know. But since working with you, I've found missing person cases interest me most. Someone wanting to find someone else, a loved one.'

'But not every missing person wants to be found. Just be careful.'

'The person seeking them might be their abuser.'

'Right. Or just too controlling, or disapproving of their lifestyle or relationships.'

'OK,' said Mack who'd heard enough.

Paz then said, 'This game ain't all glamour, as if you didn't know that already. I just got offered a case over there involving an old factory: asbestos, oil drums, everything abandoned. No-one knows who it belongs to. Some kid fell through the floor of an outbuilding. Luckily, he wasn't killed. But who does his family sue? That would be for me to find out for them. Anyway, after Mr Alitmeyer's chat, dare I ask: did you get back with Lily?'

Mack said she returned to find Lily gone. She was watching TV when Lily returned. She'd bought an expensive-looking ring, got down on her knees and formally proposed there and then. Hearing this, Paz found himself melting. At last she'd got what she wanted. 'I'm so pleased for you,' he purred.

'Oh I couldn't possibly accept it,' she replied. 'Not yet. Oh no. Too soon. Too cynical. I said I'd think about it. Of course, I meant to accept in due course, when I was satisfied she was sincere, but—'

'But what?'

'She walked out in disgust. So how was that proposal sincere?'

He banged his forehead with his fist. This was not his worst nightmare but it was close: Mack, on whom he relied so much, was in emotional freefall at the firm's expense. 'So what's happening now?' he asked wearily.

'Lily's going to California to see her friend Gloria. I haven't talked to Nikks yet, but we'll probably go to California as well. She'll show me where she used to live. I guess she feels nostalgic.'

'What about poor old Giff and his money?'

'We'll hire someone to drive us. I'll pay you back the cost of my trip, Paz. I'm truly sorry.'

'By the way,' he began tentatively. 'I may be out in the States myself.' He was being coy; the truth was that he was thinking about closing the office for a while. The question was, for how long could he get away with it? 'I'll be there next week,' he said, 'on a couple of cases.'

Chapter 29

California Pure

The main case Paz was asked to investigate in the States began for him one afternoon in Brighton with the wind and rain beating on the windows. Paz was alone and, though he wouldn't admit it, missing Mack. A woman came in - late fifties if he was being unkind - slender, well-dressed, bobbed black hair, wealthy-looking. She had an American accent - Californian probably. Her name was Janet Levino.

After removing her designer raincoat and telling him how glad she was to be inside, she revealed that she'd travelled down specially from London. She said she and her husband Franco had come to Europe on one last big trip together as he was suffering from a rare blood condition that was terminal. This was sad enough, but then she disclosed that her husband's health had declined faster than the doctors had expected; he was now in hospital and they could not return to the US.

'I'm most terribly sorry to hear that,' Paz said, already intrigued as to how she thought he could assist them.

'You will be wondering why I've come here,' she said. 'Especially on a day like this. You see, my husband is in partnership with an old family friend. It's a small financial services firm with a good reputation — of course, I'm biased when I say that.' A sad little smile appeared on her small red mouth. 'The thing is, all communication from my husband's partner has ceased. Obviously, in view of my husband's poor health, his partner, whose name is Salvatore DeLuca, has been running the business himself, letting my husband know what's going on, checking with him on any major decisions, and Franco responds as and when he feels up to it. But now there's just silence. Nothing at all. It's as though Salvatore's vanished. It's been weeks now. If he'd died, I'm sure we'd have heard. He's not on any missing persons list. We're at a loss to understand what's happened to him. Obviously we've been in touch with friends and family, and employees, but no-one seems to know anything. The police did a welfare check. To them he's just stepped away for a while. So we decided to see if you can help. I realise it will mean going out there, but we're desperate.'

Paz felt proud. He said, 'Thank you for considering me for this task. You can rest assured, it will be my top priority. Can you tell me where this firm is based?'

'Los Angeles.'

After answering his remaining questions, she gave him the contact details for her son in Ventura, should he need anything. Thanking her, he said to the extent possible he would use his assistant for internet searches and the like. After a brief discussion about what it was like living in the UK, which he told her he preferred to the US despite the weather, there was another spate of rain on the windows. He offered to order her a cab for the journey to the station but she declined, saying she would rather 'experience the weather'.

That evening, Paz phoned a lawyer friend in L.A. The lawyer was unfamiliar with the names but agreed to assist. His firm would have one of the local investigators they used check it out. The following day, Paz received an email from the lawyer stating the office Levino and DeLuca operated out of was closed. The investigator had reported there appeared to be quite a lot of new mail on the floor just inside the door. Apart from that there was nothing odd.

Next day, Paz flew to L.A. After the English cool, he found the hit of the sun's heat almost overwhelming and he immediately wondered how Mack was coping with it. From the airport he took a cab out to the clients' office to see it for himself. It was in a small but quite luxurious block in a quiet street. He found the office exactly as the other investigator had told his lawyer friend. He rang the company's phone number. No answer. He looked around and got talking to someone who worked for one of the other tenants in the building, a bridal boutique. She confirmed the Levino office had been closed for several weeks.

From his hotel he phoned Mack who was overjoyed to learn he was in America. She found Salvatore DeLuca on social media. There had been no recent posts. She tracked down a personal address for him in Thousand Oaks.

Next day, Paz went out to the house, which resembled a small French chateau. He found it deserted. On returning to his car there was a blue Chevy Blazer waiting close by with the engine running. The car had two occupants. The passenger, a young woman in a blue headscarf, called out to him. She revealed they were looking for DeLuca. He asked why. She said it was a personal matter. He suspected it was a debt but wondered why a partner in a supposedly successful financial firm would have people calling to collect personal debts, unless for something cash-based like drugs. Paz told them his involvement was a missing person's case. They suggested exchanging information. He was initially reluctant, in case they had criminal motive, but he took their phone number and gave them his contact details. He wasn't expecting any exchange to happen anyway.

He liaised further with Mack who'd found DeLuca's wife's page on Twitter. She was originally from Peru, and from her Spanish language posts they gleaned that she was there now. Mack had also located the company's law firm, Chassingers.

That afternoon, Paz called in on Chassingers. The man he met was the big, bland, stonewall type he'd encountered amongst lawyers many times: Time wasters who gave you nothing but a fixed tight smile and forced charm. Paz explained he was acting for the company since the Levinos had requested his help in locating DeLuca. The lawyer said they'd need to confirm with the Levinos, which Paz had anticipated, although he'd expected at least a veneer of urgency and concern on the law firm's part.

Mack's research found DeLuca's secretary, by name of Erin Gonzalez. There was a phone number. Paz tried it but received no answer. Mack had also located Erin's address.

Paz paid a visit to a smart condo in Hermosa Beach and met Erin and her partner Zach. They invited him in for coffee. Shy and initially looking away from him as they spoke, the dark and beautiful Erin told him she knew Levino was in London from his wife's emails but appeared shocked when he told her that her boss's partner was too ill to return to the US. She confirmed she'd been laid off and the firm closed. She then said she'd heard DeLuca had 'got religion' and joined a church. Paz found this incongruous, but perhaps it was the fact she appeared to smirk as she said it.

On leaving them, he remarked on the beautiful car, a red Maserati, that he'd seen on the drive. The broad-shouldered, muscular Zach walked outside with him and they stood admiring it like a couple of teenagers. He said, 'Yeah, it does me proud.'

'What line of work are you in?'

'Finance.'

'Really? What's your surname?'

'Everstone.' He became embarrassed. 'I should stress, I'm just a day trader. I got lucky, I guess.'

Back at his hotel, Paz talked to Mack on the phone while she did a search on Zach. She identified him as a mechanic. Paz thought it possible he was both, using investments as a sideline, but perhaps Zach thought 'finance' sounded better in the circumstances.

Next day, he received a call from a woman who used to work for Chassingers. Mrs Levino had spoken to them on her husband's behalf, insisting they tell Paz everything they knew, including 'off the record' rumours, for the purpose of helping find DeLuca. The woman said she'd been asked on an unofficial basis to ring him 'presumably because they think I know all the gossip'. She revealed a rumour that DeLuca had been having an affair with his secretary Erin. His wife had left him and returned to Peru as a result.'

'My assistant picked up that last point from social media.'

'What she wouldn't have got from it is that DeLuca was rumoured to be so obsessed with Erin that he planned to rip off the company to set up a new life with her. That's the story, though I'm not sure about it. Anyway she left him for a new boyfriend. DeLuca persisted but the new boyfriend—'

'Zach?'

'Don't know — reportedly threatened him with violence.' She added that DeLuca had a breakdown and talked about moving out to a desert community. But before doing so, he would have tried again with Erin.

'OK. Incidentally, do you happen to know anything about the car he drives?'

She didn't.

After the call, Paz checked with Mack. She downloaded a picture of DeLuca from the company website and from a second, similar photo found him on the website of a small religious group announcing a new member. He had a new ID: Louis Spickert.

Paz drove out to the church. It was on a minor road leading to the Mojave desert and represented one of the more obscure corners of the Christian faith - not exactly a personality cult, more an earnest retreat from the world. On visiting the admin office at the dusty Colonial mansion once owned by a movie mogul and now serving as the church's headquarters, he encountered a couple of tall bearded men in long white robes - 'cartoon elders' was the phrase Paz later used when telling Mack - who made it clear they were not interested in cooperating with his enquiries. Without checking their records, they denied that anyone answering the names DeLuca or Spickert had ever participated in the church's activities, or even visited there. When he pointed out the website picture, they denied all knowledge. The surprisingly aggressive sallow-faced 'monk', who did most of the talking, threatened him with calling the police.

After this he waited in his car outside, thinking about what it all meant. A brief perusal of the parking lot showed that some of the participants - elders or otherwise - had money to spend on expensive cars. He surmised that DeLuca had brought embezzled funds in and the sect were trying to cover it up to avoid sequestration.

Paz thought about gaining entrance into the church grounds to talk to a few of the members. He could see a gate leading to the commune's gardens and so he walked towards it, ostensibly on an idle stroll which in the overpowering heat was all he could manage anyway. Acting as though he were meant to be there, the moment a pickup truck loaded with tree debris came out through the gate, he strode in. Once inside, he pretended to be a philanthropic businessman interested in making a donation to support the gardens and keen to observe their 'innovative' irrigation systems. He asked a middle-aged couple whether they knew Louis Spickert, claiming he'd been inspired by the man's example after seeing him on the church's website. They said they didn't know of him, but something in their manner suggested they were being deceitful. Within a few minutes he found himself being grabbed from behind and bundled out by security. He had not reached his car before he was picked up by local law enforcement who'd been called out.

Paz made it clear to the two police officers who he was and what he was doing there. He explained that he suspected the missing person DeLuca had ripped off his company and was living at the commune. They were unimpressed, but he was so insistent, quoting the names of senior LAPD officers he knew personally who'd vouch for him, that they went to the church's office and asked for permission to search without a warrant. The church consented and the police went through the house and grounds but found no evidence of DeLuca having been there. They told a subdued Paz that the church wanted no charges brought against him, saying he'd made the church aware of a problem with their online security and they intended him no ill will, misguided though he was. He felt like an idiot initially, but then mused it was obvious they would not want to press charges as that would create bad publicity.

That evening, he discussed the situation with Mack, in part for reassurance he wasn't going crazy. How soothing her voice could be at such times! Unconcerned at the police finding no evidence, she suggested someone could have hacked the church website and imported the photograph. This idea, although fanciful, served its purpose in making him feel better.

Paz decided another trip to Erin's place was called for. He wanted to check out what Chassingers' former employee had said about DeLuca visiting Erin after he'd disappeared. He found the couple less welcoming than the previous time, as though he were interrupting a row. Erin did, however, confirm DeLuca had called round before his own visit. Why had she not told him that last time? Because he hadn't asked. Zach then interjected, saying he'd been there at the time DeLuca called round, and it had been a tense situation culminating in him telling DeLuca to leave. That was after Zach had slipped out and put a GPS tracker under DeLuca's BMW. Why had he done that? Because he knew DeLuca's disappearance was going to be a big deal. He added that the car was later found abandoned in a downtown parking lot. Zach gave Paz the address of the place. As Paz left he asked Zach where his red Maserati was that he'd seen last time. He said the car wasn't his and belonged to a customer who'd allowed him to borrow it to take Erin out in. He apologised for 'misleading' him.

'What do you have then?' Paz said.

'Just an old Camaro.'

Paz said he'd like to see it. Zach asked him why. Paz told him he liked to see everything. When outside he asked, 'What does Erin drive?' Zach pointed out a white Honda Civic.

Back at the hotel, he looked up the location of the parking lot. He found some car dealers in its vicinity. He decided DeLuca had rid himself of his BMW to buy a new car, using a different ID.

Next day, Paz went to three dealers with DeLuca's picture, but none recognised him. He tried hire companies. No joy. He concluded DeLuca had stolen a car.

Acting on another tip from Erin, he decided DeLuca may have been to see his aged mother who lived in Palm Springs. With Mack's help he found her address. He visited her at her little house on a secluded tree-lined street. A retired Mexican actress with well-preserved looks and radiant eyes, she was hesitant at first, reluctantly half-opening the door, but when he mentioned Franco Levino she gently ushered him in, leading with slow careful steps to the lounge. Over sweet tea and homemade churros, she calmly told him her son could have gone out into the desert - particularly Death Valley. Or maybe Las Vegas, although he was not the gambling kind.

Paz didn't fancy looking round Las Vegas for DeLuca, especially if he was under an alias and a disguise. Nor did he believe DeLuca had left the state in his stolen car or 'turned nature boy' out in Death Valley. For all her courteous manners, he thought she'd misled him.

Paz believed Erin and Zach knew everything and started doing surveillance on them. He changed his hire car every day in the hope they wouldn't realise he was following them. He also changed his appearance, including wearing glasses he didn't need. Even a black wig. He soon noticed Erin was regularly driving back and forth between their house and an apartment block, where he observed from the parking lot she always went to apartment five. Once, after she'd left, he went upstairs and spoke to a neighbour. She told him apartment five was empty. She said there was a woman who visited at least every other day, clearly meaning Erin.

Paz phoned a contact at the LAPD and told him he suspected 'the missing Sal DeLuca' was or had been in apartment five. They said no-one from DeLuca's family had claimed he was 'missing' and they had not been asked to do a 'welfare check' at the Thousand Oaks house. Frustrated, Paz looked up the ownership of the flats. Apartments five and seven were owned by the same person, by name of Ralph Jennings, which he suspected was fake.

Next time he went to Erin's place, he noticed only Zach's car present. He waited for Erin to return.

When Erin's Honda arrived containing both, Paz confronted them, saying he suspected they were hiding DeLuca and that he was in either apartment five or seven. Zach stepped out, looking ready for a fight, but Erin told him to relax because Paz was acting for the company. She offered to take him to the apartments to prove DeLuca wasn't there. Paz agreed and Zach, still annoyed, went indoors.

On the short drive to the apartments Erin apologised about Zach, explaining he was stressed at work. On arrival she showed him apartment seven first, which was completely empty. In apartment five there was a makeshift bed in one room and in another was a young man seated on a leather sofa sipping coffee. In other rooms were painting and decorating materials, as well as various DIY tools. There were no obvious clues of DeLuca having been there. Erin explained the young man was her cousin and he was doing work for the landlord.

On the journey back, Erin said she believed he'd gone to Brazil where the firm had important clients. They would look after him there. This was also the conclusion of Janet Levino when Paz talked to her from his hotel room. She said she and her husband now believed DeLuca had removed millions of dollars out of the firm and effectively pushed it into bankruptcy.

It was then that Mack phoned him: 'Paz, I'm sorry, I've messed up.'

He sighed, wondering what trouble her Las Vegas caper had got her into now. He was thinking her bohemian nature must have put her on the wrong side of the law. What was she phoning for: bail money? 'What is it?' he said with a heavy sigh.

'Please don't fire me.'

'I promise.'

'Erin and Zach are actually brother and sister.'

'Ah, that's perfect.'

'Why?'

'It tells me Zach is not a rival to DeLuca but in cahoots. How—'

'I discovered Erin uses the surname of her ex-husband.'

Paz went to see the sceptical LAPD contact. 'This time, I'm right,' Paz insisted. 'Haul the couple in and you'll find out where DeLuca is, and you'll find the company's been cleaned out.'

He laughed. 'I thought you said before he'd put it all in that church!'

'That was a ruse. They hacked into the church's website. Erin told me he's in Brazil. That's probably another ruse. My hunch is Erin will lead us to DeLuca and they'll go on the run. I can tail her as long as you tell me not to.'

Paz continued following Erin until one day he found she was heading out to the international airport. He wondered if she was about to catch a flight to Brazil to be with DeLuca, but then she went north, pressing on until she turned off at Ventura. Mack had discovered DeLuca had an aunt there, one of several useful connections she'd found via his mother's social media accounts. But Erin didn't go to this address and she drove east away from the city. Paz felt sure she knew he was following her and was leading him away from DeLuca. But then he realised there was a car behind him and probably had been for some time. This car was tailing Erin too. Or was it tailing him? Paz became increasingly concerned, both for himself and Erin. She suddenly took a turnoff. Paz followed, as did the other car. Paz now realised this was the couple he'd seen at the start of his investigation - the couple who'd mentioned a 'personal matter' and suggested exchanging information. They'd had no contact since. He was tempted to slow down and then follow this second car. At that moment he wished he had a gun.

Erin then left the highway for a dirt road under an archway of trees. Paz drove on to see if the second car followed her. It did. Paz turned his car around and followed. To Paz's amazement he saw a wooden sign with a smiling dazed-looking face on it indicating he'd arrived at some weird retreat. Was this dilapidated old farmhouse where DeLuca was hiding out?

A few minutes later, Paz was sitting on an ancient bamboo chair looking across a desk at the berobed figure of Salvatore DeLuca. He looked like a stoned New Age priest, shaven-headed, gently nodding, exuding calm and fortune cookie wisdom. Standing to his left, holding his hand was a grinning Erin in a plain sack-like dress; on DeLuca's right were the gawky couple who'd been in the other car. After an initial greeting with at least the pretence of warmth, DeLuca asked the others to leave. When the door had closed behind them, the host demanded, 'Why are you here?'

Paz explained about Janet Levino's request. DeLuca laughed. 'She's very sweet, but naive. I doubt her husband's even ill. No, seriously. So he's in the UK? Or he was? He'll be in Zurich or somewhere else now, cozied up amongst his bank accounts.'

Paz asked, 'Why are the cops looking for you?'

'They're not. Only you are.' He laughed again. 'Look, I took money out of the firm, but to pay it back. I wanted to set up this place. I've now paid it back with a bank loan.'

'And what is this place?'

'It's what it looks like: a retreat. It's dedicated to the mystical union of meditation and marijuana. Weed quietens the mind for meditation which is what I'm really about. And here there's also massage and yoga for those that want them. Soon there'll be a health spa. I was going to buy into that place near the Mojave - by the way, that was clever about picking up Spickert; you did well there - so I gave them a donation and was going to join but changed my mind. I wanted my own gig.'

'Why did you close the firm?'

'I had no choice. Levino drained it of funds. Then he hired a dope like you to track me down and the next step would be a hit man. I'm the number one witness, don't forget. You've been duped, my friend. If you don't believe me, find him and tell him I'll see him in court. It will never happen. Not because he's ill but because he's a crook.' They were both silent. 'Life's not so bad,' said DeLuca at last. 'Stick around here. Have a smoke, or a massage from a real honey; whatever you want.'

'No thanks,' said Paz, though not without regret.

DeLuca then summoned the other three and told them, 'Mr Wheat is leaving. He has fulfilled his assignment. He knows that if he reveals my location to his client there will be consequences. Not that it will happen. The FBI are closing in on my former partner even as we speak.'

Next day, a depressed Paz met up with Mack for drinks and a light dinner at the beach in Paradise Cove, Malibu, a venue she chose. It felt strange meeting there. Mack looked happy but tired. She said she still hadn't gotten used to the time difference or the heat. Had she taken in any of the sights? No. She asked him about DeLuca. He described the meeting. 'By the way, DeLuca was impressed at you finding Spickert.'

'But all I did was—'

'No, be kind to yourself.'

'What was all that about the apartments, by the way?'

'Erin's cousin was just doing work there so DeLuca could sell them.'

'Huh! So who do you believe: Levino or DeLuca?'

'That's like: Who would you rather trust: a rattler or a cobra?'

'What will you do now?'

'What I wished I'd done in the first place: speak to the FBI. But the Levinos looked clean. It reminds me of old Jack — you remember? With Shakes Slocombe, and the wardrobe, and all? He told me it's our assumptions that kill us.'

Mack grinned. 'Oh yes, your homicide cop buddy who was slung out of the force and you didn't even know it.'

He grimaced. 'OK, point taken. But I still want to believe in Janet Levino. If her husband's a crook, she genuinely didn't know.' He ignored Mack's raised eyebrows and said, 'So tell me about your missing person's case.'

Chapter 30

The Missing

Mack had wanted to be the hero, finding daughter Molly for new friends, the Alitmeyers. But she knew quick success was not part of the game. Instead, it meant working with others; people who knew more than her; people who'd worked on the case for months with little progress and then, if they were lucky, suddenly got a break.

Molly's disappearance sounded like a typical situation in Paz's experience. A new boyfriend the parents didn't like, and with good reason, and her rebelling with drink and / or drugs. It had been a trial of strength with one almost inevitable outcome: her leaving home. Paz had said Mack could spend a couple of days on it but stressed the priority was finding Giff's money. It would probably take months for anyone new to make much progress on Molly's case, if they ever did.

Although Paz had told her of his contact in San Diego who'd provide office space if she needed it, she decided to do everything from her iPad in her hotel room. As with other cases she'd worked on, she learnt fast. After what Paz called the 'frivolity' of her Las Vegas trip, Molly's case would provide a serious education on human nature for the fledgling private investigator.

Paz merely listened as Mack recounted what happened.

The Molly Alitmeyer case had initially attracted significant media attention in New England. Publicity flyers, ads on TV, newspaper articles, a reward offered by the family, an emotional plea to everyone to look for Molly, and a direct appeal to her to make contact. But there'd been no success. The police eventually agreed to investigate but soon lost interest due to lack of leads and the pressure of new cases that had grabbed all the attention of media and public. For the press the story quickly lost its spark; there was nothing to report. Moreover, the general opinion was that, like many young people, she had left entirely of her own accord. The world turned away, and Molly's family grieved in private. They still clung to the belief she was alive, but did not like to speculate what her life might have become. Her father had told Mack they still put up missing person posters hoping she'd see one and say, 'Hey, that's me!' and appreciate how much she was loved.

Alitmeyer had said he did not want hers to become one of those cases the police filed away and only reopened twenty years later, and he admitted that when law enforcement stopped looking, saying there was nothing to investigate, the family began to lose heart. He'd tried to obtain the police file but was denied it, lest there be a subsequent finding of a crime and resulting court proceedings. He'd been distraught on being told that.

Mack studied the early press coverage. She learnt the boyfriend had been located living under an alias. He claimed Molly had left him for another man, a guy in his thirties. No social media commentator believed him. Molly had last been seen at a truck stop near Virginia Beach, seven hundred miles south of her village in Vermont. This was also the last time there was activity on her phone.

Mack noticed there was no Facebook page dedicated to the search for Molly, so she set one up, basing it on another she found online and using information from Molly's missing person posters. Afterwards, she wondered whether she should have asked the family first. It was too late, but at least it would give Paz something to lecture her about. Within an hour Candi Alitmeyer phoned. Mack felt sure she'd complain about the Facebook page, but she didn't. She merely said, 'Do you seriously think you can find Molly?' Mack said she didn't know but would try her best. Then Candi said, 'Keep me informed of your progress. Mr Alitmeyer gets muddled sometimes.'

Mack found Candi's intervention odd, especially the comment about her husband getting 'muddled'. Muddled about what? It made her suspicious, perhaps irrationally, as though Candi were out to spike Mack's efforts. But she had learnt from Paz to always keep the client at arm's length without making them aware of it, in order to remain 'dispassionate'. She quickly realised, however, there were other people not enthusiastic about her efforts.

In response to her Facebook and Twitter posts she began receiving warning messages telling her to keep out of it. These messages disconcerted her, stirring up wilder thoughts that Molly might be in the hands of criminals. And perhaps those criminals were answerable to Candi Alitmeyer who had orchestrated the whole thing as part of a classic stepdaughter / stepmother conflict. It was possible she alone was behind the various profiles sending out these warnings. It had happened in other cases. Reading the messages with a cooler eye, however, she found them not so much threatening as protective. Their authors appeared to wish her no harm. Of course that itself could be a deception, and she understood that anyone associated with Molly's disappearance would be desperate to keep it quiet. Yet whenever she wondered whether she should have become involved, she thought of poor Harry Alitmeyer who'd been so kind in listening to her, and she committed herself to do whatever she could to help find his daughter.

She deliberated for over an hour as she went for a stroll along the shoreline at Mission Beach and the busy boardwalk, looking at any girl of Molly's approximate age: Could that blonde be her with shortened hair? Could her distinctive sunflower tattoo be hidden by that sleeve?

Mack was not one for halfhearted gestures, and having spent hours on the case already, she came back from her walk determined to see through what she'd started. Accordingly, when she returned to her room, she immediately looked up one of her new connections on Facebook; marietlx737 had sent her a brief email and Mack rang the number she provided. The woman's response was blunt and unnerving: 'Who are you and what do you think you're doing? Why are you even involved?' Mack tried to explain, but the woman was not interested: 'You're from England. This has nothing to do with you. Don't you have missing people over there, instead of coming here poking your nose in things that don't concern you?'

Mack was shocked. She became suddenly anxious, tempted to ring Paz and pour her heart out. The woman would not stop berating her. She now wished she hadn't met Harry Alitmeyer. That was Lily's fault. If she hadn't been—

'Are you even listening?' the woman complained. 'Or are you rude as well as plain dumb?'

'I...' The woman let her flounder until finally Mack recovered herself: 'Harry Alitmeyer said I could.'

'Be very careful,' the woman said, her tone lowered. 'Look, you may be well-intentioned, but you don't understand the real situation, and I'm not the one to educate you. I'll leave you with this: You obviously don't know who Candi Alitmeyer is.' Before Mack could press her for clarification the woman ended the call.

Mack felt small and useless. She was again tempted to ring Paz to make herself feel better. She was also tempted to ring Lily. She resisted both urges. Instead, she stayed focused on the case, looking at websites of missing persons, Jane Does, and unidentified deceased females. She spent further hours on it but found nothing that materially increased her knowledge. She was tempted once more to ring the unpleasant marietlx737, but she did not feel confident. Then she told herself not to be pathetic. Until now she'd been shielded by Paz, but now she was on her own. So what? She was out of her depth, but she wasn't about to let herself drown.

She took a deep breath and rang marietlx737 prepared for an argument. However, when the woman answered, she asked almost pleasantly how her investigation was going. Mack said that in the short time since they last spoke she'd learnt little new. 'Well,' said the woman, think on this one: Candi was his first wife's best friend.'

'I see,' said Mack, unsure of the significance.

'Can I ask: Are you working on your own? I mean, do you have someone you report to?'

Mack recalled Paz's words of warning about not formally doing work on behalf of the firm. 'I met the Alitmeyers, Harry and Candi, and they told me they were looking for Molly. I do internet searches for my work and thought maybe I could help in a private capacity. That's all.'

'I'm going to say, you can report back to me - but only if it helps you.'

'But I don't know you. Not even your name, except for marietlx737.'

'Marie Joiner. I'm a friend of the family.'

'I see. Which family?'

'Oh, you're cute, aren't you? The Buckleys. Liliane's family. Look it up.'

'What exactly happened to Liliane?'

'Fatal house fire. Look *that* up. By the way, what is your accent?'

'Mainly Scottish, maybe a little South Yorkshire or South East England, I don't know.'

'Teach me to ask. OK, good luck with your investigation.'

After the call, a slightly heartened but confused Mack couldn't avoid the thought that Marie was playing with her, feeding her information bit by bit. Clearly neither felt they could trust the other at this point. She looked up Marie Joiner on the internet. She found little except that Marie was a Facebook friend of Candi Alitmeyer. As regards the house fire, it sounded like a terrible accident. Liliane was staying at the family's holiday cottage in Cape Cod alone one night, waiting for friends to arrive next morning. The fire started when she was asleep in bed, and she couldn't escape in time. The cause was officially undetermined due to the extensive damage. The press reports talked about a 'family tragedy', but Mack found little additional useful information in them.

She decided to look further at Candi Alitmeyer. She found an online chat forum with some particularly scathing comments about her and how she'd stepped into Liliane's shoes immediately, almost suggesting Candi was responsible for the latter's demise. By marrying Harry so quickly, she had benefited from the multiple insurances he'd been prudent enough to take out on Liliane's life. In further research, she found Candi had previously been married to a 'domestic assault specialist' whom she divorced. Looking at Facebook posts from the time, the fact Harry was a fellow Christian was clearly an attraction. Mack sent a message to Marie: 'Did Liliane's family shun Candi after her marriage to Harry?'

Marie answered immediately: 'I didn't, but others did. It was a shock, though. Molly disappeared soon after. She couldn't get on with Candi, though Candi certainly tried hard with her.'

Further research revealed Candi was a former striptease artiste. Some people wondered whether some of the less savoury characters Candi might have met through that could have kidnapped Molly to get her out of the way. Forum chatterers claimed Molly had been shooting her mouth off, saying Candi committed adultery with Harry before Liliane died. And if Candi committed the arson that killed Liliane and Molly knew it, Candi would have plenty of motive to get rid of her.

Everything was making sense. Except it wasn't. There was no evidence against Candi and it wasn't Mack's job to second guess the police. She received more warnings and decided to challenge one of them. In response to her straight question 'Why are you warning me?', the person suggested meeting. In her head she could hear Paz frantically cautioning her, so she said she would only be prepared to meet in the lobby of her hotel and in a public area. The man, who was called

Walperts, agreed. Mack felt their meeting would either be a huge revelation or huge disappointment.

The following day, in the lobby she was met by a slight, impatient-looking man in his forties, with a neat moustache, grey plaid suit, and polo-print tie. He said he'd flown in from Carson City specially, and after minimal preliminary chat, he told her he was the estranged half-brother of Candi. 'She's on a mission to find Molly,' he immediately said.

Mack paused and looked around. The leather chairs were too comfortable for a potentially difficult conversation, and noticing two wooden chairs with a small table in a secluded spot become free she led him there.

'Harry is, too,' she said as they sat down. 'On a mission, I mean.'

He laughed nervously. 'If you say so.'

'What do you mean?'

'It's Candi pushing it while pretending not to. Harry's the opposite: only pretending to push.' Mack gave him an enquiring look, but he did not elaborate.

'So why did I get the warnings?'

'Because you're wasting your goddamned time. And you're getting embroiled in something that has nothing to do with you and could put you in harm's way.'

She was irritated. 'How so? Are you threatening me or something? It certainly sounds like it.' She leaned forward defiantly.

'Do I look like a threat?' She allowed a smile. 'You're not the only one who can use the internet,' he said, his face turning serious. 'I know who you are, where you live — Brighton, UK; who you work for — Paz Wheat.'

This startled her. 'It's nothing to do with him. He didn't ask me to get involved. It's purely my project.'

'Project? By the way, how's Lily? That is her name, isn't it? Your lover, I mean?'

Mack was flustered. She withdrew into her chair. She'd never anticipated the conversation heading down this particular alley and did not like it. 'What's your bloody game!?' she demanded.

'I think I made myself clear: back off.'

'Fuck you,' she said, and made as if about to get up and leave in disgust.

'Sit down. I have to say, you act feisty but you're really rather sweet. Are you sure detective work is your thing? You seem too sincere.'

Mack wanted to jump on his head and slam it down through the tiled floor, but she also felt weakened by his cynicism and by what he knew of her already. For now she had to put her feelings aside for the greater good, so she affected calm. 'Why do you think Candi is pushing this so hard? Is it because she wants confirmation that Molly's never coming back?'

'No, because she wants to be sure Molly's alive.'

'And is she?'

'I like you. I like the way you get to the heart of things. And I'm sorry I've patronised you. You deserve better. Yes, I'm pleased to say Molly is alive and well.'

'Really!? Doing what?'

'Looking after a couple's children and living under an assumed name.'

'This is fantastic. So can I tell Harry?'

'Harry knows already.'

This hit Mack like a fist between the eyes. 'Seriously!? No fucking way!'

Walperts told her Harry had a criminal record. When she shook her head in disbelief, he said, 'How do you think I know? Check the records yourself.'

'I will,' she said defiantly.

'Mr Alitmeyer is not what he appears. He's not even Alitmeyer. He's a conman. It's not his real name.'

Mack was angry at having her view of dear Harry so disrupted. 'Absolutely no way! So what is his real name, then?'

'I forget.'

'Well, that's convenient, isn't it? No, I don't believe you. He was so nice. So considerate.'

'Conmen always are. OK...' He sighed, looking like a card player reluctantly forced into playing his best card. 'Molly has evidence.'

'Go on.'

'She has a letter from her mother saying, "If anything happens to me, your father's responsible." Same kind of thing Candi received. Candi wants the letter Molly has. It represents a kind of power.'

'I can't believe it. But if it's true, it sounds like I shouldn't tell Candi that Molly's safe and well. The trouble is, she's going to be phoning up, asking about my research.'

'She will keep pushing to find her. The irony is, so far as I know, Candi is happily married. She believes in her heart that Harry had Liliane bumped off, but he's told her she was the one he truly loved in the first place, and she believes that too.'

She was completely flummoxed. 'What do you say I should do then?'

'Just forget about it. Say you failed to find anything.'

'But I didn't fail. I can't say that.'

'It would be irresponsible to tell anyone what I've told you. But I don't know where Molly is anyway. I make it a point not to know. I have a friend who works in witness protection and he has passed her case to a friend of his. She might not be in California. Or even the US. And she has another name now. I don't even know it. If Candi goes looking for her, Molly will merely disappear again and become someone else. And so it goes on. Happy now? You should be. It's not every day a missing person story has such a happy outcome.'

'But isn't she in danger?'

'Not if she keeps her mouth shut.'

Mack's head was spinning. 'But doesn't Molly want the truth to come out about her mother?'

'No doubt. But not at the expense of her own life. And she doesn't know what the truth is anyway. Candi might have done it. She might have faked the letters. The one Molly got didn't show up until after her mother's death. The online ranters may be right with their speculations about Candi. Besides, the letters don't mean anything without hard evidence. If Liliane hadn't perished in a fire, she could have died in a thousand other ways not connected with Harry or Candi. CCTV coverage didn't reveal anything sinister. The fire investigators found nothing.'

Walperts went on to explain that Molly would never go back to her father anyway. He was strict and religious: 'He used to chastise her as part of his faith. But it doesn't make him a killer. His criminal record was for fraud, not murder.'

He began to get up to leave, but Mack wasn't done. 'Proof,' she said. 'How do I know you didn't make all this up? Or even who you are?'

He nodded and sat down. 'I was beginning to think you wouldn't ask.' He produced his driving licence and passport. He then showed her the text of an email with the sender's address redacted, which made reference to Molly moving to a new county but with no details given. He also produced a photograph of her date-stamped two weeks earlier and showing her sunflower tattoo. Mack accepted that it looked like Molly. 'I was sent it,' Walperts said. 'The thing is this: If I knew where Molly is I could take you there; you'd meet her, but you wouldn't really know if it was her or not. It might be an impostor for all you know. That tattoo she has could be replicated.'

After he'd left, a stunned Mack went over what he'd said. She concluded that if Harry did kill Liliane there was a strange alliance of aims, with neither Molly nor her father wanting her to be found.

After telling Paz this story, Mack said her confidence had evaporated over it. 'I feel such an idiot. It's like trying to be the first person to solve a puzzle, finding out someone else has already done it, and the person who asked you to do it didn't really want you to do it in the first place. But at least now I feel satisfied she's OK. How was I so easily conned by Harry? In my defence, I only met him briefly.'

'All the more reason not to be swayed by him. So you think he pretended to be looking for her when he wasn't at all, just to please his wife? Huh! You fell for the oldest trick in the book, Mack.'

'What's that?'

'The silky words of a charming stranger.'

'So I've gone from genius to dummy? Thanks. Don't forget, he'd conned women who'd lived with him for years.'

'Don't worry,' he said. 'He fell for the second oldest trick in the book. And he fell harder. He underestimated a young woman. He thought you naive so was happy for you to investigate. The irony is that he can go on thinking you naive because you can't tell him anything. But I think you should put it aside now. You were looking to find a missing person and you've established as best you reasonably can that she's alive. The fact she never wants to be found is not your issue. Nor is what happened to her mother, which will always officially be an accident unless someone one day comes forward. So if anyone calls you about all this — Candi or Marie Whatsherface — you tell them you had to switch to other stuff: Giff's money.'

'Candi will definitely want to know what I found. Weirdly, all I really discovered was from someone in her own family.'

'Right. But it's not our business. We need to keep out of all that. As far as you know, Molly is happy in her new life. Let's drink to that. Who are we to put her in jeopardy by anything we might say or do?'

Chapter 31

Mack In L.A.

Nikks had wanted to spend more time in San Diego, even though the nexus of Giff's investment scam appeared to be further up the coast. 'She just wanted a good time,' said Mack. 'I think being back in California made her want to be living there again. And being disillusioned with policeman Robert made her want to find someone new quickly. She was keen to party. I wasn't. I wanted to work. Fortunately, in the hotel lobby of all places, Nikks met someone she liked and thought she could maybe trust, so after a couple of drinks with them in the bar, I decided I could retire to bed.'

'What happened about Lily?' said Paz.

'I know you said I should make up to her, but I was still upset. I missed her terribly, though. Alone in my room under the covers and far from home I never felt so lonely. Nikks was in the arms of her new beau Vez, while Lily was under the roof of the woman I think she really loves — platonically, I mean — Gloria. But doesn't "under the roof" sound vaguely rude?' She chuckled, but it was a lonely chuckle. Lily had worn her down. 'She's such a stuck-up little harlot these days, but it doesn't stop me aching for her. I could not sleep. I wished I'd gone out with the others for long enough to get drunk. Next morning, I had breakfast early and alone. I watched TV in my room while I was researching Molly's case. I struggled to concentrate. Later that morning, Nikks joined me. She doesn't care about a thing. She just lies there, casually watching the world's latest tragedies on TV while tanning her legs in the sun pouring through the balcony door.

'But I noticed a particular commercial kept coming up. It was like a short interview. "So you've an exciting new investment opportunity to talk to us about?" this guy, all saccharine, was saying to a suited gentleman with fake tan who was in his, say, late forties. "That's right," said the suit. Could this be the guy with Giff's money, I wondered? He looked the sort could steal your soul and sell it back to you in pennies. So smooth. Well, if all their people are like him it's no surprise Nikks' dad was caught out. The suit explained the scheme offered twenty-five percent a year interest in real estate ventures. But it was exclusive — that was the key — only a limited number could join. People of a certain net worth. Which made me wonder how a pensioner like Giff got caught up in it. It was called Jorland. At the end of the ad there was a notice saying Jorland was hosting seminars in and around L.A.

'Was Jorland the man's name?' asked Paz.

'No, Jessop. I wanted to discuss it with Nikks, but she was only interested in talking about her new boyfriend, her "hunk". She was purring, "Ex-marine, ex-FBI." I told her, "Sure."'

'Cynical,' said Paz, half-laughing.

'Xavier Vespuccio the Third. Friends call him Vez. Chilean-Italian heritage. His father owns a copper mine, and Vez drives a Lexus and plays polo. "Too good to be true," I told her. But she babbled on: Dad owns a racing car, and a racing yacht, and a stable of racehorses.'

'Yawn!'

'Right. He calls himself the Third, but I bet there's no First or Second. Every inch the dodgy entrepreneur — pricey suit, power watch, handkerchief, gold chain. A big player.'

'What does he actually do?'

'Money broking. Nikks didn't elaborate. And, I suspect, nor did he. I told her I wanted Lily to work with me on the case. She was annoyed, worried Lily would steal her new boyfriend, but she didn't argue because having her on board made sense. When I talked to Lily over the phone, she sounded pleased to hear from me, but said she wouldn't go to San Diego for any reason. Robert had texted her saying he'd be "waiting for" her there. I wasn't relaxed at that news either.'

Mack had then flown up to Anaheim to meet Lily. They were both keen to reconcile and cried in each others' arms. After lunch Lily drove her to a beach that Gloria had recommended and they had fun running around on the sand, eating ice creams and doughnuts, laughing about everything. Next day, they found a Jorland seminar in a Malibu hotel. There were about forty people there, mainly middle-aged or retired, well-dressed, all seated on red conference chairs in neat rows. Mack was expecting to see the man in the ad, but when they arrived they found someone else at the front waiting to present, also called Jessop, a decidedly not-for-TV wizened man older than most of the audience. Was he the brother or even father of the man in the commercial? Feeling out of place amongst all the glittering jewellery and beaming Botoxed faces, Mack found the talk boring and the charts stultifying. Now and then she would glance over at Lily who seemed to be taking it all in. During the break over coffee, Mack asked the presenter straight out, 'How does my friend's old man get his money out?' and told him about Giff. He told her they would need to sort it out in the UK. 'But they said to come out here,' she insisted. She was irritated and tempted to make a scene but thought better of it so as not to embarrass Lily.

In the second part of the event, 'personal testimonies' were presented, with various dreary characters telling their 'dear friends' how their investments had been in the doldrums, but 'the fund' had bucked the market trend and turned their fortunes around. One exception to the blandness was a man passing himself off as an English lord. Mack recognised him from press reports on a wine investment scam. He had bought a peerage that was fake and claimed to be a relative of the Royal Family, and even an investment manager for the Royal Estate. Lily found him hilarious and started giggling. Mack gave her a quizzical look and Lily wrote *Accent!* in large letters on her pad. Mack smiled. The impostor's English aristocratic tones were increasingly breaking into Californian, and every time he dangled yet another obscure European monarchy he was supposedly acting for, Lily began tittering. Afterwards, as they were leaving Lily said to no-one in particular, 'Tell you what: Why don't you just give your money to me? I know where there's a pot of gold. All we need's a fricking rainbow!'

Mack told Paz that later in the fancy beach-side hotel Lily had chosen, she looked up where Jessop lived online and that night the pair of them drove out to it in the San Fernando Valley.

Paz was immediately concerned: 'Woo, take it easy! Going to someone's house?'

She said they merely stood under the trees and stared at the mansion from outside the gates. They saw several classic cars on the drive. Then they left without a word, feeling foolish.

At this moment, Paz realised the whole trip was a mistake. Mack would put herself in serious danger. It reminded him of the time the awful client Alf gave him a warning, specifically mentioning her.

Mack said that back at the hotel she read up about the fund. It was clearly under pressure. The L.A. Times had an article calling into question the Jessops' reliability. In response, a spokesman for the fund insisted, 'No investor has ever lost a single cent. It's 100% guaranteed.' But it sounded false.

Lily wanted to go to another seminar which she'd learned about from a leaflet she found at the first one. It was to take place at a smart hotel in West Hollywood. Mack, who'd become disillusioned at Nikks' lack of interest in finding her father's money, did not wish to attend. Her time would be better spent online, she said. Lily therefore went alone, raising Mack's fears for her lover's safety, but she understood: Lily wanted to fully play her part and wasn't one for the online stuff.

Mack was relieved at Lily's return from the seminar and soon wished she'd accompanied her. Lily told her that the person presenting was different again. She showed Mack the picture she'd taken: Once more the man was closer to seventy than forty. Lily wondered if there'd been a boardroom coup, 'Or was it the fake death of the big boss to send the company's stocks down? And then it turns out he was alive after all, so the shares miraculously bounce back up again, yielding a nice profit.'

Mack told her, 'Lily, you're so cynical.'

Lily also reported there'd been a protester outside trying to discourage potential investors from attending. She'd spoken with him and obtained his contact details.

Mack's delight at what Lily gave her had been diluted by the news that Nikks and Vez had arrived at the hotel.

When Mack told Paz this, he put his head in his hands and said, 'The circus just hit town.'

'That's right. With Robert trailing behind them.'

'God!'

Mack then described a bizarre meeting she had with the three newcomers. Lily had refused to attend. 'Just tell me where you want me to drive,' she told Mack. It was tense because Robert had now turned his attentions back to Nikks, and he had the confidence of secret knowledge - secret knowledge about his love rival Vez.

Mack was great at research on Jorland, but she had no idea how to achieve the end result: getting Giff's money back. Vez's suggestion was to use his 'connections' amongst the underworld to stage a robbery at Jessop's place and sell off the proceeds. He envisaged a hit squad of 'PR consultants' to take direct action. It was a disturbing idea. Their imaginations ran wild about Jessop's fate. It was suggested, for example, he had become involved with a drug cartel and owed them money. Mack watched Robert, concluding that only a desire not to offend Nikks prevented him from roaring out loud with laughter at Vez's ideas. Nor was Robert persuaded by Mack's notion of 'working with' protesters. 'To what end?' he sniffed. 'Protests are intended to put people off. On the contrary, we want to encourage people to join to keep the fund going.'

Robert was playing the role of cunning strategist and suggested deceiving Jessop by promising him extra funds 'from an unnamed source' in return for a hefty introduction fee. 'He'll be desperate for cash,' he insisted.

Vez dismissed this, saying Robert's idea was too fanciful, especially as no-one knew where Jessop was; better to raid the house instead. The direct approach was always best, he insisted. At this point, as if on cue, the door burst open and in rushed three men. Mack dived to the floor.

Hearing her describe this, Paz gripped his chair in anguish but said nothing.

The men immediately handcuffed Vez. They were FBI special agents arresting him for multiple identity theft scams and possible murder. 'It's all a lie!' Vez protested. 'I'm not who you think I am!' The agents bundled him out. 'I told you so,' said Robert calmly. Nikks was in a state of shock and asked what would happen to him. Robert said they'd get him to confess, rough him up, and dump him on the beach somewhere.

Mack then explained to Paz that the agents were in reality actors Robert had hired. 'He had wanted to show Nikks what a fraud Vez was. A complete fake.'

'And is he a fraud, based on your research?' said Paz.

'You bet. And neither Chilean nor Italian. Anyway, he's gone now.'

Mack described how, after the sudden end to the meeting, she immediately returned to her room to be with Lily. She wanted to lie down on the bed in her lover's arms, but Lily had spent the last hour watching trashy TV and was desperate to go out. Irked at any possible suggestion of indifference to the cause, she wanted to return to Jessop's place. Mack was reluctant but keen to appease her. When they returned to the mansion they found the classic cars gone. The place looked abandoned. Embarrassed at their sheepishness last time, they decided to make enquiries. When they pressed the intercom button by the electric gate they were surprised by the response. It was an old man's voice. He said 'the family' had gone. Where to? 'They bugged out,' he said.

'Bugged out?' said Paz. 'I haven't heard that expression in a while.'

'Lily asked him who he thought they were bugging out from. He said, "The owners of the house, of course." He said Jessop didn't own it. Didn't own any of it: the expensive furnishings, the art on the walls, the cars.'

'Did he say why they quit?' said Paz.

'Someone threatened them. Investors, so he said. He thought we must be relatives of investors as we sounded young. Then we left.'

She revealed that as they turned from the gate a car pulled up, and the middle-aged male driver had the window down and in a gruff and threatening tone asked what they were doing there. Were they looking for Arthur Jessop, by any chance? The driver revealed he was an associate of Jessop's. Lily confirmed they were looking for him. The voice said, 'Be careful. They don't like people who hang around out here.' Lily told him they hadn't seen anything strange. He said, 'Don't misunderstand me: They don't like *anyone* hanging around out here.' The car then approached the gate to go through. The pair noted he was not someone they'd seen at either seminar. Lily said that maybe he'd come to clean up the place of any signs of the crime that might have happened there. They quickly left.

Paz had listened to all this carefully and told her he did not like the sound of it. He sensed danger. He felt protective towards them and said, 'Mack, I think you and Lily should go back to England.'

'That's what Lily wants. She said it's gone far beyond what she signed up to. I told her, "Where's your sense of adventure? This is real."' Mack said Lily acquiesced but with a caveat that if it got too dangerous for them she would insist both of them left.

'I'm all for you and Lily being brave but not at the risk of you getting killed,' said Paz. 'Especially now that harebrained Robert is back on the scene. I have to think of your wellbeing — and that of the firm.'

'But it's fun,' she said.

'This is not meant to be fun! Look, dodgy money is never far from violence. They're not going to roll over to have their tummies tickled.' To avoid further discussion on this, he changed the subject. 'So is the original group reconciled now?' It was a mischievous question because discord was never far away.

Mack revealed that, with Vez warned off, Robert assumed Vez's ideas as his own. He had the notion of tracking down the classic cars, stealing a couple of them, and using the proceeds from selling them to pay Giff.

'What!?'

'He's even thought about threatening to blow up Jessop's yacht.'

Paz could not believe this. After he had recovered himself he told her 'If you persist with this crazy venture I will have to become personally involved to stop it. It's a fiasco. And a dangerous one at that. Have you checked out this Robert? Is he even a real English bobby? Does he think these people — the Jessops — are going to say, "Hands up. You got us, gov?" Of course not. They're going to fight. They're going to fix their enemies. Are you sure you're not being followed?'

'No. How could I be sure anyway?' She looked like she'd just been punished for something she now realised was wrong but which hadn't occurred to her before. 'Do you want me to give up? I will if you want me to.'

'I'm not saying that.'

'Are you upset with me?' she said sadly, not looking at him.

'I can't be upset with you. It's my fault. I agreed to this trip. Admittedly, in a moment of weakness, but even so...'

Afterwards, he took her for a drive along the Pacific Coast Highway. 'I feel incredibly happy,' she said. 'Even though in your way you've told me off, I feel loved.'

'By Lily?'

'I don't mean Lily. Cared for, then. I feel cared for. By you, you booby. You care for my wellbeing almost above everything. Don't try and deny it.'

He didn't deny it.

Paz decided he would get a room at the team's hotel. It wasn't a cheap place. Paz was already resigned to the fact the trip would be a financial loss, and strangely, he realised he didn't care. 'I'm looking forward to meeting Lily at last,' he said as they arrived at the parking lot. The hotel was beside the sea. They could hear the waves breaking and the breeze in the palm trees as the two of them dawdled in the warm air. In the dim artificial light, Paz heard a gull cry overhead and Mack was pointing out a lizard scampering away when Paz felt something hard hit his neck. It felt like a heavy branch but then there was a blow to his leg and he collapsed. All he saw was a large shadow on the ground before him. Mack was screaming. Paz shouted 'Run!' as more hits came in. He couldn't see his assailant. And then another blow to the back of the head knocked him out.

He woke up in hospital. As he gradually pieced together his vague thoughts, he wondered where Mack was. Had she escaped the assailant? He lay drifting in and out of consciousness. He was aware his head was bandaged and his leg was elevated.

A young male doctor came to see him and advised he had several injuries including a broken leg. Later, the arrival of Mack awakened him. He was overjoyed just to know she was alive. She also seemed relieved more than anything - relieved he hadn't been killed. She was confident no-one had pursued her there, but told him she believed it was a warning to back off from the investigation. She revealed the incident had provoked more trouble in the group. Lily had announced she wanted to leave, Nikks had called her a 'coward', and Mack had then weighed in on Lily's behalf.

'You should both go home,' said Paz. 'Let Nikks and Whatshisname do what they like. From what I know, you two have done all the real work anyway.'

'I can't leave you,' she said.

'You have to. I want you to be safe. Besides, we can't run the office from here. And Lily wants out, you say?'

'She does but, bless her, she said she won't leave without me. I do think I've broken her at last, Paz. Broken her heart, but what should I do about her now?'

'Tell me, how confident is Lily driving around here?'

'Out of the city, she loves it. Big wide roads. Open skies. Scenic views.'

'OK. If you're confident you're not being followed — and only if — see if she'll drive you up the coast. Take a stop in Santa Barbara, and go on to Big Sur — you'll love it — fly home from San Francisco. I'll sponsor the extra cost. It will be good for the two of you; take a romantic break.'

'I would really like to nail this case and get Giff's money back for him, but I guess you're right.' She gently caressed his face, kissed his forehead, then held his hand in hers for a moment. She quietly wept for him as he drifted off to sleep.

Lily, perhaps still stung at the accusation of cowardice, reiterated she was prepared to stay and complete the trip as originally planned, but Mack assured her it was unnecessary. In fact, it was Nikks who left first after claiming she received a strange and threatening phone call in the room she shared with Robert. He himself was determined to stay on in the effort to reclaim the money. Thus, the 'love rat' / creep became the only one left on the frontline.

For once, something Paz had privately predicted came right. The trip north on the Pacific Coast Highway proved to be every bit as romantic as he'd hoped for Mack. It was when driving through Big Sur, just after stopping to see McWay Falls, that Lily, again spurred on to resist any thought of timidity, proposed to her. And this time Mack accepted, although she pretended not to hear so Lily had to say the words twice. On receiving Mack's text advising this, Paz was so delighted he spontaneously made as if to leap out of bed, almost causing himself further injury.

When back in England, Mack formed an unlikely alliance with 'dirty cop' Robert who remained in the US. The scam proved more intricate than either of them had thought. Mack established that the person in the original commercial she'd seen was not Jessop. The real Jessop had already made a run for it, having used the company as his piggy bank. The attendees at the seminar knew nothing about this and were content to listen to the senior gentleman doing the presentation; after all, he looked the same age or older than them, and they were keen to believe the message. Only later would they learn that the real Jessop had embezzled almost all the money.

With Mack's online assistance Robert tracked down Jessop in Miami Beach in a small hotel. Accompanied by a couple of local hoodlums he'd hired, Robert informed him he was going straight to the FBI if he didn't pay up. Jessop shook his head, saying that as soon as the FBI intervened, he'd hold them responsible because the fund was continuing to rise and they'd be preventing it. By now, working with the protester Lily had met, Mack had established there was no real investment going on. All the funds had gone direct to Jessop apart from a small amount to his assistants. Beleaguered in his hotel room surrounded by muscle hostile to him, a desperate Jessop assigned ownership of one of his luxury cars to Robert which the latter could then sell. But Robert was suddenly loathe to part with it. Mack argued with him and eventually prevailed. She pressed him, 'Do you want the girl or the car?' Frustrated, Robert sold the car and sent the proceeds to Giff's bank account. All they had to do now was hope the authorities would not shut down Jessop's operation. Otherwise, the proceeds of the car might be clawed back as the feds created a fund to pay back everyone.

Mack reminded Nikks that some of the money belonged to Paz. Nikks acknowledged this but then learned Giff had already reinvested it all. One of his barber's other customers had set up their own cryptocurrency and Giff was excited to become a supporter. Mack did not need to ask Nikks what she thought about it. To pacify Paz she told him she'd pay the entire cost of her trip herself. Paz, however, would not countenance it. The trip had been a disaster, with the only important exception being the ring on Mack's finger, but he had survived the assault and money felt less important now.

Chapter 32

Everything Turns

Paz's injuries from the incident persisted long after he was able to return to England. As well as his injured leg, he had lost mobility in his right arm and was plagued by back pain. Mack felt guilty for having involved him in the Giff investment saga, but it made him tetchy when she expressed this to him. As a result of his injuries, he was prescribed heavy doses of painkillers which made him drowsy. He was forced to give up investigation work. All he could do was write reports and conduct straightforward internet searches.

Mack visited him often at his flat. She did the majority of the work in the office with Paz giving her an experienced steer where required, to keep her and the firm out of trouble. But closure became an increasingly realistic threat, and eventually Paz felt compelled to shut down operations. Mack, devastated, accepted an invitation from Fran Owens to work for him. Paz saw this as a betrayal.

Lily and Mack were married in a small private ceremony in London. Paz was thrilled to be invited. Mack's parents managed to maintain a truce between themselves, and her father, with whom Mack's relationship had previously been strained, formally gave her away. She looked beautiful while, like almost all other men who met her, Paz fell instantly in love with Lily. This woman had not only beauty but style, he observed. In his imaginings, her deep blue eyes bore the irresistible power of a Siren who could destroy marriages and ruin lives without trying or even wanting to. He found her both imperious and vulnerable. Paz prayed that the couple would be happy, but privately feared that Lily's long-held reluctance to commit would persist in some fashion after the wedding.

Suzi resumed dropping hints to Paz about marriage, but he thought: why marry when he could have sex with her when he wanted? Not that he could enjoy it, because of the pain from his injuries. No, it would be altogether too corny for him to marry her. Besides, her bigamous 'husband' Terry would probably return at some point making trouble. Or some other creature from Suzi's past would emerge from the shadows - anyone who was the controlling type that restraining orders were meant for.

But Paz decided he would propose to Suzi after all. This became more crucial when she was diagnosed with a life-threatening heart condition. A case he reluctantly agreed to take as a favour to an underwriter friend took him to the States, and he was resolved to propose to her on his return. However, the case took longer than he expected, partly because of his own fuzzy-headedness, and on his return he was shocked to discover she'd died. Her funeral had not yet taken place, but on enquiring he learned it was to be a private affair, invitations only. Suzi had no children but was close to her nieces. Her feisty sister was the dominant force in the family, and it was she who decided who attended the funeral. Paz was not included. Despite all he'd meant to her in life, he meant nothing in death - worse than nothing, he was a reminder of her 'disreputable' occupation.

Mack called Paz to tell him that her marriage was already in trouble. Within three months Lily confessed that she had been unfaithful. She could have gotten away with it because Mack was unaware, but it had played on Lily's conscience. She had been regularly going to a hotel after work for sex with her lover before coming home to Mack. In confessing she had assumed it would follow their traditional ritual. She would put her hands out in surrender, allow Mack to slap her hard around the face, accept a harsh telling off and then be made love to until she was sore. But it was different now they were married. They had made sacred vows and she had broken hers. Mack told Lily that she always knew she was marrying a slut and if Lily had confessed to one infidelity there must have been more. Lily's facial expression indicated this was true. 'I know that guilty look,' Mack said, before announcing she was moving out to be independent of her. Mack told Paz, 'Lily kept saying the affair was over and it would never happen again. She meant it, but then she always means it.' Mack said she thought about doing surveillance on her to see if she was being faithful, but if it were a man watching her could she even trust him not to become infatuated with Lily?

Fran asked Mack what Paz was up to. She explained that since the business closed he only did the odd case now and then, and she thought he needed a new impetus. Fran said he might be interested in working with Paz. He envisaged some kind of partnership, and he made the approach through Jane. When she phoned him, Paz made it clear he was not interested. On hearing this, Mack, from her new-found position of strength, was able to force Lily to consider buying out Paz, even though it was a rickety investment that met none of her usual criteria. Lily was not happy about such a deal, and nor was Paz, but she saw it as an unavoidable act of appeasement towards Mack. Even in her weak moral position, however, Lily made it clear she would sell the business on if it could not be made viable. Paz thought Lily's tentative initial offer too cheap, but the accounts turned out to be far worse than he realised. He hadn't paid attention to them; he'd only really been interested in the cases. Often he'd forgotten to charge, and he hated chasing up unpaid bills. Jane told Mack it was one of the reasons she left; it upset her to see their work go unrewarded. The prospect of being forced to sell the business depressed Paz so much he backed out of the deal, much to Lily's relief. Combined with the painkillers' effects, his disillusionment led him to pay even less attention to the occasional freelance work he was receiving.

Mack was able to extract other concessions from her promiscuous wife, but when she tried to insist Lily have a tattoo reading 'Owned by Mack', Lily snapped, saying she wasn't owned by anyone, nor ever would be. They argued and then they wrestled, an established ritual played out on the floor, with rules Lily invariably broke. But this time she did not need to cheat; easily the stronger, and with her lover lying flat on her back, she trounced her again, with a long intense kiss that broke any last remnants of Mack's resistance. Lily then immediately left to go to the north of England to see her sick grandmother. She was to stay there for many weeks.

Paz's depression worsened and, for the first time since his teenage years, he turned to the bottle and in a big way. He felt sorry for himself. He felt Mack and Lily had tried to con him out of his business that was so much part of his identity; he was also upset at being prevented from grieving in public for Suzi, and he convinced himself that if he'd married her she would not have died. Above all, he regretted becoming increasingly distant from Mack whom he'd loved working with.

He knew what he was doing to himself was absurd. It was like a play he was both director and solo actor in. He could halt the production at any time but could not be bothered to do so. Offers of work trickled in, but he either said he was too busy or did not reply at all. Paz's self pity began to grate on Mack in their now rare interactions, as well as his drinking and the whoring she imagined he was doing - 'buying affection' as she called it. She convinced him to take a couple of surveillance cases, but they were handled sloppily. He knew Fran would see it as a victory, but Paz no longer cared.

Paz brightened, however, after a chance meeting with a woman called Flick. He'd stumbled in a car park outside a local church hall where there was a regular salsa dance class; she was the teacher there and it was she who found him. Although drunk he was able to convince her it was the effect of the painkillers. She took pity on him and he was able to turn on the charm enough for her to offer her phone number 'to let me know you got home alright'. They soon began spending time together. She invited him to hers but, embarrassed about his flat, he took her to cheap hotels. He began to feel better, but then started to realise that he kept seeing the same car about, and recognised the driver as Joe Clayton who often worked for Fran. It was clear to him Fran was using Clayton to intimidate him after his rejection of the ludicrous 'partnership' idea which he did not believe had been sincere anyway. He complained to Mack about Fran using Clayton to follow him: 'You see what your "all-caring" employer is really like?' He then took great satisfaction from the fact he stopped seeing Clayton - clearly he'd been removed after being found out - and Paz saw no-one else that might have been a substitute. But one day Flick, clearly spooked herself, dumped Paz for another man. The suddenness of it hit him hard, and he abandoned all pretence at looking after himself.

He heard nothing further from Mack and made no attempt to contact her. He distracted himself with TV all day, engrossing himself in all manner of things he didn't care about. His only daily excursion was to Suzi's favourite bar at a time when it would most likely be empty, to give homage to her in his own way - he would drink himself almost insensible, unable to think beyond the immediate future: How to get home.

Mack was upset about the use of surveillance on Paz and demanded Jane tell her the reason. She merely replied, 'For a client, of course.' With Lily away and not communicating, Mack started going out to bars to look for girls she could seduce. It was then she encountered Aja who was a student at Brighton University. Mack was smitten by the nineteen-year-old Indian beauty. They went on a few dates until Mack finally coerced her into bed. She was to be disappointed, however, because Aja told her she was not interested in sex. Frustrated at her lack of success, Mack started drinking heavily and reacquainting herself with recreational drugs.

Jane noticed a falling off in Mack's commitment to work and chided her about it. Mack in response again demanded to know why Paz had been followed. Jane refused to talk about it and Mack became unhinged. They had a fierce row, bringing back all the resentments and mutual antipathy of their early days of working together. Jane said if it hadn't been for Mack, Paz wouldn't be in his current predicament, and that enraged Mack more than anything. Their row was so loud that Fran Owens, who happened to be in the office at the time, came into Jane's room and demanded to know what was going on. Mack was immediately sent home and later that day informed she'd been suspended for a week. The situation caused uproar amongst Mack's co-workers. Mack was highly popular, while Jane was considered a bully. One of the gay co-workers complained to Fran that she'd made homophobic remarks to him.

Fran ordered Jane to 'make peace with' Mack. She made a point of visiting Mack after work the next day but was appalled to find her stoned out of her mind. Jane told Fran she could not work with Mack again and recommended she be sacked. Instead, Fran summoned a contrite Mack to his office, told her the reason why Paz was being followed, said in future she would report direct to him and that he had a 'special project' for her. He ordered Mack to apologise in writing to Jane, which she willingly did. He then challenged Jane on her alleged homophobia and told her to apologise to Mack and her male gay co-worker and 'deal with' her own overly aggressive management style. Jane agreed to this, though somewhat grudgingly.

Eventually Mack called round to see Paz again. True to character, she simply turned up unannounced one evening. 'Why have you come?' was how he greeted her. He did not want her to enter the flat. He felt ashamed - ashamed at the state of everything: his flat, his appearance, his life. She was not easily fobbed off, and he was forced to let her in. 'Oh Paz!' she sighed, 'What have you done to yourself?' He looked like a much older man than even recently.

She asked him about Flick and warned him about her. 'I'm not with her anymore,' he said.

'She was the correspondent in two divorce cases. And you could be a correspondent in hers.'

'What?' It hadn't occurred to him she was married.

'That's why you were being watched.'

'Eh? After all these years of surveillance, maybe I should be flattered to be considered an appropriate subject myself, but I'm not.' He was angry at all concerned.

'But it's not the first time for her, I bet,' she said. 'And I reckon she was with you to cover up her other affairs. But what would an innocent girl like me know? Why did you choose another old slapper anyway.' He gave her an angry look, and she immediately apologised for the insensitivity of 'another', though not 'slapper'.

'Believe it or not, an old slapper as you call it is all I can expect at my age. But she's neither old, nor a slapper.'

Next, she broached the idea she had of *Paz & Mack* as a new investigation company. He thought she was joking. When it was clear she wasn't, he said he couldn't do it. She challenged him, claiming what he meant was that he was too full of self pity.

'Is Fran Owen behind this? I bet he is. He would like nothing more than to set me up in what sounds like an end-of-a-very-long-pier double act.'

'He is prepared to support it.'

'Then I want nothing to do with it. He's sent you here and this is a con. You're conning me out of the business.'

'What business? Lily didn't want the firm because she said, "What am I buying? A name, that's all. And the person who owns the name is doing nothing with it."'

He argued. She told him he was paranoid. 'Paranoid Paz' she called him. He was infuriated by this, perhaps recognising it was true.

In the end she lost her patience, 'Fuck it, then. Fuck it. You think everyone's out to get you and where are you?' She stood up as if to leave and began putting on her coat. He watched her as she bustled out with her overnight bag. 'Come back!' he called.

'What's the point?'

'Please.'

She paused, relenting, exactly as she'd planned to. Relieved, she put her arms around his neck and told him she'd give him time to make a decision about the company. He felt nostalgic, realising that this precocious young woman was sometimes even now that same bohemian girl who, not even knowing where she was, had wandered into his office that first day. He agreed to at least think about it.

She said, 'I can honestly say I've never felt happier in my life.'

'Why so?'

'Because I am in love — and, believe it or not, with a man.'

'Really? Who's the lucky one?' For one vain moment he wondered if it might be himself.

'You'll never guess.'

'Tell me then.'

'Rafe Lasche.'

'Eh? Not that pretentious, pompous artist fellow?'

'Yes, And I used to think that. But he's a sweetheart. And he's madly in love with me.'

'How on earth?'

'I saw him one day in the street, and for a laugh I said 'Hello'. Of course — remember that meal at English's where he was blindfolded — he'd never seen my face. He was intrigued and said, "Say it again," which I did. He said, "So you must be Mack. How divine is this!?" He took me for coffee. And so our unlikely romance began. He adores me. He takes me everywhere. He shows me off. He tells me how beautiful I am, even though I know I'm not. He says I'm "transgressive" and calls me Ali Cat. It's liberating, like being a new person. I have so much fun.'

'What about sex?'

'Trust you to ask. So prurient. He's impotent and doesn't care. All he wants is for me to talk dirty to him over the phone now and then.'

'So you're a sex worker now?'

She was offended but resisted showing it. 'He's my boyfriend, so no. I'm just so happy and I've decided I want to marry him.'

'But you're already married.'

'We're not compatible. The tart turned up at the flat tonight with a travel case, talking about reconciling and trying again. I told her I now accepted she and I could not ultimately be together. I said, "You can't deny your biology." She looked at me with those pleading eyes and said, "And I can't deny my heart," or some such cornball—'

'It's not.'

'I sent her away. I told her I was coming here.'

'Oh no.'

'But I'll phone her tomorrow. And when I do, Paz, I'm going to tell her I'm divorcing her.'

'Why!?'

'I'm tired of that little whore.'

'Are you mad? Is this all some joke? You've loved her since you were thirteen, wanted to marry her for years, and now you want to end it for that frivolous idiot?'

'But I'm having so much fun.'

'Fun? It's not about bloody fun! It's about living through the highs and lows of life with a special someone else. Mack, are you stoned or something?'

'But you've never married so how—'

'Look, most of the cases I've ever dealt with are about people not happy with what they've got, wanting something else, getting it, and then being unhappy with that. What happens when he tires of you, when you're no fun for him anymore? And, anyway, remember when Lily took you back after that Jude nonsense? She'll pick you up when that oaf dumps you. She'll forgive you, and you should forgive her now. That's what love is, not this other trivia.'

Trivia? She'd heard enough. 'Oh, fuck you, Paz!' She strode out of the room and, after slamming several doors, went to bed. Bemused, he sat up watching TV and drinking wine for an hour before retiring.

Mack couldn't sleep. She was shocked at what Paz had said. She'd expected him to be happy for her. Why wasn't he? She reflected upon it. It wasn't mere jealousy of Rafe. It wasn't his infatuation with Lily, or his belief she could do no wrong. He thought Rafe had played on her vanity, and maybe he was right. She'd once told Paz off for treating her like a sex object but wasn't she encouraging Rafe to make her into one? Why was she doing that? With Rafe it was like being in a different world. A fantasy world. And why did reality have to grind down your very soul all the time? Rafe lifted her up and gave her wings, but what if, like Icarus, the stupid wax on them melted?

In the middle of the night, she left her bed and went into Paz's room in her pyjamas. It was hot and stank of drink and sweat and Paz. He was lying on his side in the middle of the bed, gently snoring. She opened the window and breathed in the city air. His phone was flashing on his bedside table. Feeling nosy she checked and saw it was a text from Flick: 'It would be good to meet up'. She was tempted to respond with 'Fuck off!' but she restrained herself. She wanted him to find someone and be happy.

She removed her pyjamas and, naked, lay down beside him, gently massaging his shoulders and upper back. 'Scooch over, baby,' she said, pressing harder. He stirred. 'Mack?' Responding to her nudge he shuffled over. 'I love you, Mack.' He immediately resumed his slumber but she talked to him anyway: 'So you finally said it. And I'm sorry for what I said to you. You're right. I'll take Lily back. I'll let her beg but really it'll be me that's begging. I know I'm no better than she is. Worse in some ways. I'll tell her about Rafe. What she doesn't know already she'll be OK with. And we'll have a laugh about it. You're so damned wise — and boring. But God, how I wish I could have married a younger version of you with just a dash of Rafe to make me laugh! But the *Paz & Mack* show — that could be our marriage. Yes it could.' She leaned over, kissed his neck and whispered 'Frivolous idiot!', giggled, rolled onto her back, and then over to her side of the bed. Contented at last, in less than a minute she had tumbled into the warm, forgiving arms of deep sleep.

Thank You

Thank You For Reading My Book!

I really appreciate it.

Please leave a helpful review on Amazon letting others know what you thought of the book.

Thank you so much!
John Holmes

HAPPY
SELF PUBLISHING

Happy Self Publishing is a one-stop destination for publishing services such as book cover design, editing, formatting, audiobook narration, website design, and marketing. At Happy Self Publishing we help authors find their voice and self-publish professionally.

▶ **WHAT WE DO:** We help coaches, consultants, trainers, speakers, and entrepreneurs who aspire to position themselves as the trusted experts in their field by helping them become bestselling authors within 6 months or less, even if they hate writing.

▶ **HOW WE DO IT:** We show you how to build a profitable author funnel and use the book as the lead magnet in the funnel to give you expert positioning and attract qualified leads for your business.

▶ **WHY IT WORKS:** After working with over 400 authors from 35 countries, we've been able to simplify the process and show you the easiest and fastest way to publish your book. It doesn't matter at what stage of your author journey you are currently - we have the tools & resources to take you to the next step and help you publish a world-class book.

▶ **SERVICES WE PROVIDE:**

✓ book writing aka angel writing
✓ book coaching
✓ editing
✓ book cover design
✓ formatting
✓ publishing ebooks, paperback & audiobooks
✓ global distribution
✓ author websites
✓ book trailers
✓ bestseller promotions

🌐 www.happyselfpublishing.com
✉ writetous@happyselfpublishing.com

Schedule a free Book Strategy
Call with us to discuss your book project:
www.happyselfpublishing.com/call

Printed in Great Britain
by Amazon

10022356R00178